TEMPTING

SUSAN JOHNSON

TEMPTING

KENSINGTON BOOKS

KENSINGTON BOOKS are published by

Kensington Publishing Corp.
850 Third Avenue
New York, NY 10022

ISBN 0-7394-1597-2

Printed in the United States of America

Chapter 1

Leicester, England
November 1892

Princess Christina arrived a day late for her friend Shelagh's country house party. She had needed to see her boys off to school that morning and also take leave of her parents, who were on their way back to Wales. The train ride north had taken longer than usual due to some difficulty with the engine, and feeling tired and harried, she tried not to snap at her maid, who was helping her change into a tea gown.

A short time later, on entering the drawing room to join the other guests, she resisted the urge to scream. Gina Campbell, ex-actress, the new Lady Fane, lover to a great many men—her husband, Hans, included—was holding court, her retinue entirely male.

And suddenly, Christina dreaded the coming weekend.

Already weary from the hectic pace of her day and the long journey, she wasn't up to a sparring match with Gina, who always managed to address her with some rude remark. She would plead fatigue to Shelagh and escape upstairs till dinner.

Her hostess was understanding, and very soon Christina was ascending the broad marble staircase, liberated from conversation about the day's hunting *and* the notorious Lady Fane. The thought of a short nap before dinner held blissful appeal, for she had risen at five that morning. Once rested, she felt assured Gina Campbell's smug impudence could be more easily ignored.

Not that she was unsophisticated about the leisure activities of her class. Christina understood that amorous peccadilloes were not unusual, but rather, were commonplace with many of her friends. And while she had never felt the urge to be unfaithful, she didn't consider herself particularly virtuous or moral. Everyone simply dealt with life in his or her own way. Her marriage was no worse than others; she had two wonderful sons, and if Hans wasn't perfect, who among her friends could boast of a devoted husband or a love-match?

When she reached the top of the stairs, she felt as though she had gained safe haven. The corridor was quiet, shadowed, her footsteps muffled by the plush carpet. Looking forward to lying down and relaxing, she came to a stop opposite the Cavendish portrait of an admiral—her reference point for her room—and, grasping the doorknob, pushed open the door.

Her eyes widened in shock.

Lulu, Baroness Kellie, her best friend, was clinging to the broad shoulders of a powerfully muscled, dark-haired man. Her legs were wrapped around his waist, her riding habit rucked up over her thighs as he pressed her against the mirrored wardrobe. The taut strength of the man's biceps was starkly evident as he supported Lulu's weight in his arms. Nude from the waist up, his discarded shirt lay at his feet. His half-undone chamois pants clung to his hips like a second skin.

They both still wore their riding boots.

Apparently, they preferred sex to tea after the hunt.

At Christina's entrance, Lulu squealed in surprise. The man stopped in midstroke and glanced toward the door. No more than a fleeting second passed; then turning back, he murmured something to Lulu and resumed his rhythm.

With the man's shockingly cool gaze pervading her consciousness, Christina jerked the door shut. Flushed and embarrassed, she quickly glanced up and down the corridor.

Thankfully, no one was in sight.

She would have to apologize to Lulu, although the man's patent indifference suggested this wasn't the first time he had been caught in flagrante delicto.

Moving down the hall to the next bedroom, she cautiously eased the door open, peeked inside, recognized her cosmetics tray on the bureau and only then entered the room. Her faux pas was understandable in a country home with forty bedrooms and perhaps too many portraits of admirals—although had Lulu or her friend been more discreet, one of them *might* have had the presence of mind to lock the door.

As she entered her room, Lulu's squeals of delight were immediately audible, the shared wall inadequate to muffle the graphic cries. And while Christina did not begrudge her friend her enjoyment, any thought of a nap was completely out of the question. Nor could she return downstairs after having pleaded a headache—which meant she was temporarily a prisoner in her room.

For the next hour, Christina was mercilessly bombarded with the noisy evidence of Lulu's rapture until finally, thankfully, silence prevailed. Setting aside the book she had erratically perused between pleasure cries, she lay down on her bed for her much needed rest.

A short-lived one, as it turned out.

Lulu slipped into her room a few minutes later, leaned against the door and offered her friend a smile of beatific satisfaction. "I just wanted you to know that I've glimpsed the glories of paradise," she purred. "He's unbelievable . . ."

Understanding her nap was over, Christina eased into a seated position. "It did rather sound as though he was being very good to you," the princess drolly noted, "and I *do* apologize for barging in."

"Sorry about the screams." The Baroness Kellie grinned as she strolled to a chair and dropped into it with a look of happy exhaustion. "Actually, I'm not sorry in the least," she corrected, one brow arching in sportive emphasis. "And you needn't apologize. Your entrance didn't bother us, because Vale's so beautifully *focused*. And much, much, *much* better than one could ever imagine—even after hearing all the extravagant reports on him."

The princess had heard the gossip as well. "Is he better than your darling Teddy?" Lulu had been as enthused about Lord Cliden last month.

"Pooh! There's no comparison! Dear Max is absolutely godlike!"

"So it's *dear Max* now," Christina noted with a teasing flicker of her brows, "although I suppose under the circumstances . . . a certain intimacy is allowed."

"The most excellent intimacy, I assure you," Lulu maintained, grinning. She held her hands apart, indicating a sizeable length.

"I'll keep it in mind when I meet the marquis. It will add a certain flavor to our conversation," Christina remarked. She and Lulu had been friends since childhood, and even though the princess didn't share Lulu's propensity for serial love affairs, she was generally regaled with all the lurid details.

"Really, Christa, when are you going to consider indulging yourself? Husbands and children and charity work aren't enough. And life passes by quickly, darling." The baroness pursed her lips in a fleeting grimace. "Think, we'll be thirty-one next year."

"I'm content enough, Lulu. I don't require the excitement of infidelity."

The baroness gazed at her from under her auburn lashes that

matched the auburn splendor of her hair. "You've never found anyone to excite you, you mean."

Christina shrugged. "Perhaps. Nor do I expect to, after having met hundreds of men."

"All of whom you've turned down," her friend pointed out. "It's not normal, darling, being so faithful. God knows our husbands aren't."

"Don't start, Lulu. You know how I dislike that subject."

As well she should, the baroness thought. The Prince of Zeiss was known for his dalliances as well as for his infrequent appearances at home. "Well, at any rate, you can enjoy the riding here at Shelagh's. The Belvoir Hunt offers the best sport. Did you bring Tremaine with you?"

"Would I leave my favorite jumper behind? My groom brought him up yesterday."

"I heard a rumor that Hans is actually joining you this time." The German prince rarely accompanied his English wife on her holidays home.

"So he said. He likes to ride with Eddie, so I expect to see him. Late tonight, actually."

"Max rides as well as Eddie, better perhaps. I saw him at Cheltenham where he took first over a rough course. Hans may find Max an interesting challenge."

The princess smiled faintly. "The marquis might be too tired to compete if you keep him busy making love to you."

"Apparently he can do both without loss to either sport. Or so Sophie tells me," the baroness added with an arch look. "She met Max in Baden last year and spent a blissful month with him while he was riding the international circuit."

"Good God, Lulu, you *must* find some other form of entertainment."

Lulu wrinkled her perfect nose. "Plenty of time for that when I'm old, darling. Although, considering our long friendship"—she opened her arms wide in an expansive gesture—"I'm willing to share the darling Maxwell Falconer with you. I'm sure he'll be capable of servicing us both."

"While I appreciate your generosity," Christina pleasantly replied, "I don't find Vale of interest, nor do I wish to add myself to his rumored list of conquests."

"Nor do you have an amorous bone in your body, sweet darling. For if you did, you couldn't resist him."

"You're right, I'm sure," the princess agreed, the discussion of possible liaisons for her not of recent origin. Lulu had been indulging her sensual appetite and trying to convince her best friend to join in the adventure for a very long time.

"Your prim mother's to blame for rearing such dutiful daughters."

Christina smiled. "This isn't a blameable offense, for I gladly leave all the amorous adventuring to you. I'm really not interested. My life is quite busy enough. For instance," she pointedly said, "I rose at five this morning and I'd very dearly love a nap before dinner."

Lulu lazily stretched. "Then, I'll leave you in peace." She rose. "I'm going to soak in a nice warm bath before dinner and think of a way to see Max tonight."

"That might be slightly difficult with your husband in bed with you."

Lulu grinned. "Then again, maybe Charles will find Lady Duff as interesting as he did Ascot week. She's here, you know."

"Along with Gina Campbell," Christina noted with a grimace.

"You have to ignore Gina, darling. She loves to taunt if you allow it. And if she hasn't slept with every man here this weekend, it's not from lack of trying."

"Don't remind me," the princess gloomily replied, fully aware of the gossip about her husband and Lady Fane.

"If it helps, she means nothing to any of them." The baroness moved to the door. "So ignore the little slut. That's what every other woman here will do."

"While the men will flock around her."

"Because she'll sleep with any one of them. I'm telling you, darling, give illicit love a try one of these days. Not like Gina, of course, but dip your toe into the water at least." She waved as she left. "I'll see you at dinner."

Chapter 2

Christina found herself seated beside the Marquis of Vale that evening, and she wondered for a moment whether Lulu had changed the place cards. But she was soon disabused of that notion when her hostess, Shelagh Cavendish, winked at her from her place at the head of the table and unobtrusively pointed to the marquis, who was engaged in conversation with the lady on his right.

Shelagh, a longtime friend like Lulu, considered Christina an aberration in the faithless world of the beau monde. Apparently, tonight, she was intent on introducing her to the marquis's renowned charm.

Bracing herself to receive unwanted advances, Christina responded to the marquis's first conversational parleys with coolness.

He seemed not to notice, turning to Lady Moffet on his right, listening at great length and with enormous courtesy to her monologue concerning salmon fishing and the merits of gillies who knew their place.

When next he spoke to Christina, the main course had been served. She had been bored to tears by Admiral Galworthy's observations on the superiority of the English navy, and when the marquis said, "I'd be more than happy to apologize to you, if you require it," she couldn't help but smile at his beguiling expression.

"I should apologize to you," she replied with a small sigh. "I already did to Lulu. I'm terribly embarrassed."

"As well you should be." His faint smile lit up his beautiful dark eyes, revealing an alluring boyishness beneath his harsh good looks. "I haven't seen you at Shelagh's before."

"While I've heard of you even in Silesia."

He grinned. "Good reports, no doubt."

"My friends all like you enormously. It must be your American charm."

"You mean I can't claim any of my father's qualities. Not that I'd want to." The previous marquis had not been known for his benevolence, preferring the hard-drinking country life of a hunting squire.

"You ride well, I'm told. Perhaps you could claim that trait from your father."

"Actually, I learned to ride out west. My stepfather owned gold mines in Montana."

"You left England at an early age, didn't you?" The aristocratic world was small. Everyone knew everyone. Everyone knew that the American heiress, Millicent Carter, had walked out on her husband the moment she inherited her father's fortune.

"We left when I was four. My mother decided she preferred her native land," he blandly said.

"And how do you feel about England?"

"I like Minster Hill. My father kept a prime stable. I can't fault him there."

"Will you make your home in England now?"

"Perhaps for part of the year. It depends on business. My stepfather and I are developing a new oil field in the States."

"My husband's family owns coal fields in Silesia. Even with good managers, a certain amount of overseeing is required, it seems."

"My mother speaks for me in my absence." He smiled. "She's probably better at finding oil than either Ted or I."

"She sounds an unusual woman."

"Meaning?" A slight defensiveness echoed in his tone.

"I envy her such freedom."

"She's always been independent," he said with pride. "It helps to have one's own money, she tells me."

"She's very right."

He took note of the faint poignancy in the princess's reply. Even though he had visited England rarely while his father lived, he knew of her. With no doweries other than their splendid looks, the pale blond beauty of the Grey sisters' had brought them both titles of rank. But not happy marriages, according to gossip. "Are you au courant on the British navy now?" he softly queried, tactfully changing the subject.

"To the last coastal freighter," Christina murmured. "And I perceive you've been suitably informed as to how a gillie should be treated."

"With a stern hand and an almighty arrogance."

His voice was low and deliciously husky, she noted with an uncharacteristic frisson of pleasure. "I trust you will take Lady Moffet's advice," she primly said with a touch of drama to cover up her unusual reaction to this man.

But he saw her sudden blush and felt his own odd pleasure, when blushing women weren't his style, no more than virtuous wives. He signaled for more wine, needing to mask his remarkable response. "Would you like more?" he asked as a footman leaped forward to serve them.

"I shouldn't."

He found her reply startlingly provocative, as though he were fifteen again and about to seduce his first woman. Inhaling, he cautioned himself against such rash feelings toward a woman who believed in the sanctity of marriage. As he was about to reply with a suitable politesse, she said, "Maybe just a little."

Immediately tantalized, he just as instantly chided himself for crassness. With all the available women here this weekend, he didn't have to corrupt such innocence. Besides, she reminded him of his half sister, not only in her pale beauty, but in her unblemished virtue. And for the remainder of dinner, he consciously conversed as though Celia were seated beside him.

After dinner, with the men left behind for their port and cigars, the ladies retired to the drawing room, where Lulu drew Christina aside and breathlessly said, "Isn't Max wonderful?"

"He's very kind—almost benevolent. I was struck by his decency."

"He's benevolent, all right," Lulu murmured with a teasing leer. "Are you intrigued?"

"This was Shelagh's doing, wasn't it? Putting him next to me."

"She's matchmaking. He'll change your world if you'll let him."

"I didn't get the impression he was interested. Nor am I," Christina quickly added. "We spoke mostly of the oil business and his mother—and of my boys."

"Really."

"Don't look so surprised. I'm sure he doesn't constantly play the Lothario."

The marquis had been in England since August, when he had come for his father's funeral. And in those months, he had not been known for his temperance. "He didn't try and seduce you?"

"Good heavens, Lulu, sometimes I think you're obsessed with sex."

Several women in the vicinity turned in their direction at the sibilant word.

"Pray, talk of something else," the princess murmured.

"I need more champagne," Lulu decisively remarked. "Unless Shelagh wants to add some brandy to this tea. But, darling, I don't mean to importune. As long as you're happy, I wish you the best." Waving a footman over, she glanced at her friend. "Some champagne for you, too?"

As Christina hesitated, Gina Campbell's trilling laughter suddenly rose above the swell of conversation. She abruptly nodded in acquiescence.

"Now there's a sensible answer," Lulu noted, leaning back in her chair. "Particularly if we have to sleep with our husbands tonight. What train is Hans coming in on?"

Prince Hans Heinrich XV arrived shortly before eleven, after the men had rejoined the ladies in the drawing room, when everyone had already been drinking for hours. He stood in the doorway for a moment, still dressed in his traveling suit, surveying the various members of Shelagh's house party, smiling at his hostess as she quickly approached him. He spoke with her for some time and then to several other guests before he came over to where Christina was seated with Lulu. Lightly kissing her on the cheek, he immediately moved on to the entourage with Gina Campbell at its center.

Christina tried not to be hurt by his casual disregard, or take undue notice of his marked attention to Gina as the evening progressed, but she failed miserably.

"Darling, I don't see the sense of your staunch loyalty," Lulu said, casting a glance at Hans and Gina, their heads almost touching as they sat together on a secluded sofa, their conversation obviously intimate.

"Would it do any good to make a scene?"

"I was thinking more of getting even."

"In *your* way."

"In the only way that matters."

Christina grimaced. "Does it become a contest at some point? Does one eventually keep score?"

"I'm not talking about trying to best your husband at his own game." Knowing Hans's proclivities, Lulu doubted it possible. "Rather, I was thinking about you enjoying yourself for a change, laughing with someone, making love out of pleasure, not duty, allowing some happiness into your life."

"I adore my boys, Lulu—you know that. They're my greatest happiness."

"You have to consider some personal happiness, too. Do you want to look back on your life with regret twenty years from now?"

"And you won't?"

"I'm trying not to. Look, we both understood the reasons we married."

"But I really loved Hans." He was tall, handsome, so attentive all those years ago when she had dreamed young girl dreams.

"Good for you. Do you now?" When Christina didn't answer, Lulu said, "If it's any consolation, we aren't alone in our loveless marriages. In fact, we're probably the rule rather than the exception."

"My parents were happy—*are* happy together," Christina maintained. "It's not impossible."

"Well, mine are not. Nor are you. And if your parents happen to be happy together, they certainly didn't offer much objection to either you or Charlotte marrying well."

Christina sighed. "They were hoping Charlotte and I would have the money they'd never had."

"But it's poor recompense, isn't it?" Lulu's husband, while only a baron, was one of the wealthiest men in Ireland and England thanks to his family's foresight in purchasing large tracts of west London real estate.

"I'm not sure. I don't know. God, Lulu, don't ask me to weigh my sons against Hans's infidelities."

"Except for them, you'd leave, wouldn't you?"

"The point is, I can't. We could discuss this till doomsday without changing the facts."

"So take a lover."

"And be happy. It's that simple? Are you?"

"At times. More than you, sweet," Lulu gently admonished.

"Why don't you at least think about Max? I'm being generous because you're my dearest friend and he's utter perfection. And if you mean to dip your toes in, as it were, who better to lead you into deeper water," she finished with a smile.

"He's yours to give me?"

She shook her head. "But if he's interested in you"—Lulu grinned—"I wouldn't put up a fight."

"But he isn't." Christina glanced across the room. "It looks as though May is more his style tonight. Shouldn't you step in and make your claim?"

"I don't want to own him, darling. I only want to make love to him. And I'd say he has enough stamina to service a harem. We both came several times this afternoon. And he was ready for more."

Christina blushed. "For heaven's sake, Lulu, keep your voice down." But for the first time since Hans's appearance, she forgot her resentment and anger, the memory of the marquis's magnificent body prominent in her thoughts, their conversation over dinner strangely intimate, as though they claimed previous friendship. Recalling the deep velvet of his voice brought added color to her cheeks.

"Think of him, darling. Think of how he could make you feel." Lulu's smile was playful. "Have you ever screamed when you've climaxed?"

"I'm not about to discuss my sex life in Shelagh's drawing room," Christina whispered, embarrassed and at the same time chagrined. Hans wouldn't approve of her screaming, she knew.

"Very well, but how long has it been since Hans has come to your bed? I just don't want you to die of frustration." Leaning over, she patted Christina's knee. "And that's the end of my scolding. I'm going to see if I can win some money at bridge," she said, rising. "Do you care to join me?"

"Not just yet. I'll observe the foibles of our incestuous society over the rest of my champagne."

"And you'll think about indulging in some fun, too, won't you?" Lulu teased.

Christina grinned. "Almost exclusively."

But as Lulu walked away in a cloud of violet scent, Christina found it difficult to avoid the sight of her husband and his current flirt, understanding now why he had suggested joining her for the hunt when he normally did not. Apparently, he was in correspondence with Gina or with someone else who knew of the guest list this weekend. She felt useless and de trop and apart from all the flirtatious banter so typical of country house parties, where husbands and wives discreetly looked the other way, where hostesses spent as much time arranging the placement of bedrooms as they did the dinner table seating. Where one never knew who might bump into whom in the darkened halls at night.

"You look as though you might need another drink."

Glancing up, Christina saw the Marquis of Vale with a champagne bottle in his hand, his smile so kind she almost burst into tears.

"May I join you?" Without waiting for an answer, he sat down in Lulu's vacated chair, conscious of the tears welling in Christina's eyes, wishing to give her a moment to compose herself without his gaze on her. He set down the fresh glasses he held in his hand and took his time opening the bottle. Only when he began to fill the stemmed goblets did he speak again. "I don't know about you, but I'm hopelessly sober while everyone else seems to be well into their cups. Do you think we should attempt to catch up?"

"A splendid idea." The smile she offered him was tentative; but her voice was collected, and she had brushed the tears from her eyes with the back of her glove.

"Lulu seems a good friend. Have you known her long?" He intended to speak only of pleasant topics, her sorrow so evident, he had been drawn to her side like some knight errant.

"Since we were girls. Although she's much braver than I."

Suddenly blushing, she added in a nervous rush, "Not that I meant—I mean . . . whatever Lulu does is no concern of mine. Oh, dear, I'm making a botch of this, aren't I?"

"I didn't realize our rooms were adjacent," he calmly said. "Anyone could have mistaken one door for another." The thought that she would be sleeping only a few feet away from him struck him with an ungovernable rush of pleasure. "Are you hunting in the morning?" he quickly interjected, uneasy over such intemperate feelings when impersonal lust was much more familiar.

"I'm looking forward to it," she said, a new elation in her tone. "I just love the early morning runs when the air is clean and the sun is glowingly fresh. It reminds me of the simple joys in life."

"Then, we should drink only one bottle more," he sportively noted. "I've given my man orders to wake me at six."

"In that case, I'll be up before you. My maid is waking me at five-thirty."

"Would you like to join me in an early morning ride?" He spoke spontaneously, the shock of his words vibrating in his ears, when he had only intended to offer her comfort in her loneliness.

She looked away, and he chided himself for taking such liberties.

"Forgive me. Perhaps I had more to drink than I thought."

"I would like to ride," she slowly said, as though testing her wings with each word.

And for a moment he was speechless because he didn't wish to involve himself with so saintly a woman. She was blushing again, like an untried maid, and rather than further embarrass her, he nodded. "Good. Fine, then." Suddenly he felt in unfamiliar waters, caught, not sure he cared to play the gentleman so early in the morning. "Should I wait for you downstairs or at the stables in the morning?"

"The stables," she quickly replied, catching sight of her husband exiting the room with Lady Fane. "If you'll excuse me."

She was gone in a soft swish of burgundy velvet, leaving him strangely rattled. Refilling his glass, he decided his unease was due to the oddity of a virtuous woman in his life. He had to make sure he didn't say or do anything tomorrow to further encourage her.

The last thing he was interested in was virtue.

Chapter 3

Christina found her husband and Gina locked in a heated embrace just outside the drawing room door.

"I'd appreciate it, Hans, if you'd move more than five feet from the drawing room before you have intercourse."

He quickly stepped back, his hands dropping away from Lady Fane.

"And really, Gina, wouldn't you prefer a bed?" Christina caustically added.

The door to the drawing room suddenly opened, and several men exited.

"Hans!" one of them cried. "Come shoot some billiards with us. Teddy thinks he can win back the money he lost last night."

"If you'll excuse me." The prince bowed to Gina, glared at his wife and walked away.

"Now you'll have to wait, Gina. Such a shame," the princess murmured, surprised at the degree of her anger when she had known for years what Hans was like. "Although, surely, there must be enough men still left in the drawing room to service your needs."

"Something you wouldn't know anything about."

"Sleeping with other women's husbands? You're right, I don't."

"Sleeping with anyone at all, darling," Gina mocked. "Including your husband."

"We can't all be as generous as you . . . and your husband," she replied, ignoring the barb. "I understand Lord Fane is more than willing to share you."

"I doubt Hans would mind sharing you."

"Whether he would or not doesn't concern me. *I* would mind. Good hunting tonight, darling. But then, you're readily available to anyone, aren't you?"

"I'm not the only one Hans fucks," Gina snapped, resenting the slur.

"But I'm the only one he married," Christina softly replied, and turning, she walked away.

Hans returned to their bedchamber very late, but Christina was still awake, unable to sleep after the scene in the hallway. Finding Hans with Gina was a kind of culmination of years of betrayal, a final sticking point. She had decided as she lay waiting for him to return that she no longer cared to overlook his blatant infidelities. She wished some resolution to the casual detachment of their marriage. Sitting up, she quietly said, "I don't care to live like this anymore, Hans."

Aware of possible repercussions to the scene with Gina, the prince had dismissed his valet and was undressing himself. Looking up from unclasping his cuff links, he coolly surveyed his wife. "Don't lecture me, Christina. I'm not in the mood."

"Then, you'll have to get in the mood, because I have no intention of being dismissed. I'm weary of your blatant indiscretions, and I want them to stop."

"You can't be serious?" He set the diamond cuff links down on the bureau top and began shrugging out of his evening jacket.

"I'm dead serious."

Throwing his jacket on a chair, he slipped his embroidered

suspenders off his shoulders. "What the hell does that mean?" But he spoke without emotion, as though he were disinterested in her answer.

"It means I wish you to stop your philandering."

Pulling his white tie apart, he slid it from around his neck and gazed at her, the tie suspended from his fingertips. "I have no intention of stopping."

She felt her heart skip a beat. "Then I'll divorce you."

"Of course you won't. You'd lose the boys." Dropping the tie, he kicked off his shoes.

"Maybe I won't."

"Darling." He addressed her with chill disparagement. "You don't have a penny of your own, and divorces are costly. Not to mention, our marriage settlement very clearly states that any children born of our union are mine. Now, I'd appreciate it if we could discontinue this senseless discussion." He stripped off his shirt.

"How would you like it if I slept with any man I fancied?"

"Jesus, Christina, stop acting like a petulant child." Whether his indifference was real or based on the assumption she would not indulge in adultery, he obviously dismissed her pronouncement. His trousers followed his shirt to the floor, and he stood before her in his silk underwear.

She used to be enthralled by his tall, muscled body and blond Nordic handsomeness. The feeling was so distant now, she couldn't remember when she had begun to despise him. "Maybe I'll sleep around, too. If you can do it, why can't I?"

His smile was patronizing. "Probably, because your mother would disapprove, and you're ever the dutiful daughter, aren't you?"

"And *your* mother doesn't disapprove?"

"She understands the prerogatives of princely rank," he brusquely said. "Now, are we done?"

"I wish you all the best with Gina," the princess snapped, sliding from the bed as he approached, checkmated, as always, with access to her sons in the balance. "Although, surely, all you men must be no more than a blur to her."

"I'm not looking for exclusivity, my sweet," he pronounced with spurious affection, "only for an accomplished fuck."

"We're all looking for something, aren't we?" Christina tartly declared, stalking toward the dressing room. Slamming the door behind her, she walked to the chaise and angrily punched the cushioned headrest—an act so out of character even she understood she had reached a saturation point of conjugal insult. Maybe Lulu was right. Maybe the only way to retaliate was in kind.

But as she lay on the narrow chaise, the darkness as black as her mood, she didn't know if she was actually capable of such revenge. How would one start, and ultimately, how would one deal with the commonplace act of adultery? Would such reciprocity spiral into endless acrimony, with bitterness piled onto bitterness? Or did Lulu's search for self-gratification indeed offer the possibility of happiness? Happiness and illicit love—it seemed an untrustworthy hope. Although, certainly, there was little enough happiness in her life, she thought, other than her joy in her children.

Sleep eluded her with her fury and frustration at fever pitch, her thoughts in continuous tumult, her sensibilities touched by some inchoate call to action. And for the first time, she found herself seriously considering Lulu's words about regret. Twenty years from now, how would she feel about having settled for so little? Twenty years from now, with her sons grown and living their own lives, what would she do to maintain her sanity? Would she and Hans still exist, barely speaking, seeing each other so rarely one felt almost a stranger?

The Marquis of Vale had talked with her about her sons.

The unexpected memory broke into the turmoil convulsing her brain.

She smiled. They had shared anecdotes about boyish pleasures. How pleasant he was. And then, unbidden, the image of him half-nude, pleasuring Lulu sprang into her mind, and she felt herself blushing in the dark.

When she shouldn't be thinking of Vale and sex or Lulu and sex or sex at all.

When she should be contemplating a solution to her arid life instead.

But her emotions couldn't be so easily controlled, and recall that the marquis and her youngest son, Fritz, had the same middle name drifted into her consciousness. As though their common name mattered in the debacle of her life, or such a small similarity was of any import in the misery of her marriage. They had both laughed over the coincidence. Even as she smiled again, she chided herself for such incautious musing. But caution notwithstanding, she next remembered how Max had invited the boys to ride at Minster Hill next time they were in England.

And that his stamina in bed was rumored to be prodigious.

Good God! Shamed, shocked by the perverse juxtaposition of ideas, she shook her head, as though physically negating such infamous reflections. And forcibly reminding herself that the marquis used women much as her husband did, she tried to bring her senses into order, intentionally concentrating on her next week's busy schedule. But regardless that she deliberately recalled each London appointment, the seductive image of the handsome marquis continuously reappeared in her mind. Shaken and confused, bewildered by her unmanageable feelings and the realities of a man like Vale, she decided to cancel her morning ride.

But no sooner was the decision made than Hans's smug declaration of princely prerogatives reminded her of her future. Of the long line of infidelities yet to come.

And she changed her mind once again.

Perhaps the marquis would be the perfect antidote to her frustration and indecision—as well as a match for her husband's prodigality.

She took a deep breath.

Would she have the nerve to enter the unknown world of casual amours?

Chapter 4

As if she needed encouragement for her first adulterous deed, when she crept into the bedroom early that morning, searching for her gloves, she found the bed empty.

She hadn't realized it was possible to still feel such anger after so many betrayals, but she found her heart racing and her hands shaking at the flagrant insult. Hans didn't even have the decency to appease her for a single night. And so their life would continue—unless . . .

Returning to the dressing room, she stripped off her nightgown with trembling hands and pulled a riding habit from the armoire, any further indecision about right and wrong, morality and affairs, banished from her mind. When her maid came to wake her a few moments later, she sent her away, not inclined to have Hans's absence the stuff of gossip below stairs. She was capable of dressing herself.

But for a brief minute after Rosie left, she stood in the center of the dressing room, numbed by the enormity of her intent.

Could she really bring herself to do this?

Regardless of Hans's provocation, regardless of the level of her frustration, was she capable of such a calculated act? Then Lulu's words about regret echoed in her mind, the empty bed leaped into her consciousness, and stirred into action, she moved toward the bureau and jerked open a drawer.

The meek did not inherit the earth. And if discretion and duty were the means to happiness, she wouldn't have spent last night in tears.

So . . . she mused, staring at the neatly piled silks and linens, about to embark on her first intrepid journey of self-discovery. Did one wear the normal utilitarian undergarments for riding or something more provocative for an assignation? Although, she noted, their morning ride wasn't technically an assignation with the marquis yet unaware of his role. Rifling through her lingerie, she ultimately disposed of the plain linen things, selecting instead a chemise and drawers of pale yellow silk to complement her favorite green velvet riding habit. And illicit amour no doubt required some subtly placed fragrance, she decided. Spraying a goodly amount of perfume here and there and in the most unlikely places should those unlikely places be called into play before the morning was over, she felt simultaneously fearful and exhilarated as the scent of lily of the valley pervaded the air.

Although, how exactly would this consummation be achieved while out riding? she suddenly wondered.

Momentarily nonplused, she stared at her image in the mirror. Would they make love on the ground or standing up? Would he hold her as he had held Lulu? Or would he take her to some nearby inn? Feeling an absolute tyro, were it not five-thirty in the morning, she would wake Lulu and ask for advice. But it *was* five-thirty in the morning, and at age thirty, she decided with a small sigh, she should be able to engage in sex without an instruction book.

In any event, she would find out soon enough where the Marquis of Vale preferred making love while out riding. He was a man of prodigal sexual habits; no further conjecture was required. Stepping into her lacy drawers, she focused on her toilette rather than on the unknown, and before long, she was dressed and exiting her room. Walking down the long, quiet corridor, she briefly speculated on who was sleeping with whom this morning—with the exception of her husband, of course, who had made his inclinations plain enough last night. Still, as of this morning, she, too, had made a selection for the first time in her life. It only remained to be seen, she thought, moving down the stairs, whether she could embrace the sophisticated world of amour with the necessary aplomb. Resolved to at least try, she lifted her chin and crossed the large entrance hall to where the night porter held open the door for her. Walking out into the bright sunshine, she inhaled deeply of the pungent fall air and smiled.

Was that the smell of freedom?

Unable to sleep, Max had arrived at the stables early. He had instructed their mounts be saddled and brought out, and then dismissing the groom, he had paced and checked his watch and paced some more, as though he had never waited for a woman before, as though he were a green, untried youth about to be alone with a woman for the first time. As he crossed and re-crossed the stable yard, his riding boots crunching on the raked gravel, he reminded himself that this was *just* a morning ride, that the Princess of Zeiss was *just* another woman, that he was years beyond such restless trepidation, that he was acting the fool. But regardless of such sound logic and admonition, his errant senses failed to calm.

Nor did it help when the princess strode into view around the curve of the stable drive, looking like some svelte, slender Diana of the Hunt, dressed in lush forest green, the morning sun heightening the pale gold of her hair. The sway of her hips was particularly tantalizing beneath the figure-hugging lines of her riding skirt, and the flaunting thrust of her lavish breasts—even constrained beneath her severely tailored jacket—was impossible to ignore.

What the hell was he going to do? He could feel his erection surge, and gritting his teeth, he forced his gaze away—anywhere but on those plump, bouncing breasts and the enticing juncture of her thighs so manifestly evident with her long-legged stride.

His voice was almost curt when he greeted her, and she stammered in response, her voice trailing away, her smile fading.

"Forgive me," he quickly apologized, her instant hurt touching him to the quick. "I just woke a few minutes ago," he lied, when he had hardly slept last night for thinking of her. "My vocal chords haven't warmed up yet. If I sounded brusque, I didn't mean it in the least."

How starkly handsome he was, regardless of his brusqueness and slight frown. How tall and powerful, like a praetorian guard, selected for his physical prowess. And dark—his hair and eyes, the color of his skin—she liked that he was so different from her husband. "It *is* rather early," she agreed, feeling strangely giddy standing so close to him. "I hope you don't mind going for a ride with me."

Her tone was so tremulous and tentative he didn't have the heart to be honest. Smiling, he curbed his lecherous impulses with an iron will. "No, not at all."

His voice sounded odd even to his own ears, and a small silence fell—tense, awkward—the sound of birdsong suddenly loud in the stillness.

He was debating how best to keep his distance or even how to renege.

"Will you make love to me?" she blurted out, instant color pinking her cheeks.

Caught unaware, his instinctive impulse was to sweep her up into his arms and carry her back to his room; but reason reasserted itself a second later, and he quickly glanced around, concerned a groom may have heard. But no one was in sight.

"It's just that Lulu . . . you know her"—Christina's blush heightened as she recalled how well he did know her—"I mean," she rushed on, "we *both* know her . . . she's my best friend . . . and she said the other day . . . Oh, God, I've never been so embarrassed in my life, and if you think me mad you may be right."

She took a deep breath, thinking it was too late to pretend this was just a casual conversation, and if she intended to taste freedom or even get within hailing distance of it, she couldn't cry off now. "You see," she quickly went on, thinking the marquis was either stunned or exceedingly polite not to interrupt, "I've never slept with anyone other than my husband. And I've come to the conclusion," she added with a shaky smile, "that it's about time I did, and if you'd accommodate me, I'd be ever so grateful." She blew out a small breath and looked up at him with such a hopeful expression, he thought for a moment he should simply say yes and accommodate them both.

But he was not a tyro in matters of amour, nor did he ruin women to accommodate anyone. "Don't let Gina bother you," he kindly said. "She's not worth it."

"How would you know?"

He didn't respond.

"Of course," she muttered, humiliated by her ineptitude and naivete, mortified by his rejection.

"Let's just say Gina's friendly with a lot of people," he gently said, wishing to be as benevolent as possible in a situation that didn't concern him. "But that doesn't mean you should change your way of life."

"Maybe I *want* to."

"Neither of them are worth it," he offered, in an attempt to relieve her distress. "Believe me."

Her gaze came up. "You know my husband?"

"We competed on the Continent last summer—in the steeplechase championships."

"And he's not worth my rancor?"

Max shook his head.

"You know what he's like, and yet you counsel me to duty? That sounds like a male point of view."

His gaze narrowed for a moment. "I'm the last man to talk to about male point of view; I like women."

"So rumor has it."

"I'm not going to apologize for my life. And that's the point. You're angry now. But you live a different life. Don't rush into something you'll regret."

"Maybe I won't regret it."

He drew in a constrained breath. "That's not quite helpful to my rare fit of conscience."

She felt her humiliation ease. "You're not refusing me because you don't like me, then."

"On the contrary . . ."

She smiled. "I'm glad."

And suddenly it seemed that she was standing much too close, the scent of her overwhelming his senses, her eyes filled with an innocence and expectation so sweet he could almost taste it.

"At least take me for a ride," she softly implored.

And so Eve might have spoken, he thought, trying to resist. "We shouldn't."

"We don't have to go far."

Regardless how innocent her remark, all he could think of was the more explicit act of plunging in as far as possible. "I'm not virtuous," he gruffly said.

"We'll take along my groom."

A threesome, he perversely reflected. "As a chaperon," he more decorously noted.

She arched her brows faintly. "If you need one."

What he needed, he shouldn't have. "You're damned tempting. You know that."

"I don't, actually. I've never thought about another man—in those terms."

"I'm honored," he drawled.

"But not willing."

"I'm intimidated by purity," he lightly replied.

"Perhaps I could endeavor to be less pure."

He held up his hand. "Please—don't."

"I understand."

"I doubt you do, because I'm having a devil of a time understanding it myself."

"At least let's enjoy a morning ride. If I bring Dieter along, will you agree?"

"I suppose," he slowly said, thinking, *How can it hurt with her groom along?* "It's a shame to waste such a beautiful day."

"We *are* both up and dressed," she pointed out, admiring his silky black hair, gleaming with blue highlights in the sun.

He grinned. "So why be difficult?"

Her smile was dazzling. "I didn't want to say it."

And on that harmonious note, Max called for their horses and the princess's groom, and in short order they were cantering over frost-tinged fields.

Chapter 5

They rode a considerable distance because the morning was beautiful, their horses primed to run, and in truth, they both found themselves susceptible to feelings of rare well-being. Tremaine wanted to gallop full out after traveling in a boxcar from London, and Max's huge black kept pace with ease. Christina was a skilled rider, taking Tremaine over the jumps with an effortless grace. After a particularly high hedgerow that she and her mount executed with finesse, Max saluted her.

She waved back and shouted, "I'll race you to Digby!"

They flew across the fields, their two hunters well-matched, the horses' long-legged strides leaving Dieter and his mount far behind. A church bell chimed in the distance, a clear and silvery sound on the bright, frosty morning, and Christina felt joyously alive for the first time in ages. Prone to intemperate stimuli that reminded him quite often that he was alive, the marquis experienced instead a novel sense of contentment.

They smiled at each other, a conspiratorial intimacy in the gesture, as though they alone were cognizant of the blissful wonder in living.

Coming over a rise a short time later, Max pointed toward a cluster of buildings in the distance. Raising his voice enough to be heard above the galloping hooves, he shouted, "I'll take you to breakfast!"

"I'd love it!"

"Last one there has to sit by Lady Moffet at dinner tonight!"

Christina whipped Tremaine, urging her hunter to more speed, and they raced down the slope, neck and neck. At the last, with the cobbled street in view, Max's mount surged ahead and took the victory by a half dozen strides.

He had been holding his thoroughbred back, Christina realized, the powerful black's sprint for the finish effortless. But she enjoyed the exhilaration of racing, win or lose, and as they reined their lathered horses to a walk, she cast him a teasing glance. "I thought a gentleman always lets a lady win."

"Sorry." Max's dark brows flickered upward. "I had more incentive."

"What makes you think you're Lady Moffet's dinner partner again tonight?"

"She informed me I was such a superb conversationalist she would request my company."

"I see." Christina's eyes sparkled with amusement. "Your charm is universal."

"It wasn't charm, but my silence, that was irresistible," he replied. "Lady Moffet prefers the sound of her own voice."

"And now I'm to save you."

"You lost. You have to."

"Truly you knew I'd lose against that huge brute you ride. But I'm gracious in defeat." She grinned. "Actually, Lady Moffet and my mother are friends."

"Perfect. I shall repay you for the favor, of course."

"How nice."

His eyes narrowed at her purr. "I *meant*—I would repay you with some social courtesy."

"What I have in mind is of a social nature, my lord."

"What *I* had in mind," he sardonically noted, "was in the nature of a gift—like flowers."

"Or maybe another kind of gift. I hear you have a remarkable reputation for giving."

"But not to women who are only intent on wreaking vengeance on their husbands."

"Do you normally ask first?" she archly inquired. "I doubt I'm the only lady so motivated."

"But the first of such alarming innocence."

"So if I were not so innocent?"

"I would have fucked you last night." He was intentionally blunt, wanting her to understand what she was asking for wasn't moonbeams and roses.

She colored at the lewd word. "I see," she replied on a small inhalation.

"You're very beautiful, Princess—and desirable—but I'm not in the market for novice paramours."

"I'll have to find someone else, then."

He was surprised at his aversion to her statement. But well trained in avoiding personal entanglements, he only said, "Suit yourself."

"You're very annoying." She wrinkled her nose and then suddenly smiled. "You're not at all like your reputation."

"Only because you're out of your league, darling." He grinned. "Now, let's have breakfast and talk of something else besides your quest for vengeance."

"Very well," she agreed, but her quest for vengeance had taken second place to her increasing attraction to this man whom all the world saw as a libertine and she found only extremely kind.

As they were dismounting before the inn, Dieter caught up with them and took over the horses, leading them to the stables for a much needed rest. The marquis and Christina found the parlor bustling with locals when they entered, the timber and beamed room filled to overflowing. But a table was quickly brought in for such fine gentry, several parties were squeezed closer together, and very soon, Max and the princess found themselves seated before the crackling fire.

"I just love early mornings." Taking off her gloves, Christina smiled. "Don't you?"

"Sometimes. Particularly this morning," he graciously added. "And if I have some food soon, life will be perfect."

"I agree. The simple pleasures—fresh air, bright sunshine, good food."

"And pleasant company."

She was lifting off her hat, and for a fleeting moment, she felt as though they were alone in the noisy parlor—in the world.

Perhaps he felt it, too, and in response, deliberately changed the subject. "I do thank you for saving me from Lady Moffet tonight."

"I don't mind in the least." The spell broken, Christina removed her hat and placed it beside her gloves on the table. "I'll ask her about her daughter's new baby, and then all I'll have to do is listen." Catching sight of Dieter at the entrance to the parlor, she said, "Excuse me a moment," and went to speak to him. Returning shortly, she smiled at Max as she sat down. "They've managed to find room for him in the kitchen, even in this mad crowd. Apparently, it's market day. It's warm in here, isn't it?" She began unbuttoning her jacket. "Are you as hungry as I? It must be the brisk air." Sliding off her jacket, she tossed it on the chair back.

She shouldn't have done that, he was thinking, his gaze on the swell of her breasts beneath the delicate white silk of her blouse, and it took him a fraction of a second to recall her question. "I'm always hungry"—the word suddenly ambiguous in meaning—"brisk air or not," he crisply finished, cautioning himself to constraint.

She surveyed him briefly. "You look as though you have a hearty appetite."

Everything she said or did struck him as suggestive, and he chided himself for having such lewd thoughts when her reason for being here had already been put to rest. In any event, she wasn't practiced enough for seduction. "Would you like tea or coffee first?" he asked, consciously diverting the conversation to a neutral topic.

"What would you like?"

There. Again. It didn't bear thinking what he would like with so many bedrooms conveniently above them. She was off limits. "I prefer coffee," he said, disconcerted at the surge of desire warming his blood.

"Coffee would be fine."

"Have tea if you like." He didn't wish her to be so obliging when lust was taking center stage in his brain.

"Coffee actually sounds good on a cold morning. I like mine hot and sweet, with only a little cream."

Good God, was she some experienced courtesan in disguise? Hot and sweet and creamy sounded damned enticing—like her. And for an ungovernable moment, he thought of jettisoning common sense and sending Dieter away.

Fortunately a young maid came to take their order just then, for he wasn't sure he could continue to act the gentleman, regardless of the fact they were in a parlor filled with people and she was a babe in the woods of adulterous intrigue. And when the young girl left, he began talking of Christina's sons in an effort to curb his unbridled impulses.

They spoke of her boys' school, of the teachers and subjects they liked best, and for all the world, the marquis could have been an interested parent, his comments pertinent and apt, insightful at times. And when the coffee came and then the food, they ate with hearty appetites and a level of comfort generally given only to those of long acquaintance.

The coffee was, indeed, hot and sweet and overtly stimulating to senses that in truth required no other stimulus, proximity alone sufficient spur. And before Christina had finished her first cup of coffee and omelet, she was experiencing a heated pulsing deep inside she had never felt before. She shifted slightly in her seat, but the movement only heightened the pleasurable sensation, the lush tingling between her thighs increasing in intensity.

He noticed. Her small stirring, the flush on her cheeks, the compelling fragrance of her perfume as her skin heated. Expert at recognizing the signs of female arousal, he was faced with a difficult dilemma.

He had never refused a lady who intrigued him—never. And the question of her inexperience and motive no longer seemed as germane as it had even a half hour ago.

How much did it really matter—whether he played the gallant? Was his refusal chivalrous or simply expedient? Had he posed the gentleman for her sake or because, in truth, he didn't relish teaching in bed?

"Are you almost finished eating?" Her voice held a questioning note distinct from the words.

"If you wish." He put down his flatware. "Would you like to leave? I could fetch Dieter," he offered, trying to read her tone, her expression, unsure of his own feelings.

"I sent Dieter back to Shelagh's."

His pulse leaped.

"I hope you don't mind."

Fucking you? he thought. *Not likely.* The question was more one of frightening the hell out of her with the increasing violence of his need. He glanced around the room, wondering how closely everyone was monitoring their conversation.

"Have I embarrassed you?"

He softly snorted, and when she smiled back, he abruptly grinned. "To hell with decency it seems. Although I blame you completely," he sardonically added.

She didn't look disconcerted; she looked pleased. "You've overcome your scruples?"

"More or less." His dark gaze took on a predatory cast. "As long as you understand the rules."

"You have rules?"

"There are always rules, darling. For everything."

"You don't look like the type to abide authority."

"Call it custom, then, convention, like your role of virtuous wife. Are you sure you want to do this?" One dark brow rose in speculation. "Last chance."

She nodded. "I've never felt this way before, tingly and heated, restless. I blame you completely." Her smile was playful as she repeated his phrase. "Feel my hand; feel how warm I am."

He drew back slightly, uncomfortable with the degree of his longing.

Emboldened by the small initiatives she had taken, pleased she had sent Dieter away, she disregarded his withdrawal and leaned across the table. "Then, I'll touch you." Placing her palm on the back of his hand, she gazed up at him. "See?"

It felt as though her flesh was melting into his, and whatever last reservations he may have harbored evaporated in the heat of that startling fusion. "I'll get us a room," he brusquely said, abruptly coming to his feet, his chair almost toppling over with his swift rise. He had already taken a step when he turned back and smiled. "Don't go away."

"You don't know how far I've come for this," she softly replied. "I'm not going anywhere."

He nodded, acknowledging the parity of their need. "I'll be right back."

She watched him thread his way through the thronged room, his progress closely attended. It wasn't often a fine gentleman was seen in the parlor of the Digby inn, and rarely one so handsome, although his air of confidence was equally attractive. He exuded an intrinsic competence quite apart from his tall, broad-shouldered physicality—as though he were capable of taking on anyone or anything. And in terms of pleasing the ladies, according to gossip and Lulu, his confidence was well-founded, she mused, anticipation warming her senses.

Just looking at him sent a tremor up her spine, and she wondered whether it was the novelty of the circumstances or her inexperience or simply his potent allure that made her feel so fevered. And were she not so overwhelmed with desire, she might have questioned the stark difference between her current emotions and those she had experienced in the conjugal bed.

But he was almost instantly back, striding toward her with a faint smile on his face, and all she could think of was how gloriously beautiful he was. "Everything's ready," he murmured, lifting her hat and gloves from the table, her jacket from the back of her chair, before helping her to her feet. "This way." His voice was low, aware of the attention they attracted, and with his hand at the back of her waist, he guided her through the staring patrons.

No one spoke to them in the small lobby, although Christina was conscious of the landlord's scrutiny. "He won't say anything," Max quietly noted, as though reading her thoughts. "A few more steps and we're out of sight." The carved balustrade shielded them on their ascent, and as they reached the top of the stairs, he kissed her—a light, butterfly kiss on her cheek. When she looked up in surprise, he pulled her close and kissed her again—on the mouth—and this time there was nothing delicate or trifling in the pressure of his lips. This time he invaded her mouth and tasted, slowly savored, his tongue exploring, teasing, probing, eliciting deep-felt, blissful sighs from the lady. Bringing his erection hard between them, he reminded them both that gratification had many guises.

But it disturbed him that he felt such enchantment from mere kisses. It was a critical matter of independence, perhaps, or a libertine's fear of such wholesome emotion. Releasing her, he stepped back. "I'm not used to this," he ambiguously said.

"Nor I." Immune to his ambiguity, she was trembling with desire, her voice barely audible. "I'm going to melt right here."

"No, you're not," he quickly said, galvanized by selfish motive, on familiar ground once again. Handing her her hat and gloves, her jacket, he lifted her into his arms and carried her down the hall to the room he had engaged. Shoving the door open with his booted foot, he quickly crossed the threshold and kicked the door shut. Setting Christina on her feet, he turned to lock the door.

"You remembered this time."

"Don't remind me," he muttered. "You shouldn't have seen that."

"So, you're not an exhibitionist."

"Hardly." His voice was curt, annoyed at her reminder of other women when he was feeling such unprecedented, almost adolescent lust.

"Don't be angry. Please."

And then he felt a brute—like her bloody husband, probably, who had made her so damned timid. "I'm not—angry. I'm sorry . . . really. Here"—he held out his hand—"come sit with me."

"I don't know if I can."

"Just over here," he said, taking her hand, thinking her afraid.

"I mean"—she lifted her free hand so he could see the tremor—"I don't know if I can move."

"Jesus . . ." After all the technically proficient ladies in his life, he was momentarily dumfounded. "You're sure?" He had assumed so innocent a lover would require lengthy foreplay. "You won't be frightened?"

She shook her head, clearly teetering on the brink.

If she wanted instant gratification, he was more than willing. Quickly carrying her to the bed, he gently lowered her to the quilted coverlet.

"Hurry!" she whispered.

Pushing her riding skirt up over her thighs with a sweep of his hand, he reached for the ties of her drawers, pulled open the bow, eased the yellow silk garment down her legs and tossed it aside.

But the instant his fingers touched her pulsing labia, she uttered a small sob and began climaxing. Quickly slipping two fingers up her hot, slick vagina, he stroked and massaged with the expertise of much practice, matched the undulating rhythm of her hips with deftness, penetrated the exact distance most beneficial to sensation. She was dripping wet; his fingers slid over her throbbing tissue like silk on silk, and he longed to bury himself in her hot, sweet interior and fuck himself to death.

And he would just as soon as her orgasm was complete.

He waited until her last shudder subsided—just barely—and then driven by the same urgent need that had brought her impetuously to climax, he tore open the buttons of his riding pants, climbed between her legs, boots and all, and plunged inside her. He shouldn't have, he knew. He was never precipitate; his reputation, in part, based on his aptitude for artful foreplay. But he wasn't expert now, or discreet or interested in finesse. Impelled by a ravenous lust, he drove into her like a man possessed, fiercely, ferociously, mindlessly. But even in the throes of an unbridled, predacious frenzy, his natural talent for fornication, the expert rhythm of his lower body cultivated in numerous boudoirs around the world, afforded the princess ravishing, untrammeled pleasure. Transported to a sensual paradise previously unknown to her, she greedily clung to him, melted around him, opened her thighs wider to each powerful thrust, absorbing the entirety of his superlative length with small, panting cries of ravishment and bliss.

He heard it finally, his sensibilities attuned to female cries of passion regardless of his delirium and struggling to regain a modicum of control, suppressing his urgent need to plunge forward again only with supreme effort, he paused. "Have I hurt you?" he whispered, unsure of her cries.

She shook her head and arched her hips upward, exquisite rapture beginning to peak once more.

Relieved, gratified, desperately thankful, he drove in again, impaling her on the flowered coverlet, holding her prisoner with the rigid length of his erection, stretching her for a savage, pitiless moment before withdrawing marginally for the next downstroke.

"Don't, don't . . . Don't you dare!" Her hands pressed hard on his back, her voice harsh with need, any previous trace of innocence burned away.

His fingers splayed wider as he tightened his grip on her hips, the feel of her soft, pliant flesh heavenly, like the heated silk of her cunt, and he gave her what she wanted, what he wanted, ravished her, gorged her, unequivocally filled her—her wild screams a gauge, a measure, a yardstick for the extreme limits of penetration. And when she began climaxing again, he hoped the landlord was sufficiently dégagé to overlook cries of passion.

But he prudently glanced at the door to make sure the latch was in place.

Once her orgasm had diminished to the whispery sighs of fulfillment, he allowed himself his own release, withdrawing at the last possible moment and coming on her belly, arching his back against the excessive violence of his ejaculations. For endless, fevered moments, he forgot where he was, forgot to breathe, forgot everything but the wild, pulsing orgasm jolting his body, each spasm pouring through him with such shocking intensity he shut his eyes against the agonizing pleasure.

Chapter 6

For a lengthy time, only the sound of labored breathing broke the silence.

And then the marquis opened his eyes. "The quilt is pink," he murmured.

Christina's lashes slowly lifted. "So is the canopy."

His gaze moved to her face, and he smiled. "Hello there."

"Now that I've returned to the world," she breathed, her voice redolent with pleasure, "hello back."

"There are those moments," he softly agreed.

"*Now* I know why Lulu does what she does."

He felt a small, niggling resistance to the idea she follow in Lulu's footsteps. "I wouldn't recommend it."

"And why is that?" Her gaze was amused. "Coming from a man of your repute."

"Never mind." He didn't know, himself, why the notion bothered him.

"I suppose they're not all like you."

"I didn't mean that."

Feeling blissfully at peace with the world, she was immune to equivocation and uncertainty. "I promise not to ask any more difficult questions. Except perhaps for one." Her smile was lush.

"Later. And if you don't think me overly bold, I'd like to say you have too many clothes on."

His brows rose. "Forgive me. I was under the impression speed was critical."

She grinned. "I'm no better than Lulu. Do you ever get a chance to take off your boots first?"

It wasn't a question he was about to answer. "Give me a minute to catch my breath and I'll take them off."

"I apologize for pressing you so, but everything felt so wonderful and I was afraid I'd lose those fabulous sensations and I'd never feel like that again and well . . . I've never climaxed before; so you see I couldn't be expected to just stop and wait and hope that maybe . . ." Her voice trailed off.

"I see," he mildly said, masking his surprise. Either Prince Hans didn't believe in giving pleasure to a wife or he perceived sex as an act of self-gratification. Although, knowing Gina, he doubted she would allow such selfishness in a lover.

"So if you're not too . . . er, tired—or finished or something—I was hoping we might do it again. If you don't mind, of course," she quickly added, in the manner a young child might ask for a second piece of cake.

"Why would I mind?"

Her eyes widened. After sex, Hans had always immediately left her bed. "Really. How very tempting you are."

"No more than you," he murmured, gazing at her. Her cheeks were pink with the afterglow of passion, her pale hair curling in unruly tendrils at her temples. She looked dew fresh, vulnerable as a young girl with her startled gaze, and he found himself curiously tempted to protect her.

"I'm so very glad you asked me riding."

It took him a moment to reply because his original reservations aside, he was faced now with further complications having to do with sensibilities other than sex. Unnerving feelings of fondness, or worse—affection.

"Don't worry," she said, recognizing his hesitation. "I won't cling."

"It's not that. It's just that I'm—"

"Much in demand. I understand."

"No. Rather, you attract me more than I'd like," he said, questioning his sanity; honesty was always a disadvantage in matters of amour.

"And you dislike anything emotional. I understand. I shan't be demanding, although, if you don't mind too much, I'm still tingly and throbbing with this delicious aching need, and I want you very much . . . and *very* soon." She wrinkled her nose. "I'm so sorry, and after I said I wouldn't be demanding."

He laughed. "You needn't apologize. I'm more than happy to oblige." Time enough to concern himself with novel feelings after he was done fucking her.

"I'd be ever so grateful." She smiled up at him. "Would you mind if I kissed you? I have this overwhelming desire to kiss you and touch you and hold you and stay in this bed with you forever and—"

He interrupted her wishful litany with a kiss, wanting what she wanted, even though sex wasn't just sex this time, even though he should be questioning the significance of tender feelings, even though the word "forever" was frightening the hell out of him.

When his mouth lifted from hers a leisurely time later, she whispered, "How can you make me feel like this with only a kiss?"

He didn't know, no more than he understood why it wasn't possible to view this encounter as simple sex. "I'll be right back," he murmured, rising from the bed, thinking he should walk away—from her, from the room, from the weekend party.

Had she said something wrong? Was he leaving? In a moment of panic, she tried to decipher his brief comment, his tone of voice.

But he only walked a few steps to the washstand, rinsed himself, set his riding breeches to rights, wet another towel, grabbed a dry one from the rack, returned to the bed and without comment wiped his semen from her stomach. Were they leaving? Had he changed his mind about more sex? Was this the only climax she would ever have? Unfamiliar with the protocol of sexual affairs, dismayed at the possible curtailment of the most wonderful pleasure she had ever experienced, she watched him as though she might glimpse a clue in his actions.

"Now then," he said, avoiding any further enigmatic dilemmas, reverting to type with practiced ease, "you also have a great deal too many clothes on." He dropped the towels on the floor and stripped off his jacket. "Lift one foot," he softly ordered, reaching for her boot.

She raised her leg. "I thought you might want to leave. I don't want to go back."

"Not ever?" Not sure what she meant, he was equally unsure why he was pursuing the subject. Dropping her boot on the floor, he cautioned himself against becoming involved.

"At least not soon. For purely selfish reasons," she added, lifting her other leg for him.

"We could go somewhere else." Easing off her second boot, he seriously considered he had lost his mind. What the hell had come over him?

"We could?"

She looked so hopeful, he heard himself saying, "I could send Shelagh a note—make some excuse," as though some stranger were occupying his body and brain and speaking with utter disregard for his principles of noninvolvement. But in the process of sliding her white lace garter and stocking down her leg, he decided bizarre as the idea was, having those long, shapely legs wrapped around him for an extended time was motive enough. And the bizarre suddenly took on the aspect of a workable premise.

"Dieter knows we're here, though."

He took off her second garter and stocking. "We won't stay long."

"Do you do this often? And I don't know why I'm even asking, except I feel as though I'm stepping off the edge of the world and—"

"I'm walking over the edge with you," he softly said. "And don't ask me why because I haven't a clue. Except I want to make love to you until I can't make love anymore, until I don't have breath to move." His expression went grim for a moment. "And I'm not exceedingly happy about it."

"I'm sorry."

"Don't be." His sudden smile was open, boyish. "Actually, I'm looking forward to it."

She sat up and threw her arms around him. "You're absolutely wonderful—perfect and wonderful and I feel as though I'm fifteen again." She paused because she wouldn't have dared do what she was doing at fifteen, but then she hadn't been betrayed a thousand times yet either. Consciously repressing such unhappy thoughts, she smiled at the man who had offered her a delicious new kind of liberation. "So tell me how long we can stay in this lovely pink bed, and how often you'll make love to me—and tell me, tell me, *tell* me this isn't a dream."

Leaning back so he could see her face, he smiled at her enthusiasm. "If it's a dream, don't wake me." He had his own pronounced feelings of delight. "And we can safely stay here at least another hour. No one will miss us until lunch. And since we have a limited time, I'll only make love to you a thousand million times."

The joy in her eyes was unmistakable."You're much too good to me."

"This isn't an unselfish act, darling. Not even slightly. Now, sit back and I'll unbutton these very small buttons on your blouse."

"Let me. I can do it faster." She slipped her arms from his shoulders and reached for the blouse buttons. "If we only have an hour . . ."

He took her hands in his, eased them down, held them in place for a moment. "We're not racing this time. Dieter won't arrive back at the house for another half hour, and even if someone were to come looking for us—"

She opened her mouth to speak, and he stopped her protest with a quick, brushing kiss. "This time," he murmured, his mouth warm, grazing her lips, "I'm going to make you come—very slowly."

She smiled, took a deep breath. "I'll try to relax. I don't even know how to thank you for this—for this incredible wonder. I'm thirty years old. I've been married for twelve years and I never knew what I was missing."

Releasing her hands, he dipped his head and grinned. "Pleased to be of service, ma'am."

"Not as pleased as I," she purred.

"Wait till next time."

"It's better? No!"

He laughed. "It *will* be better . . . and longer"—his voice turned soft—"and deeper and slower, and I hope you don't bring the landlord up here with your screams."

Her eyes flared wide with shock. "I didn't scream."

He gently nodded.

"Oh, my God . . ."

Amusement gleamed in his eyes. "It's not a problem so long as the door's locked."

"You don't mind?"

"Why should I mind?"

She blushed. "It seems so—"

"Hot and sexy?"

"Really? Sexy?" She said the word hesitantly, as though it were foreign to her tongue.

"It's all right to be sexy, darling. In fact, it's a real asset. And you have plenty of natural talent."

"I do?"

He was dealing with an ingenue regardless of the fact she had been married so long. "You really do," he whispered.

"Suddenly, I feel as though I have to make up for lost time."

He couldn't tell if she was teasing or serious, her words so softly put. "I'm available," he offered, sliding a hairpin from her chignon. "For lost time or making up time or any time at all." He pulled another hairpin out.

"I may turn out to be demanding after all," she said, clearly pleased with the prospect.

"I'll do my best to accommodate you." His wink was deliciously wicked.

She softly sighed. "You must be every woman's dream come true."

Uncomfortable with such allusions, he said, "Here, you hold the pins," and cupping her fingers, he placed the hairpins in her palm.

"I warn you," she playfully noted, warmed by his close proximity, by his modesty, by tremulous anticipation, "I may no longer be as compliant as I once was. I climaxed, you see, and I'm feeling empowered by the sheer delight of that accomplishment."

"Interesting," he said, this man who had always felt empowered. "Are you going to take charge?" His tone had turned roguish.

"I might." She grinned. "Just as soon as I learn how to swim a little better—metaphorically speaking. Lulu said you'd be the perfect person to teach me how to swim. And she was right. Oh, dear"—a fleeting expression of surprise had crossed his face—"I suppose I shouldn't have said that. Do men talk like that with their friends?"

"I don't know. I don't." Two more hairpins came free and her pale hair tumbled to her shoulders.

"I suppose with all the ladies in your life, there's no need to discuss—" Her breath caught in her throat.

He was sliding his fingers through her hair, the delicacy of his touch triggering paradoxically forceful ripples through her vagina. She shut her eyes against the sublime sensation.

Content he had averted further discussion of the ladies in his life, more content with the sensuous feel of her hair slipping through his fingers, he was looking forward to the prospect of feeling more of the voluptuous lady he had taken riding this morning—the lady who would soon be riding him. Twining his fingers in her hair, he tugged her closer.

She leaned forward at the slight pressure, and he licked her lips. "I don't really care who's in charge," he whispered, "so long as we agree on the agenda."

"Which is?" She touched his tongue with hers.

"Whatever you want—twice," he murmured, his smile close.

"How nice," she breathed. "Perhaps I could return the compliment and raise you one."

Such unqualified license brought his erection surging upward, and through the soft leather chamois, she felt it against her thigh. Reaching down, she stroked the length of it with her palm, his prodigal size warming her with a rush of pleasure. "I'll try to be good. I'll try not to hurry, but"—she took a deep breath at the sudden movement beneath her hand—"I can't promise . . ."

He felt for a moment as though he might be incapable of restraint as well, the feel of her small hand impacting his desires more than he wished, but understanding the merit in delay, he eased her hand away. "Later," he said, grasping her around the waist, lifting her away, setting her against the pillows at the head of the bed. "Be patient for a minute and I'll be right with you."

Bending over, he quickly removed his boots and stockings and then turned back to her. "Now we're essentially at the same place. I'll take off your blouse, you take off my shirt, and so on," he said, smiling faintly, "and we'll see if it's possible to actually get undressed before we come."

"So I'm not the only impatient one."

His lashes lowered fractionally. "My friends would be shocked."

"As would mine."

"I'm not complaining."

"Nor am I. On the contrary," she noted, lazily stretching so her large breasts rose provocatively before his eyes, "I find this paradise of the senses so exquisite, I'm tempted to disregard everything else my mother told me as well."

"So she told you nothing of these pleasures?" Reaching over, he touched a peaked nipple prominent beneath the fabric of her blouse. "In a way, I'm glad," he whispered, delicately squeezing the taut bud between his thumb and forefinger. He couldn't bring himself to say he would have been jealous of the men before him. "I'm glad this was all saved for me," he said instead.

"And this," she whispered, lifting her other breast, offering the nipple to him, the sweet ache between her thighs encouraging an unguarded behavior she couldn't have imagined prior to meeting the marquis.

He took the other nipple as well, lightly squeezing, feeling the distended tissue swell beneath his fingers, harden, and when she swayed into his hands and softly moaned, he pushed her away so her nipples stretched taut under the pressure.

She was going to come, she thought, with his touch alone, fully dressed, not even kissed. She said very softly, "Please . . . ," and he knew what she wanted.

He released her, and she whimpered in protest.

But he gently kissed her and laid her back on the pillows and said, "Soon."

Unfastening the buttons on her blouse with expertise, he eased the garment off her shoulders, down her arms, his large hands holding hers until the last when he slipped the blouse over her fingers.

The air should have been cool on her skin, but she was so heated, she felt relieved. But not relieved enough, she began to unbutton the waistband of her skirt.

"You can't." He lifted her hands away. "I won't let you."

Her heated gaze held his for a still moment. "You have to."

He knew what she meant. "As soon as I undress you," he softly promised, freeing her skirt buttons.

"I wish I could tell you to go to hell," she whispered, taut with nerves and wanting.

His brows rose faintly. "You surprise me, Princess." He hadn't heard her swear before; indeed, she had appeared proper, even docile, yesterday.

"Maybe I'll make *you* wait when I undress you."

"If you last that long." Lifting her hips slightly, he pulled her skirt down and threw it over the footboard. "Ummm . . . nice." She was naked below the waist, the gentle curve of her hips, the pale curls on her mons, her soft pink thighs exposed in all their beauty, her willingness not in question with the glisten of moisture on her labia. And then she flexed her spine, an unconscious courtesan's gesture, and her plump breasts thrust upward, quivered. "You don't wear a corset," he said, as though taking note of some technicality. Her chemise stretched tightly across her ostentatious bosom.

"Not when I'm riding."

"Riding what?" he suggestively murmured, his erection increasing in length at such a pleasant prospect.

"You, of course," she whispered, as though she had planned this, as though she knew she would be lying here, her thighs spread, waiting for him to enter her.

"We'll have to see how well you ride."

"And whether you can handle me."

He laughed. "That should be interesting." He pulled his shirt over his head, too much in haste to unbutton it.

"I was supposed to do that."

"I changed my mind."

"You can and I can't?"

"I'm bigger than you. Stronger."

"That's not fair."

"I think you'll like it anyway. Move over."

She held his gaze for a taut moment.

"Be a good girl," he whispered.

After another moment of hesitation, she complied.

He settled beside her, lounging back against the headboard. "I'm ready if you're ready." Part teasing, part sparring discord, all sardonic drawl, his dark gaze was shuttered.

"You're annoying me."

His grin flashed white, but it was sportive more than playful. "How much?" he asked, unbuttoning his breeches and sliding them off.

His erection was enormous. She could almost feel it sinking deep inside her, the spiking rush of pleasure effectively muting her resentments.

"Feeling better?" he murmured, as though her emotions were transparent.

"Moderately . . ." She could be dégagé, too.

He held out his hand to her. "This is new for both of us—this inordinate, perhaps unwise desire. But come, darling." And this time his smile filled his eyes. "I can't wait either."

"You make me wild with wanting," she whispered, taking his hand. And quivering with need, she allowed him to lift her over his legs until she was straddling his thighs. Wondering if others felt such unbridled longing, she softly sighed as he raised her and steadied her while she slowly eased down his rigid length. Her tissue slowly yielded, slowly absorbed his length, his hands at her waist allowing only a circumspect descent until she was fully impaled.

And at that moment of consummate saturation, they both caught their breath.

He was sober. It was ten o'clock in the morning. And he was obsessed, he thought, the wild, unmitigated pleasure he felt beyond compare.

Awed, trembling, overcome by delirious sensation, she thanked destiny and all the mystical, astral fates that she had decided to go riding.

He moved. Infinitesimally.

And she screamed.

For a riveting moment neither could distinguish the perimeters of reality. And then she felt the strength of his shoulders beneath her hands, and he, the small flexing of her fingers. When she panted, "More . . . more," he indulged her and himself as well, wondering for the first time in his life whether one could die of pleasure. He almost immediately wished to argue against it, preferring less emotion with his lust. But then she leaned forward the slightest distance, her warm breasts flattening against his chest, and she licked a path up his cheek. "I want more . . ."

He flexed his hips and thighs, thrust upward with all his strength, and she instantly came, her face against his, her sighs warm on his cheek, the ripples of her vagina adding new dimension to his erection.

It took enormous self-control to resist climaxing with her; but he couldn't with safety, and she wasn't finished yet. And he would have leisurely brought her to orgasm a few more times, had he not been obsessed.

But he was, desperation a new phenomenon for the man who held records for stamina at a good many brothels here and abroad. And when she was at last replete, he rolled over her and made love to her again—for her, for himself, for obsession.

She was wet, slippery wet, and her long legs fit his hips to perfection. He slid into her with such ease, they could have been the matrix for making love, for consummation, for primal mating.

"I'm never letting you go," she whispered, heated, near orgasmic again, so near to paradise, she could smell the lilies. "I'm sorry . . ."

"And I'm going to fuck you for a hundred years," he breathed, not sure a century would be long enough, feeling the way he was feeling now. "Sorry . . ."

And then she lifted her hips to draw him in deeper, and he gasped and counted to ten in Arabic and then whispered, "Hurry, because I can't wait much longer."

But gentleman that he was, and as well-trained as he was, he managed to curtail his orgasm until she had come again, and with the merest hairsbreadth of control remaining, he pulled out and braced on his hands to come on her stomach in an endless convulsion, his heart beating like a drum, his brain on hold, rapture flooding over him like liquid sunshine.

She kissed him afterward, pulling his face down and covering it with kisses, on his eyes and nose, his chin and mouth, on his fine dark brows, on his smile.

"Those are all thank-yous." She gazed into the warmth of his eyes. "And I've lots more when you have time."

"For that, I'll make time." His kissed the slender bridge of her nose. "But if you'll excuse me for a minute, I need a towel, you need a towel . . . we both—"

A soft knock on the door gave rise to a look of terror on Christina's face.

Putting a finger to his mouth in warning, Max climbed from the bed. "Who is it?" His voice was cool, unruffled, but he was reaching for a towel and his breeches as he spoke.

"It's me, boss."

"I'll be right there." Turning to Christina, he smiled in reassurance as he pulled on his pants. "It's my valet, Danny, and don't worry, he's always one step ahead of everyone."

But Max was frowning slightly when he stepped out into the hall a few moments later. After making sure the door was closed behind him, he quickly inquired, "Is someone looking for us?"

"No, boss, it ain't that. I got better news. Thought you'd like to know that Prince Hans took off this morning with that there actress you know—the Campbell woman."

The marquis's frown vanished, and he slowly smiled. "You don't say."

"Damned right. Around eight, eight-thirty. Off they went in

his carriage, half-dressed, if you know what I mean. It didn't look as though they'd slept."

"I suppose Shelagh's is too crowded for them."

"I heard tell his wife rang a peal over him." Danny shrugged. "Might put a crimp in his fucking—along with all the people. Then when the princess's groom came back after they drove away, I figgered you'd decided to stay—for a while . . . like you do sometimes. So I asked Dieter a few questions. Nothin' he'd take no notice of, but enough so I could tell where you were at. Just in case that prince guy's leaving mattered a'tall."

"It does. Very much," Max affirmed. "Thank you." He glanced down the hall at the sound of a door opening, conscious of their vulnerability to gossip so close to Shelagh's. "Has anyone at the house missed us yet?"

Danny shook his head. "Most of them are out huntin', and the ladies who stayed behind—half of them ain't out of bed yet."

"Perfect." While he hadn't been overly concerned with playing truant from Shelagh's house party, he was pleased Hans was gone—for Christina's sake.

"Figgered you'd like to know what was goin' on. You didn't sleep too well last night, did ya?"

Danny probably knew Max as well as anyone. Max had found the tearful five-year-old on a bench outside the coach office in Helena, waiting for his stepfather to return. Danny's mother had been buried the day before, the boy had said through his tears, and his stepfather was coming right back. But the man had never been found.

"I suppose I kept you awake," Max acknowledged. "Sorry about that."

"Na . . . ya didn't, but I coulda helped you saddle up this morning."

"The lady was skittish." Max waggled his fingers in equivocation. "She still is. But I could use your help now. We're going to leave here and go"—he shrugged—"somewhere. I'm not sure where. I'll send a note to Lady Temple with some suitable story.

With the prince gone, our absence shouldn't be a problem, but I'm—*we're* going to need some clothes. You'll have to be discreet."

"The princess's maid is right friendly. Shouldn't be a problem there."

Danny was never at a loss endearing himself to a female he fancied.

"Even then," Max warned, "be careful not to tell her anything."

"Don't worry, boss. I'll get the clothes and she won't be none the wiser."

"I'll send you a message with our direction." Max nodded toward the door. "I can't stay. The princess is nervous."

"Right, boss."

Danny was already halfway down the hall by the time Max closed the door and turned to Christina.

"Do they know?" she nervously asked. "Is someone looking for us?" Partially dressed in her skirt and blouse, she was seated on a chair, pulling on her boot.

"No one's looking for us."

Leaning back, she visibly relaxed and dropped the boot, only to look up with suspicion a moment later. "Why did your valet come here, then? And why aren't you smiling?"

"Danny brought some news. Good news, bad news—I'm not sure. You decide."

She frowned faintly. "That sounds apprehensive."

"It's about your husband."

"Hardly good news, then." She straightened her shoulders. "Tell me."

"He left Shelagh's about eight this morning—"

Her face lit up. "Wonderful. Good God, that's very good news."

"I didn't finish."

"You mean the bad news . . ."

"It depends how you look at it. He left with Gina."

"Ah." She smoothed a wrinkle from her skirt. "In the present circumstances, I can hardly take issue with that, can I?"

"Probably not. But if you'd rather—"

She shook her head. "I wouldn't. It's amazing how little Hans matters now, and I don't mean to put any pressure on you in any way. I only mean, I don't have to sit and wait any longer, sit and wait and hope he'll change." She smiled faintly. "I have you to thank for that."

"Don't thank me. You made that decision yourself when you sent Dieter away."

She pursed her lips. "I did, didn't I? So I have delivered *myself* from conjugal purgatory—taken the first step, as it were."

His dark gaze was serene; his calmness, an antidote to the dysfunction of her marriage.

"I consider myself fortunate to have been in the neighborhood."

"You *are* the neighborhood, darling. And the county, country and world at the moment. Not that I wish to alarm you," she courteously amended. "It's only for a weekend, and then we both go back to our lives."

"I'm not alarmed." And strangely he wasn't, when he had spent the greater part of his adult life taking instant alarm at territorial females. "So, are you interested in another venue, my liberated sweetheart? A larger bed perhaps, a different view out the window? More soundproof walls?" he teased.

"Am I your sweetheart?" She liked the sound of the word, liked the warm intonation, liked the man who had uttered it. And she had never actually been anyone's sweetheart, she realized—that truth not immediately apparent to a young woman who had married twelve years ago with stars in her eyes.

"Yes," he simply said, not questioning the staggering pronouncement.

"Then, I'm definitely interested in another venue so long as you're there with me."

"Count on it."

"Not *too* far away," she implored, the look in his eyes warming her blood, stirring all the familiar receptors. "Actually, something close would be nice . . ." She glanced at the bed.

"No." A brusque, soft command.

"You said they weren't looking for us."

"But they might."

"Send Shelagh a note."

"Be sensible, darling. Dieter knows."

"Do we have to leave right this instant?" She shifted slightly in the chair, the exquisite pulsing between her thighs potent blandishment to linger. "Couldn't we stay here just a little longer?" Grasping the heavy green velvet of her skirt, she lifted it upward, impelled by new and breathless desires, helpless against a seemingly insatiable longing. She slipped the hem over her feet, past her knees, pulling it higher until her bare thighs and nest of blond curls were fully exposed.

"Where are your drawers?"

"I don't know."

"Were you planning on riding without them?"

"How gruff you sound. Don't be angry with me." How irrelevant his questions were against the heated urgency of her need. "Let me feel you inside me once more before we go," she softly said. "Please . . ."

He should ignore her, see that they left as they should, but what man could withstand such blatant temptation? "Just once," he cautioned. "Dieter might return."

"I'd be ever so grateful," she whispered, oblivious to his caveats. "See how wet I am, how much I need you?"

A tiny rivulet of pearly fluid oozed down her inner thigh.

He took a deep breath. "You understand. We can't stay long."

"Whatever you say. I'll do whatever you say."

A score of salacious possibilities flooded his brain; but he knew better than to gamble with her reputation, and he wasn't so new at this game that he couldn't wait.

But she was and she couldn't.

So he went to her. Kneeling between her legs, he eased her thighs wider, moved in closer, and slid his fingers slowly down the slick folds of her labia, opening her. As he bent forward, she stopped him, tugging on his hair, raising his head. "What are you doing?"

His hands slid away. "Making you come."

"You can't do that. I—that is . . . you—can't."

"It's up to you." He shifted slightly, as though he might rise. "We should go anyway."

"I didn't mean that." She had not released him, her fingers still twined in his hair.

"It's up to you." His gaze was bland. "We don't have much time."

"It's just that I've never . . ."

"It's an orgasm, darling. You like those . . ."

"Couldn't you—"

"This is faster." Reaching up, he unclasped her fingers from his hair, brought her hands to his mouth and gently kissed her knuckles. "Trust me," he whispered, placing her hands on his shoulders. "Now hold on."

It wasn't as though she could constrain her desires. She was trembling, flushed, and if she didn't know how close she was to climax, he did.

His fingers were cool on her throbbing flesh, and she felt a quiver race through her senses when he touched her heated cleft. She tensed under the slight pressure, all her mother's admonitions about propriety and decorum recalled with a vengeance. He felt her stiffen and looked up. "It's just you and me, and I'm going to taste your sweet cunt whether you like it or not . . ."

Shamed, at his words, at his coercion, at her rush of pleasure, she breathed, "No . . ." A futile protest—a sop, perhaps, to motherly admonitions.

"But you like when I touch you—here . . ." And bending, he delicately licked the swollen nub of her clitoris.

She arched her back and choked back a scream as she felt a river of desire melt downward to the imprint of his tongue.

"Now, if you promise not to scream, I'll let you come twice." Spreading the verges of her labia wider, he circled the sleek, pulsing tissue with his fingertips. "And if you're very quiet, I'll fuck you in the carriage as soon as we leave here." Slipping two fingers up her vagina, he forced his palm hard against her clitoris and gently rotated his hand.

She whimpered at the first flowing ripples convulsing her fevered tissue.

"You can't scream . . ." He could almost feel her orgasm begin, and leaning forward, he tipped his head, drew her taut, throbbing clitoris into his mouth and gently suckled.

She tried not to cry out, moaning as the ecstasy jolted through her belly and thighs and aching genitals where the marquis's mouth and tongue were presently ensconced. But he continued sucking, and irrepressible rapture soared higher and higher—treacherous, hammering, rash, incautious pleasure. And lost to all reason, even the forfeiture of another orgasm melted in the hot flames of passion.

She screamed, a high, keening sound of release, and he smiled through the scent and taste of her.

He had been counting on her unbridled sensuality.

Now they could leave.

And their new lodgings—unknown to others—would afford the opportunity to explore their sexual compatibility at leisure.

Chapter 7

The marquis rented a small carriage—something he could drive himself—had their mounts tied on behind and then escorted Christina down a back stairway to the stable yard. In the lull between breakfast and lunch, with most of the village in the market square, they were able to depart the inn with a minimum of scrutiny. Max had also paid the innkeeper sufficiently well to erase recall of them from his mind should anyone inquire, and they drove north—away from the Temple estate.

"Where are you taking me?" With Max's arm around her shoulder, she leaned into his side, his solid warmth both comforting and enticing. "Not too far, I hope?"

Glancing down at her, he grinned. "I'm *not* stopping along the road."

Her smile was tantalizing. "Well then . . . I hope you find an inn soon."

"At the next village, I promise. The landlord at Digby said The Red Oak is only five miles north—off the main road a half mile and very secluded."

"Did he say 'very secluded' like that?"

"No," Max lied, her discomfort plain. Actually the landlord had uttered the words with a leer. But the man also recognized the jeopardy in compromising the Marquise of Vale's privacy. "If you're concerned with propriety, though, why don't I introduce you as my wife? It would avoid any undue curiosity."

"You don't mind?"

"Why should I mind? We don't know anyone at The Red Oak. Or God willing we won't."

"You don't think—someone, I mean—"

"No, darling. No," he firmly declared. "We're going to have all the privacy we wish. Shelagh's assuaged with a suitable excuse—my horse went lame, and we're resting him before coming back. Danny will bring us a change of clothes—surreptitiously," he quickly added at her look of alarm. "Really, he's very competent."

"Because you do this all the time, I suppose."

"No, because he's trustworthy; he's like part of the family."

"Unlike my family, who couldn't be trusted to understand this—"

"Sexual holiday?"

She laughed. "They couldn't even utter such an indecent phrase."

"Your sister, too?" He happened to be acquainted with Charlotte's husband, and the duke wasn't known for his faithfulness.

"I'm not so sure. When we had lunch last week, Charlotte said something that seemed strange to me at the time. She talked about Joe Harley and his hunting box—and his paintings. It sounded as though she'd been there."

"You two don't discuss your lives?"

"I thought we did. On the same hand, I doubt I'll tell her about you."

"Because of gossip?"

"Because I want to keep these memories for myself, and once you tell someone . . ."

"There might be rumors anyway. Just a warning." He shook

his head. "Not from me. I'd never discuss this with anyone, but there's a crush of people at Shelagh's." He shrugged. "You know what they're like."

"Bored and jaded and sometimes very dull. Not everyone, of course," she added with a grin. "You, for instance. Definitely not boring or dull."

"And jaded is only bad press," he observed with a twitch of his lips.

"I'm enjoying all your jaded expertise, my lord. I'm not complaining."

"And I'm enjoying your delightful innocence. It's been a long time."

"Since you've bedded a tyro?"

"Since I felt like I do now."

"I never have."

"We're fortunate," he softly said.

She took a small breath. "Indeed."

"With luck, we can hold this rare contentment—"

"At least until the party's over on Tuesday."

"So cynical." He was surprised it mattered.

"Just practical."

"You're not allowed to be practical until Tuesday morning."

"I don't want to be—I'd like to say, ever again—but I know better. Still, you've given me more than pleasure alone. . . . You've given me hope."

"For?"

He had this strange feeling he wished her to say something that would include him and just as quickly rejected such sentiment. Their lives were too disparate, too distant, their only compatibility transient pleasure.

"A life of more freedom. It's exhilarating. I'll be forever in your debt."

Did she mean sexual liberation? Would she become like so many women of her class—a participant in serial love affairs?

"What kind of freedom?" he deliberately asked, as if he had the right.

"Freedom to not wait anymore for something to happen in my life. Freedom to find my own path and my own pleasures."

"Are you staying in England long?" He shouldn't ask; he shouldn't care. He shouldn't want to be part of those pleasures.

"For another fortnight. And then my boys come home for the holidays. We always have snow in Silesia at Christmas. Will you be in England long?" she quickly interjected, searching for a less disconcerting topic than her home and children.

"I'm not sure." He had tickets to sail back to the States on Thursday.

A moment of awkward silence ensued as the world intruded into their rash and impromptu adventure.

Suddenly burdened with a heavy weight of guilt and accountability, Christina sat up straighter, distancing herself from Max as much as possible on the narrow carriage seat. "Maybe we should go back to Shelagh's."

"No." He may be unsure of his feelings and his future plans, but of one thing he was sure.

"What if I insist?"

"Then, I'll change your mind."

"Maybe you can't."

He noticed the equivocation. "Look, we're almost there." The small lane to the inn was in sight.

"I don't want to go."

"Because you know I can change your mind."

"Very well. Because of that. You're right. Are you happy?"

"I don't want to be right. I just want to be with you where no one is going to intrude."

"No." She shook her head. "I can't."

He turned down the country road, ignoring her protest.

"If you insist on this," she tartly said, "I'll embarrass you in front of everyone."

His laughter rang out. “You could try.”

Her mouth set in a prim line. “You’re beyond embarrassment? Is that it?”

“Long ago, darling.” He grinned. “But I doubt *you* are.”

“Are you threatening me?”

“I’m only pointing out that I’m more careless of my reputation than you,” he said with a teasing smile. “And if I’m in the mood to indulge myself, I might just carry you up the stairs to one of the empty rooms and lock the door behind us. And you couldn’t do much about it.”

“You’d abduct me against my will? What of the proprietor? Would he stand by and allow it?”

“For enough money, he would.”

“You’re familiar with the scenario, then, although a man of your prodigal habits no doubt is.”

“No, I’m not. I don’t abduct women as a rule. I don’t have to,” he softly added.

She was momentarily speechless, checkmated by his simple assertion, recognizing herself in the long line of females succumbing to his allure. And sudden recall of the rapture they had shared brought her face-to-face with the undeniable truth that she was no different from all the rest. Bracing herself to withstand temptation, she said with what she hoped was composure, “Am I to become the exception?”

It took him a lengthy interval to answer, his emotions in turmoil, her tone open to interpretation. He didn’t force women, but he didn’t believe in blind duty like she did, either. “You’re not the exception if you don’t want to be.”

“I doubt I do.”

There. That tentativeness again. It didn’t sound like forceful resistance to him, and if she was in doubt, he was more than certain for both of them. “Why don’t I find us a really large bed this time,” he suggested, the promise in his voice enticing. “Something big enough so we’d have plenty of room to play, so I could show you a dozen different ways to come. Have you ever been tied up?" he asked, watching her face. "Apparently not," he murmured, at the blush rising to her cheeks. "Perhaps you'd rather tie me up. Have you ever given orders to a man in bed?" He smiled faintly at her shocked look. "No to that, too, it seems. Or I could just kiss you all over from your tiny pink toes to the sweet beauty of your eyes, and we could see how many times you could come with kisses alone . . ."

"Damn you," she whispered, her voice tight with restraint, the suggestive images stirring her desires.

"If you prefer something else"—impudence gleamed in his eyes—"just let me know."

"I prefer you take me back to Shelagh's."

"You mean it?"

"Yes." A breathy, suppressed sound.

"What a shame, darling . . . when I'd much prefer driving my hard cock into you so slowly you'd feel it in every hot-blooded, tingling inch of your luscious pussy. And when I was finally buried so deep, so damned deep you could feel it in your throat, I'd keep you filled like that, saturated, gorged until your hot little cunt was exhausted." Leaning over, he brushed a kiss down her cheek. "I'd make you come so many times you'd lose count—we'd lose count—and then I'd fuck you some more . . ."

She was desperate, ravenous, the pulsing of her vagina so powerful it felt as though he had already driven deep inside her. "I shouldn't," she whispered, her hands clenched in her lap. "We shouldn't . . ."

He drew her close, his arm hard on her shoulders. "Yes we should, and don't think about"—frustrated, he blew out a breath—"all the things you think about. Nothing matters but this. You and me and this . . ."

"I should have more sense," she breathed, dizzy with longing. "Consider the consequences . . ."

"As should I," he whispered. "I've always been able to walk away."

The intensity in his voice gave her courage or perhaps just banished the fear or maybe only paralleled her own incomprehensible desires. "I can't believe I'm doing this—that I'm so hot in rut . . . Lord, Max—everyone will know when we get there."

"No one will know," he soothed. "They're in business to accommodate guests. People drive up every day and ask for a room. And I can be as proper as the Pope. Just watch."

And he was, when he bespoke a room, his tone appropriately deferential when addressing his blushing wife, his manner unutterably correct.

"What a fine young lord," the proprietor declared with a satisfied nod to his wife when he returned from ushering his guests to his best chamber. "I wonder if he's a churchman, he were so gentle and mild."

"If he be a marquis, he be too busy. Men like him pay some parson to do good works on their estates. Did he say what they be wanting for supper? I wonder. I better send Jimmy to Farmer Watts for some fresh chickens."

"He didn't say nothing about supper, but he wants bathwater. They been riding some today, he said."

"They're a right pretty couple, they are. And in love, I'd say," the elderly woman noted. "Did you see the way he looked at her? Didn't look churchy to me."

"He paid me twice what I asked—for privacy—so I don't care what he is. His wife's tired and wants to sleep, he said."

"At this hour of the day. There's no accounting for the gentry. They please themselves, they do."

"And they can please themselves here as long as they like with the money he's payin'."

"I'll take that," his wife firmly said, holding out her hand. "Just in case you feel the urge to sit down and play a hand of cards tonight. I don't want Tom Bailey to be takin' this money home."

* * *

"Did I do well?" Max drew Christina into his arms the moment the landlord closed the door. "Did I treat my darling wife with the courtesy she deserves?"

"You were everything a wife could ask for," she murmured, enchanted by the whimsical fantasy. "You are definitely the joy of my life."

"While you are the jubilation in mine."

How he delighted her, how easily she could find herself deep in love if she didn't take care. Her voice took on a teasing note because it would never do to consider their weekend play as anything but sport—particularly with a man like Max. "You found us our very large bed, my lord."

"The better to please you . . . and me. And us." His voice was soft with suggestion at the last, a tenderness in his eyes.

What graceful charm. Was he ever at a loss when making love? How often had he said that in the course of his amusements? she wondered.

He saw the fleeting melancholy in her eyes. "Did I say something?"

"I'm not as practiced—at this amorous repartee and sport. I feel out of my depth." She pulled away slightly. "I'm not sure I can summon the necessary nonchalance."

"You're wrong."

"I doubt it. Really, Max, how often have you been here before—like this—with a woman who wants you?"

"Never. Look," he said on a small exhalation, "honesty is rare . . . in these situations, but so are the feelings you evoke in me. And I could no more summon nonchalance than you. Truly."

More than his words, the look in his eyes offered her solace, but the strictures of a lifetime weren't so easily jettisoned. And while she may have succumbed to her need for vengeance as well as her desires at Digby, this was different. This wasn't some spontaneous whim pressured by rage and betrayal. They were in this room with single-minded purpose. And she was filled with doubts. "I want you desperately, and as desperately, I don't. Do you understand? I want to stay here with you forever or leave this second before I won't be able to, before my life—"

"Is changed forever. I know." The circle of his arms tightened. "You asked me when I was leaving England. I should have said Thursday, but I didn't because I'm not sure I can leave you. So don't talk to me of nonchalance."

The solid feel of him was comforting even as the world spun out of control. "I didn't even know you yesterday," she murmured, bewilderment in her gaze. "What's happening?"

He didn't reply for a very long time, and it frightened her that his answer meant so much to her.

"Whatever it is, we'll deal with it," he finally said.

How did one translate such bland equivocation? More to the point, how did Max deal with possessive women? Or she with a man who would be gone from her life as suddenly as he had appeared.

"To begin with, I won't be leaving Thursday."

She felt as though the sun had risen after a lifetime of darkness, and this time she didn't question the glory. "You don't know how wonderful that makes me feel."

"Yeah, I do," he murmured, his American drawl velvety and low. "I sure as hell do . . ."

Overwhelmed with emotion, she leaned into his large frame, laid her cheek against his chest and cried.

"Hey, hey . . . ," he whispered, gently stroking her back. "None of that when we have another two weeks together."

She looked up, tears trailing down her cheeks. "Together?"

"I'd suggest you cancel your engagements. You won't have time."

"Truly?"

He was shocked at the disbelief in her eyes, and he wondered how many times she had been betrayed. "Word of honor." He smiled. "We'll go to Minster Hill, and afterward, I may even decide to see the sights in Silesia."

"No! You can't!" It was impossible with Hans's family in residence.

She was clearly frightened. "We'll talk about it."

"No, Max." She pushed on his chest. "We *won't* talk about it. It's out of the question. Do you understand?"

"Whatever you say."

He was too obliging. "I mean it, Max. Promise me."

"I won't do anything you don't want me to do."

Vague, ambiguous, alarming words. "Promise me you won't come to Silesia. Say it."

"I won't come to Silesia," he repeated. *But I might* go *to Silesia,* he silently noted, *should the occasion warrant.* For a man raised in the West at a time when the law was loosely interpreted and often enforced at gun point, he knew how to take care of himself.

"Thank you," she breathed, her relief patent.

"And thank you for deciding you like the accommodations at The Red Oak today." Their time was limited; he had no intention of spending it in argument. "Now, what do you think?" he lazily drawled. "Sex first or a bath first. You decide, because I'm trying like hell to be the perfect gentleman right now and I wouldn't want to impose in any way."

"Other than in the most delightful of impositions, I hope."

"That goes without saying, *chou chou.* I was speaking of the order of events only."

She smiled. "Then, I don't have to decide about sex."

He grinned. "I already made that decision."

"And I must oblige?"

"Or I must oblige you; it depends on your point of view."

"Are you implying I'm demanding?"

"Only in the most delightful way. In that heaven-on-earth kind of way."

"You like me, then?"

"Fuck yes. So don't toy with me," he growled, and then struck by the full extent of such earnestness, of the possible obligations incumbent on him, he softly swore. Abruptly displacing her hands from his chest, he stepped back, physically distancing himself from the bondage he had always associated with a sincere relationship. He had spent most of his adult life avoiding female entanglements, and now he was willingly yielding? "I need a drink. Do you need a drink?" Surveying the room, he searched for the nonexistent liquor table, and then without waiting for an answer, he crisply said, "I'll be right back."

When the door slammed a second later, Christina walked to the windows and leaned her forehead against the cool pane. The notorious marquis was clearly shaken. She understood the feeling. Her secure world had been shattered as well, all the tradition and rules, the conduct and manner of her life swept away by a man who made her feel so happy she wondered that she could have been so deceived by the mockery of her former existence. A man who would disappear in two weeks, she reminded herself. Or sooner, she reconsidered, given his recent, sudden departure. She sighed, her small exhalation leaving a light mist on the window.

He was obviously disturbed or unsettled enough to need a drink.

Which hardly suggested an imperturbable acceptance of the events—of the situation, of them—whatever that meant.

She sighed again and then drew a heart in the condensation, like some lovesick girl wanting and hoping, willing to ignore harsh reality for a blissful fantasy. And in the time he was gone, she drew a pattern of hearts on the numerous panes, as though she could weave a spell of happiness—each heart an omen of good fortune, romantic hope and wishful dreams. But at the sound of his returning footfall, she quickly rubbed away the evidence of her foolish conjuring with swift, broad sweeps of her arm, and having eradicated any evidence of her foolishness, she turned to the door just as Max entered the room.

He was laden with a bowl of shiny red apples curiously topped with a sponge, a bottle of brandy and two glasses. And his face was wreathed in smiles. "I come bearing gifts. Mrs. Bagshot thought my lady wife should have some of her special apples, the sponge is for—well . . . I told her our bath—and it must be new, I said. Although I advised Mr. Bagshot to wait on the bathwater. I hope you don't mind, but it would only get cold. I told him you were sleeping. It's amazing how lie piles upon lie in situations like this. Not that I've done this before—let me quickly correct that statement. But anyway, I decided on my way downstairs that I wanted to hold you above all things and be with you and to hell with everything else. So there you have it. I hope you don't mind, and if you do, I happen to be double your weight at least and a foot taller; so what you think is not of immediate consequence." He grinned. "And I say that with the greatest respect."

He could put the world to rights with his smile, she thought, and vanquish the most confirmed skeptic in her. "And *I* think I shall need very much more than you just holding me," she replied. "I hope you don't mind, but if you do, I'm inclined to rip off your clothes with utter disregard for your wishes and make love to you whether you like it or not." Her smile was sunshine bright. "And I say that with the greatest respect."

"So I won't be needing this bottle after all," he said, placing the items he held on the table.

"I don't think you'll have time to drink, unless you're very, very dextrous."

"Actually, I am, but I can think of much more pleasant ways to put those talents to use."

"And I don't care what you say this time; I'm taking my clothes off faster than you."

He teasingly took a step toward her, but she warded him off

with crossed fingers and a wanton swish of her hips. "I'd hurry if I were you."

"Don't worry about me, my darling *wife*. I can keep up with you any day."

"We'll see about that, won't we, my darling *husband*." And the designation, no matter how playful, tasted sweet on her tongue.

Chapter 8

It was a close thing, but Max disposed of his clothing a fraction of a second faster.

"Practice makes perfect, I suppose," Christina teased, throwing her chemise at him—her last item of clothing.

Ignoring a comment that could only lead to controversy, he caught the filmy garment in midair and tossed it aside. "You won't be needing that anymore. I'm inclined to keep you naked in my cozy lair. The better to serve my purposes," he silkily drawled, moving toward her.

Her brows flickered. "Or mine."

He smiled. "Where have you been all my life?"

"Waiting for you to ask."

"Damn, I've been wasting my time."

"While I've got a lot of making-up-for-lost-time to do."

"A perfect combination, are we not?" Taking her hand, he drew her to the bed. "Could I interest you in this very large bed, Miss Making-Up-For-Lost-Time?"

"Did you mean it about me tying you up?"

He turned to her, a flicker of astonishment in his gaze. "Of course."

"You wouldn't mind?"

"Whatever you want, darling." While he wasn't adverse, he hadn't often submitted to bondage. Rarely, in fact. Only once actually—a long time ago. "Does that appeal to you?"

"I don't know . . . if you don't mind, the concept is intriguing . . . with you. Of course, everything is intriguing with you—sexual, nonsexual, clothed or unclothed. You see how enamored I am." Her smile was rueful. "Infatuated would be more accurate, I suppose, considering how short our acquaintance. And you're always so appealingly ready," she murmured, glancing at his erection.

Her words "tying you up" had provoked an instant response, and his arousal was in full ramming mode. "It must have been something you said," he noted with a grin, sitting down on the bed and drawing her between his legs.

"Oh, good—although you must help me with this. For instance, what should I use to tie you?"

He glanced around the room. "Why not those curtain fastenings?"

She turned to look. The bank of windows was hung in simple white muslin, gathered away from the panes with wide grosgrain ribbons. Swiveling back, she leaned over to kiss his cheek. "You're very sweet to let me do this."

"I have one request prior to this shackling."

"Oh, dear, you don't want to." His pronunciation of the word "shackling" had held a hint of reserve.

"Not at all." His smile was graceful and full of charm. "But depending on circumstances, I may not be able to withdraw in time. The sponge would be helpful—in you," he added at her perplexed look.

"So the sponge wasn't for our bath."

"No." He was surprised at her naivete. With no comprehension of the contraceptive value of sponges and only two children in twelve years of marriage, he began to wonder at the sexual extent of her relationship with her husband. A pleasant thought, actually—that apparently limited contact. "We should probably do that first."

"You'll be able to climax in me without unwanted consequences?"

He felt like a hygiene teacher. "You see my selfish motivation."

"Oh, I'd like it as well." She blushed. "I mean . . . it feels so very good when you're in—"

Even her breasts had turned pink. "Sit here," he suggested, swinging her onto the bed. Coming to his feet, he smiled. "And we'll get you ready for sex."

"Oh, my God, Max . . . saying it like that, I can feel—" She shut her eyes against the molten heat shimmering through her vagina.

He bent to lightly kiss her closed eyes. "This is new territory for us both," he murmured, lifting her chin with a crooked finger. And when her lashes lifted, he said, "I don't as a rule allow myself to be bound."

"But you will for me?"

"I'd do anything for you."

"Don't offer me so much. I'm greedy."

His grin was heated and close and licentious in the extreme. "I'm planning on getting my share, darling, believe me."

"And we won't be interrupted?" She felt so extravagantly wanton, she couldn't imagine having enough time.

"The Bagshots have been well paid for our privacy."

"Then, hurry, show me. Show me this sponge that will give me my freedom of you."

He strode to the table, retrieved the sponge from the apple bowl and, taking a small gold pocket knife from his jacket, proceeded to cut out an egg-shaped portion. Pouring some brandy into a glass, he dipped the sponge, then squeezed it dry.

Enamored as she was, she watched him with fascination, every movement, every gesture precious, intoxicating. Even someone less infatuated would have to agree he was male perfection, she thought. His muscles were honed and taut, material evidence of an athletic life, his tall, lean form so elegantly proportioned he could have been the sculptor's model for the golden mean. And how splendidly dark he was, his bronzed skin and jet black hair, his swarthy coloring graphically different from all she had ever known in a man.

Returning to the bed with the fragment of sponge on his palm, he said, "I should probably do this."

"Would you? I'm not sure I could—properly." Lulu had talked of a small rubber cap she used, and of French letters, but never a sponge, and none of the devices were familiar to a woman like she who rarely had sex. "I'm afraid I've never paid attention to—such things."

He felt a moment of pure possessiveness, pleased with her ignorance of sexual apparatus—astonished at his sudden scruple when he had always subscribed to the principle of equality in these amorous games.

"I've heard of French letters though. You don't have any?"

"I wasn't planning on—"

"Doing more than riding. I know." Her slow smile curved upward. "And I corrupted you."

He chuckled. "For which I'm deeply grateful."

"And now you're going to let me have my way with you," she murmured, delighting in playing the coquette for the first time in her life.

"I'll expect a quid pro quo. Just a warning," he teased, gently pushing her on her back.

"You're going to tie me up, too?"

"Or something . . . ," he said with a wicked grin, lifting her knees, easing her thighs apart. "I'll see what I'm in the mood for."

"At least you know. Everything's so new to me—oh, Lord, including that . . ." She arched her back and softly moaned, Max's long fingers sliding up her vagina, his delicate penetration skimming over her throbbing tissue, depositing the sponge at the mouth of her womb . . . holding it there with the lightest pressure while a fierce jolt vibrated through her innermost recesses.

Only sheer willpower kept him from mounting her, the possibility of coming in her now the most provocative incentive. His nostrils flared at the necessity of curbing his urges, and he abruptly pulled his fingers out. "This is going to be damned hard," he growled, moving a short distance away, struggling against an overwhelming impulse to ravish her.

Christina's fevered gaze held his. "I can't wait. I'm sorry. I feel so gauche and unsophisticated, but I can't . . ."

Thank God, he silently thought, only seconds away from losing control. "It's been too long for both of us," he murmured, settling between her legs in a graceful ripple of muscle and sinew, guiding his swollen crest to her wet sex, ignoring the fact that only an hour had passed since they had made love.

Wild with wanting, she lifted her hips in welcome, and he plunged in with a scarcely repressed violence. "I'm going to fill you with come this time." His voice was harsh, ragged, proprietary.

"Every time . . ." She understood ownership as well, and she wanted him with a fierceness that would have been unfathomable a day ago.

"Every time," he vowed, his words challenge rather than assent, and forcing her legs wider, he drove into her with a powerful, soul-shattering down thrust.

Awareness disappeared for a moment.

And when she could breathe again, she whispered. "Fill me full . . ."

He made a sound deep in his throat and, slipping his hands under her bottom, hauled her solidly upward, brute authority in the exacting response, defense perhaps to his compelling need.

Abandoned to all but riveting sensation, unaware of the contentious subtleties impelling Max, she moved against him, wanting more. His breath caught, she could feel the tension in his spine, and then his fingers tightened to gain better purchase as his lower body shifted into a rhythm of overt demand.

It was a combustible joining, turbulent, frenzied, ravenous.

He was no longer thinking clearly—an astonishing aberration for a man who had always equated sex with casual sport. She didn't know it was possible to lapse into insensibility in the throes of passion. And at the end when she clung to him, uttering wild, inarticulate cries, and his rasping breath matched the measured cadence of his powerful ejaculations, the bed and inn, the November day, retreated from the realm of consciousness.

Moments later, postcoital torpor reigned, their bodies indolent with contentment, the sound of doors banging downstairs distant, irrelevant, the coolness of the room disregarded, the bright sunshine outside the windows unrecorded by brains replete with bliss.

One can actually bask in pleasure, she thought.

And sex was no longer just sex, he vaguely perceived.

He roused himself first . . . out of habit perhaps; he often made love in boudoirs where husbands might unexpectedly appear. And instinct prevailed.

She looked up when his body shifted above her.

"A dead heat," he said with a smile. "We'll have to practice that again."

She hadn't known such glorious harmony existed. "It must be one of God's miracles."

He smiled. "Apparently, it can be."

"I'm not inclined to move for a decade," she murmured, the warmth, the faint weight of his body sweet delight.

His mouth quirked in a grin. "I'll send Shelagh a note."

"If only . . ."

A man of action, he was less unsure. "You can do whatever you want."

"*Men* can do whatever they want."

He shrugged. "Some women do as well." Dropping a kiss on her nose, he rolled away to reach for a towel, indifferent to gender conundrums.

She shivered at the sudden coolness on her body.

Taking note, he quickly came to his feet. "I'll stoke the fire." And folding the quilt over her, he reached across the bed to tuck it around her shoulders. Handing her a towel, he slid his hand under the quilt and removed the sponge in a swift, accommodating gesture finished almost before her surprise registered. "Until you become more proficient," he murmured, gallant and smiling. Walking to the washstand, he opened the doors below and disposed of the sponge. After wiping himself dry with a small towel, he tossed it under the washstand as well, not only familiar but comfortable with all the mundane particulars of amorous rendezvous.

He was at ease with his nakedness, the practicalities of sex, and she watched him walk toward the fireplace with both fascination and a novitiate's interest. Then, unbidden, recall of her first glimpse of him *en flagrante* at Shelagh's came to mind—his dismissive glance, lack of embarrassment—and a wave of discomfort washed over her. She was no different from the long list of willing and eager ladies preceding her. But he happened to turn and smile at her just then, and without reason she found herself instantly mollified.

"I'll have you warm in no time," he said, squatting down, placing two logs on the dying embers. "We've enough wood here to barbecue a steer. I don't suppose you have barbecues in Silesia."

She found she didn't care whether she was one of his harem—her happiness too great. "Nor in England either," she said, wanting to run her hands down the long, beautiful sweep of his back, wanting to feel the great strength and power.

"You'd enjoy our ranch in Montana—especially in summer when the wild roses are in bloom. They line the river for miles. There." Satisfied with the small blaze, he rose to his feet. "That should take the chill off."

"I've never been to America. All one hears of is the enormity of the land."

"Sail back with me. I'll show you."

"Just like that."

"Bring your boys."

"You're mad, of course."

"Probably." *For certain*, he thought, when he was inviting a woman he had just met and her sons he had never met to come home with him. Feeling the need for a drink or two or six to settle his obviously fevered brain, he took a short detour to the table, picked up the brandy bottle and glasses and carried them to the bed. "A little more heat, my lady," he drawled, sprawling next to her, intent on ignoring his disconcerting thoughts. Uncorking the bottle with his teeth, he leaned over and dropped the cork on the floor, poured the liquor into the glasses he held in the palm of his hand and offered her one.

"It's a little early."

His brows rose. "Then, don't drink it all."

She took a glass because she realized it was perhaps less irregular to have a drink at noon than to lie in bed with a man she had met only yesterday.

"And if you're feeling guilty," he noted with a faint smile, as though he could read her mind, "consider—we could be listening to Lady Moffet's advice this evening ad nauseam."

She couldn't help but smile. "Reason enough to be enjoying myself in bed with you."

"One of the reasons . . ." He regarded her over the rim of his glass with a cheeky impudence.

"One of many, I hope." She tipped her glass faintly.

"Count on it, darling. Just as soon as the room warms up. I wouldn't want my sweetheart to catch a chill." Lifting his glass to his mouth, he emptied it.

"Not likely with you in close proximity. I'm shamelessly in heat within a foot of you. Do you always drink like that so early in the day?"

"Are you my mother?" He refilled his glass and as quickly drained it.

"I much prefer not being your mother, if you know what I mean."

He did, and suddenly motivated to other more pleasurable activities, he took her glass from her. "That's enough conversation."

"You're in command?"

"It's a matter of size," he said with a grin.

"Speaking of size," she murmured, her gaze drifting lower.

"We're available," he offered, his voice husky. "For anything at all . . ."

"Like tying you up?" she softly suggested.

"Or me you," he said as softly.

She made a small moue. "Are you going to renege? That's not fair when I've never in my life—" His instant scowl stopped her.

"Don't remind me of your pig of a husband."

Surprised at the harshness of his tone, she stared at him. "You're hardly the man to take issue."

"I hope you're not defending him."

She wasn't. She couldn't. "You've no reason to be angry with me."

And if there was reason, he frankly wasn't ready to face it. "You're right," he quietly conceded. "Forgive me."

"Perhaps, I might"—her brows rose in teasing conjecture—"on one condition."

He laughed. "You're going to insist on this, aren't you?"

"Think of it as a lesson in life for me. And I'd adore you as a teacher."

An interesting concept, he cheerfully reflected, his focus back on track. "Then, I should be giving the orders."

"You don't take orders?"

"Not usually."

"Would you, for me?" A gentle entreaty, gently put. She was testing her newfound skills at dalliance.

He slid lower on the pillows and gazed at her for a lengthy moment. "Oh, hell, why not? But I can't guarantee my docility for long."

"Once you're tied, darling, you won't have to guarantee it."

He groaned. "The things I do to please you."

"If you'd rather go."

"You don't actually think I'd let you leave, do you?"

"So?"

She looked much too cheerful, he thought, but he was willing to humor her because she pleased him immensely—in an unabashedly novel way without precedent in his life. "All right, you're in charge," he grudgingly murmured.

"Tell me what to do first."

His brows flickered. "Hell no. You're on your own."

"Then, I'll improvise."

He offered her a wicked smile. "This should be interesting."

He drank two more swift drinks while she untied the ribbons from the curtains, not entirely sure why he was going through with this when he disliked restraints of any kind. No more could he recall ever having taken orders from a woman.

"There now, you'll look darling in blue grosgrain."

His eyes narrowed as she approached. "You're really having fun, aren't you?"

She nodded, her pale hair drifting on her shoulders. "I can't remember enjoying myself so. I'm completely and comfortably nude before someone other than my maid. I'm about to tie up a lusciously, powerful man . . ."

"Could we personalize this, darling. Just for my peace of mind."

"A luscious, powerful, *darling* man I adore," she corrected with a smile. "When I shouldn't adore you, when I shouldn't be here, when I'm doing both with exultation."

She hadn't been nude before her husband? Mildly shocked, but gratified, he prudently didn't voice his thoughts. This wasn't the time or place to remind her she had a husband. Although the prince clearly was unmoved by the concept of marital fidelity. On the steeplechase circuit last summer, he had kept company with a different woman every night. "I like that adoring part," Max teased. "Does that mean I can tell you what to do, instead?"

"Not *that* adoring, darling. Consider, you're doing me an immense favor. Think what I'm learning."

"So this is a scholarly endeavor?"

"Absolutely. I shall become as accomplished as you."

"Like hell you will." And at her sudden start, he gently added, "Strike that last remark. I'm struggling with this curious sense of ownership."

"Exactly." She smiled again, pleased she wasn't alone in the uniqueness of her feelings. "I'm thinking about keeping you shackled to my bed," she purred, trailing the blue ribbons down his legs. "So I'll test the limits of ownership as well."

That wasn't what he meant; but what he meant didn't bear thinking of, considering their hindered circumstances, so he relaxed against the pillows and said, "Let's see who owns whom."

"Me first, of course."

"I don't mind being last. I'll have more time."

"But *I* have you now. Hold out your hand, darling."

He graciously did, and soon his wrist was circled by a ribbon of blue, neatly tied in a double bow. He should have known she would tie bows.

"How pretty you look—all wrapped up for me," she observed with a contented smile. "Your other hand, please."

His other wrist was soon similarly adorned.

"Now lie down. Do you want a pillow under your head?"

"I can think of something I'd like over my face. Does that count?"

"Really." Her eyes flared wide for a moment. "What a nice idea. You see, I'm learning already."

In short order, his wrists were tied to the bedposts, he had a pillow under his head, and the Princess of Zeiss was having a very good time tying his ankles to the footboard. And if he hadn't been shackled, he would have been equally content. On the other hand, he was looking forward to the coming events, his carnal urges apparently immune to the finer nuances of confinement. Fully aroused, his erection was lying taut against his belly, very much ready for whatever education the lady required.

"I find this stimulating in the extreme," Christina murmured, standing beside the bed, admiring her handiwork. "I'm wet just thinking of feeling this"—she ran her fingertip up his penis, slid it gently over the distended veins— "inside me."

"Let me see how wet you are," he whispered, arching his back against the exquisite sensations her touch incited.

"See." She stroked her silky mons.

"I can't see from here."

"How close would you like me?"

"About here." He stuck out his tongue and grinned.

A spiral of heat spread upward at his lascivious suggestion, but she forced herself to concentrate on the enticing game. "Maybe I don't want to right now," she flirtatiously replied.

"We could just try."

"An experiment."

"An experiment," he murmured, this man with the golden tongue.

"What if I said I wanted to be the first?" Playful and coy, she smiled at him.

"Then, I'd say you're the first."

Her brows rose faintly at the blunt reminder of a master's charm. "How amenable you are."

"How delectably hot *you are*, darling. Come closer," he cajoled, his voice soft with suggestion. "Let me see if you're hot everywhere."

"What if I told you to wait?"

There was the smallest pause. "Then, I'd wait."

"For how long?"

Another brief hesitation ensued while he debated the strength of the ribbons and his affability. "For a while," he finally said.

"Not until I gave you leave?"

He smiled, a cool, provisional smile. "I said you could tie me up, darling, not torture me."

She opened her eyes wide in artful innocence. "Oh, dear, have I been naughty?"

His gaze narrowed at her sarcasm. "I'm not sure this is going to work out."

"Of course it will, because I'm thinking of letting you see how wet I am."

His tension visibly lessened.

"Is that better?"

"Just wait," he whispered, flexing his arms, testing the play in the ribbons.

"When it's my turn."

"I may keep you tied up for a very long time."

"No you won't."

"So you're just indulging me?"

"You might say that."

"What if I disagreed?"

He abruptly flexed his arms, jerking on his bonds, his muscles coiling and rippling in a convulsive display of brute strength. Wrenching upward, his pectorals bulged with the violence of his effort, his abdominal muscles stood out in high relief, his entire upper body seemed to rise from the bed in a great surge of power . . . and the ribbons snapped. Lunging into a seated position, he stretched for the bows at his ankles, ripped them open and seized Christina's hand while she stood in shock.

"Sorry," he whispered. "I don't have much patience."

"You don't have any," she gasped.

"Then, we're a good pair, aren't we?" He pulled her closer, his grip on her wrist steel hard, his heated gaze only inches from hers. "*Aren't* we?"

"You should know better than I," she asserted, not certain whether she was flattered or annoyed by his forcefulness.

"I do. And I'm going to taste your hot little pussy now," he murmured. "With your leave, of course," he added in a whisper.

If she had been annoyed, that feeling had given way to tremulous desire at the blunt lasciviousness of his words, at the scandalous promise in his husky voice, and when he tugged her closer, when the warmth of his body was so near she could feel the heat, she coyly said, in the manner of the most wanton seductress, "And if I don't give you leave?"

"I'd have to find a way to persuade you." He glanced downward to his erection and back again to her.

"I *might* be persuaded . . ."

He recognized the agitation beneath the apparent calm of her utterance, but he was cultivated in this game. "That would save time," he pleasantly said.

"Is our time limited?"

"Only by your schedule. Mine's free."

Part drama, part pettishness toward a man who was too confident of his appeal, she looked at him for a considering moment. "I *suppose* I might have a moment or two for you."

He chuckled, but his manners were beyond reproach. "I'm honored, Princess. Are you ready, then?" And without waiting for an answer, he swung his legs over the side of the bed, lifted her up and gently placed her on the quilted cover. Her eyes went shut. A frisson of anticipation raced up her spine as he positioned himself between her legs, the solid warmth of his shoulders brushing her inner thighs. She felt his hands on her hips, the width of his shoulders forcing her thighs wider, and she felt both shamed and shameless at wanting to experience such dissolute pleasures. For a fleeting moment, she thought she heard her mother's voice, but a second later she felt the warmth of his palms drift over her stomach, the delicate friction leaving a shimmer of heat in its wake, and her senses refocused on the blissful immediacy of voluptuous sensation. Max stroked the pale curls of mons, slid his finger down her dew-wet cleft with exquisite slowness, and she gently moaned. "I need you . . ."

"Let's see how much," he whispered, shifting to grip her waist.

His words were a caress to her senses, the act of possession implied and imminent. Half opening her eyes, she saw him lying between her legs, his dark gaze heated. "Oceans full and mountains high . . . ," she breathed, reaching down to touch the black silk of his hair.

"Lucky me." And then he slowly pulled her down until her wet sex rested against his mouth, her female scent filled his nostrils and desire echoed in the feverish beat of their hearts. She was temptation incarnate, passionate and eager, fresh, new lure to his jaded lust, and as he moved his hands downward, gently separated the outer folds of her labia and touched his tongue to her heated flesh, he reflected on the delectable merits of Leicestershire hunts. He licked a path up the plump, sleek tissue and then down, in a slow, gliding pattern, the flutter of her pulse beat palpable beneath his tongue, her fingers tightening their hold on his hair as his lambent massage inflamed every glossy surface. Penetrating deeper, he licked, nibbled, teased, concentrating on the turgid, taut nub of her clitoris, suckling with an expertise he had honed to perfection years ago.

He liked the taste of women, their fragrance and voluptuous softness, their desire and ardent need, and while still young, he had learned how foreplay whetted the appetite, brought paradise closer, incited carnal passions to fever pitch.

Which fact the princess was currently appreciating, he noted, her hands viselike on his head, her hips writhing against his provocative manipulation, her passions liquid in his mouth. Gently, he forced her pulsing tissue wider, parting her succulent flesh with his slender fingers to gain better access, and when his mouth made contact with her throbbing clitoris once more and his lips closed with particular competence and precision, she gasped and came in a sudden wondrous rush.

He lay motionless until she quieted, until her fingers loosened in his hair, and then he raised his head and rested his chin lightly on her mons. "Was it worth a moment of your time?"

She exhaled in a low, contented sigh. "I'm taking you home."

And for the first time in his life, he might have gone. "Or I'll take you home," he offered, because her husband would be less likely to walk into his drawing room.

She stroked his face, her fingertips fluttering over his cheeks and nose, his brows. "Darling Max . . . I'm awash in sexual desire—because of you, thanks to you. And I'm not willing to relinquish this—just yet."

"Nor do you have to," he lazily drawled, perhaps relieved she had ignored what he could only consider a moment of lunacy.

She gently smiled. "So gallant."

Rolling up into a seated position, he shrugged away any notion of benevolence. "It's damned easy, darling, when we both want the same thing."

"I never knew," she said in breathless awe. "I never knew anything about this—about feeling like this—wanting this. I always thought Lulu mad or bored or disillusioned when she amused herself with sex."

"And so she might be. What we're experiencing is"—he struggled to find the appropriate word—"just . . . different," he impotently finished.

"How? Tell me—I have no comparison in this world."

"It's something other than carnal amusement. That's all I know. Don't expect me to be poetic."

"Do women ask for that?"

He shrugged again. "Sometimes." His expression took on a roguish cast. "And if you wouldn't think me completely unpoetic and graceless, might we continue this discussion later? I'm still damned horny."

She grinned. "You shock me. You mean *my* gratification isn't enough?"

He looked amused. "I'm not that charitable, darling."

"Sometimes you are . . ."

"The operative word is 'sometimes.' Now don't go away. I have plans for you."

"Am I at your beck and call?" In the most benevolent of humors at the moment, her query was teasing.

"Definitely." He was already halfway to the table where he tore off a piece of sponge. "And I apologize for not being better prepared," he added, returning to the bed. "I wasn't anticipating—"

"Your rare fit of conscience?"

"Yes, that," he agreed, sitting down. "Who would have thought?" He grinned. "After all this time."

"You actually are very sweet . . ."

His brows arched in droll response. "Thank you—I think. Although, in my current state of lust, I apologize in advance for any lack of—" He softly swore at the sharp knock on the door. Quickly soothing Christina's panic with a reminder they were well away from Shelagh's, he rose from the bed and walked to the door

"Yes?" His voice was brusque; he wasn't in the mood for interruptions.

"Sorry, boss."

Max experienced a moment of consternation. How the hell did Danny find them, and more importantly—why? When he opened the door enough to speak to his valet, he kept his voice low. "How did you find us?"

"The guy at Digby liked the color of my money, and I'm here 'cuz the countess is near apoplectic. Wales showed up and wants to see you."

"Now?"

"You know what Bertie's like when he wants something. The countess is tearing her hair out. I got orders to have you back by the time they all come in from huntin'."

"What time is it?"

"Goin' on one-thirty. I brought fresh horses in case you needed them."

"What I need is some damned peace and quiet, but apparently that's not going to happen."

"Wales likes your company, boss. The countess said he came up special 'cuz he heard you were here."

"How damned fortunate," Max sullenly observed.

Christina could see Max's scowl even from her vantage point. "What's going on?"

"We're summoned back."

"We are?" Her mind raced with all the possible difficulties and embarrassments.

"Nothing serious. Wales wants our company."

"He's here?"

"Unfortunately. Look," Max said, turning back to Danny. "Wait for us downstairs. We'll be down in an hour or so. That should still give us time to reach Shelagh's by teatime."

"Yes, sir." Danny knew that dismissive tone as well as he knew his master's propensity for female company.

"And tell the owner I want bathwater brought up in a half hour." Shutting the door, he returned to the bed, his expression moody. "Apparently, we're not going to have the leisure we sought. Damn Bertie and his need for company."

"A royal summons is difficult to ignore."

"But damned tempting to ignore."

"We can't."

He grimaced. "I know."

"We still have a *little* time."

His frustration dissipated before such winsomeness. He smiled faintly. "Time enough."

"For *your* gratification."

"For both of ours."

"I was trying not to be greedy."

"Before this is over, darling, we can both be as selfish as we wish, because Bertie's only a minor inconvenience. And once he's assuaged and we're away from this hunt weekend, I intend to monopolize your time."

"Think how much I'm going to learn," she teased.

"Starting right now. Although I'm vividly reminded of my ado-

lematical discussion of their disparate lives and once the tub had been filled—with a grudging eye on the time—Max resisted joining Christina in her bath.

"You're sure?" she said, sliding deeper in the steaming water, invitation in her velvety tone.

"Not sure, but sensible," he muttered, moving to the washstand for a less desirable but more prudent alternative.

"The water's lovely and warm," she murmured, the sight of his gloriously nude body tantalizing.

"You're going to have to wait until tonight, darling." And while his voice was composed, only sheer willpower kept him from joining her.

"You're cruel." She pouted, watching him, the silken skin of his glorious penis gleaming wet as he washed.

His dark gaze was stark with need when he turned to her. "And you're a wanton little bitch," he silkily whispered. "But you're going to have to wait because I don't want every gossip at Shelagh's talking about you. Because I want to take you away just as soon as I can, and I don't want a flood of rumor following us. Is that clear?"

"It makes me tingle when you talk like that . . . with such brusque authority."

"I'll make you more than tingle when I fuck you tonight," he gruffly said, reaching for his breeches. "And if Wales wasn't waiting for us along with all the bated-breath guests at Shelagh's, I'd fuck you right now."

"I wish you would . . ."

He paused in the buttoning of his breeches, swiftly reviewing the possibilities, before coming to his senses. "It's damned tempting, but we don't even have five minutes. So get your hot little body out of that tub, and when I come back from talking to Danny, you'd better be ready."

"I adore that commanding tone," she purred.

He inhaled deeply and picked up his shirt. "Good try."

"What if I got out of this tub and came over there all wet and slippery and desperate for you?"

"I'd spank your luscious ass and tell you to get dressed."

"Would you really?" Her voice was tremulous as she rose from the water.

There were limits to his self-control. Picking up his boots and jacket, he bolted for the door.

Chapter 9

"You stole him from me, you little seductress."

Recognizing Lulu's voice, Christina turned from the dressing table to see her friend walking into her bedroom at Shelagh's. "That will be all, Rosie," she said, dismissing her maid. "We'll finish my hair later." Once the servant departed, she immediately apologized. "I'm truly sorry, Lulu. You have every right to take—"

"No, no, I'm absolutely *thrilled* for you!" Lulu interrupted, her smile accompanied by a suggestive wink. Taking a chair near Christina, she surveyed the princess with an assessing glance. "You're positively glowing, darling. And it's all because of lovely Max, isn't it? Now, tell me everything—every little detail."

Christina colored under her friend's scrutiny. "Lulu, please . . ."

The baroness assumed a look of mock sternness. "Don't even consider playing coy with me. I have no intention of leaving here until I hear a minute accounting of your rendezvous."

"And I as well," Shelagh asserted, having entered the room on Lulu's pointed demand. She smiled. "I want to know everything."

Not as blasé as her friends, who discussed their sex lives as casually as their dinner menus, Christina flushed under their scrutiny. "Max was very, very nice."

"In what way was he nice, darling?" Lulu inquired with a wicked grin.

"In every possible way as you well know. I have a new appreciation for desire"—she grinned—"lust perhaps, and that's all I'm going to say."

Lulu gazed at Christina from under her luxurious lashes. "I had a feeling you two would be perfect together."

"Because he's so kind," Shelagh asserted. "When many men aren't. When Christa needed someone to be kind to her because Hans isn't. And don't jump to his defense." She held up her hand to curtail Christina's response. "We know him too well."

Christina sighed. "You're right. I don't know why I bother."

"Because your mother taught you to be a dutiful wife," Lulu pointed out. "Which is why it took you so long to find some pleasure of your own."

"And then I had to go and spoil it," Shelagh lamented. "But Bertie must have his way, and he's always had a tendre for you, you know."

"While I find portly men with numerous mistresses of little interest."

"Unlike virile young men with numerous mistresses."

Christina frowned. "Don't remind me, Lulu."

"It's not necessarily a defect. Those amusements have made Max as virtuoso and charming as he is."

"On the other hand, he may just have had a natural talent for sexual play," Shelagh noted, sending a warning glance Lulu's way. "He hasn't been *that* profligate."

Christina grimaced faintly. "You needn't try and console me, Shelagh. I'm well aware of Max's reputation."

"Remember, he's sweet and generous as well."

"*Too* sweet and generous."

"You like him, then."

"Much, much too much." Christina shook her head. "When I should know better."

Lulu waggled her finger at Christina. "Don't start that again. It doesn't hurt to have some fun."

"At least while I may," Christina ruefully observed. "Max is scheduled to return to the States soon, and I must be home for the holidays."

"Then, enjoy him here and now," Shelagh declared. "I'll put him beside you at dinner."

"And I'll see that Wales has someone else to ogle tonight," Lulu offered. "Lady Brooke isn't with him, so I'll play the flirt."

"Oh, darling, don't make the sacrifice for me. I'll manage to elude Wales as I have any time these past ten years."

"There's some talk Lady Brooke may arrive tomorrow," Shelagh noted.

Christina made a small moue. "One can but hope."

Lulu threw her arms open in a dramatic pose. "Haven't we been friends forever? So all for one and one for all and we shall keep you free from Wales's unwanted attentions tonight, won't we, Shelagh?"

"Of course we will. You're much too busy, Christa darling, to contend with Bertie's demands."

"You're dear friends, but I'm capable of managing Bertie. However, I *would* be grateful to have Max seated beside me."

"Consider it done. And now we must dress." Shelagh came to her feet. "May I say, Max has brought a wonderful glow to your eyes."

"To every part of me," Christina murmured, her smile winsome.

"Good for him. Good for you." Shelagh nodded decisively. "It's about time."

Neither Lulu nor Shelagh was required to protect Christina from the Prince of Wales's attentions, for Max made it eminently clear he wouldn't allow poaching on his territory. And the Princess of Zeiss was plainly acknowledged as his the moment she walked into the drawing room. Christina had no more than crossed the threshold than he was at her side, his hand at her waist, the look in his eyes that of a man if not in love, then patently infatuated.

Those who knew him best were shocked.

Others—female in gender—were dismayed.

Even the Prince of Wales, not known for his perspicuity, realized the Marquis of Vale had posted a no trespassing sign on his newest lady love.

Unaware of the full range of Max's conquests since his return to England, Christina didn't understand the full significance of Max's unusual attention. But she did appreciate his solicitude, having been fearful that she alone was enamored and their time together might have been nothing more than a bagatelle to a man of his reputation.

"I missed you," he whispered, bending low so his breath brushed her ear. "And I adore when you blush," he added, smiling faintly.

"You're embarrassing me, but I don't care," she whispered back. "And I missed you dreadfully, too."

"Shelagh's smirking," he said in an undertone, his gaze on their hostess. "I suppose she was full of questions."

"I'm afraid so. Do you mind?"

"No. I wouldn't mind kissing you right now, either, if you could withstand the stares."

"Don't you dare!" And she would have stepped away had not his hand at her waist arrested her movement.

"Be warned," he murmured. "I intend to kiss you later."

"But not in the middle of the drawing room."

"In the middle of my bed, I was thinking."

"Please"—she resisted the rush of longing—"don't say such things when I have to survive an entire evening in company."

"You *could* suddenly get a headache."

"I'm not yet as audacious as you."

"Admit, it's tempting," he whispered.

"How am I going to last through this?" she softly wailed, knowing they were the cynosure of all eyes since their return.

"Because I promise to make love to you all night if you do."

Her gaze held his for a heated moment.

"All night," he repeated in a low, husky murmur.

Shivering, she took a sustaining breath.

His grip on her waist tightened faintly. "Smile, darling. Here comes Bertie."

Dinner was torture.

Beginning with the seating. Christina had been placed to the left of the Prince of Wales at his request, and he chose to discuss the steeplechase championships that Max and Hans had competed in last summer. Whether out of playful spite—the prince was famous for his prankster mentality—or because two of his horses had garnered metals at the competition, Christina was forced to listen to Max and Bertie and show interest when she would have preferred talking about anything else.

"A shame Hans left early," the prince remarked, signaling the footman to refill his wineglass. "I was looking forward to seeing him."

"Hans keeps his own schedule," Christina replied, knowing full well Bertie knew with whom her husband had left.

"Well, tell him we missed his company."

"I shall, Your Highness, when next I see him."

The prince looked up from his turbot at her tone of voice and, after the merest pause, asked, "Will you be hunting with us in the morning?"

"I'm not sure."

"*You* will, won't you, Vale? We need a good shot in the stand."

"I promised the princess I'd show her the jumps at Grammont."

"I see. Brought Tremaine with you, did you, Christina?"

"He's looking forward to the exercise, sir."

"I daresay," the prince murmured with what could only be construed a leer.

"If you'd care to join us, sir," Max offered, plainly not meaning it.

"Perhaps some other time, Vale." The prince smiled at Max, his look one of masculine understanding.

And the tedious meal went on, course after course, with the Prince of Wales becoming more intoxicated and his comments more pointed. Max finally said, very quietly, "I think the princess is becoming ill, Your Highness."

Christina glared at Max. "I'm fine, really."

"You look pale," he said, ignoring her glowering look. "Perhaps it was the lobster. Would you like to rest for a moment?"

"It's nothing. I feel perfectly well."

"I know you'll excuse us, sir. I'd hate for the princess to get sick here at the table."

The Prince of Wales glanced from one to the other, trying to decipher the nuances, but Max was already helping Christina to her feet, his hand under her arm literally lifting her from her chair. "Of course . . . yes—of course," Bertie stammered.

Offering his apologies to Shelagh as they left, Max led Christina from the room, and once they were outside in the hall, he said, "You can argue with me later, but I couldn't stand another minute. I wasn't in the mood to listen to inanities for another four hours and watch Bertie get drunk. He's not *my* royal family, so I can be rude with immunity. You're welcome to blame me completely if anyone should ask."

"And what exactly would be my reason for leaving with you, pray tell, should someone ask?"

"Who cares?"

"I might."

"Jesus, Christina . . . you didn't actually want to sit through that meal and then play baccarat with Wales till two in the morning, did you?"

"I may worry about gossip more than you."

"Why?"

She hesitated, none of the proprieties as important as they once were.

"You see," Max affirmed. "And think, darling, we'll have the rest of the night to ourselves. Or if you really feel brave, we could leave tonight."

"How? Bertie would be furious."

"He'll understand."

Suddenly she didn't care who understood and who didn't. Suddenly she wanted something simple with no rules and strictures.

She wanted to be held in Max's arms.

She wanted to be happy.

Taking a deep breath because simplicity wasn't so easily won, nor duty discarded on a whim, she debated the ramifications of flight.

"Think—we could be alone . . . far away from here."

Temptation stood before her, sinfully beautiful in full evening rig, offering her the happiness she craved. For a brief moment more she hesitated, and then self-denial gave way to desire. "Let's go right now," she said in a rush.

He didn't question or hesitate or even show a glimmer of shock. "There's my girl," he softly said, and taking her hand, he began walking toward the main entrance.

"Max? What are you doing? We need our things packed. We have to leave a note for Shelagh—an apology for Bertie."

He glanced at her and smiled, but he didn't slow his pace as they crossed the large entrance hall. "I'll take care of it." He signaled for the door to be opened.

"How? Max . . . Max!"

A footman was opening the door for them.

"Darling, don't worry." He nodded his thanks to the flunkey and drew her out into the chill night. "You *will* need a coat, though," he murmured, slipping off his evening jacket and covering her bare shoulders. "And someone to keep you warm," he added, lifting her into his arms and striding down the moonlit drive. He winked, a boyish warmth in his eyes. "And I'm the man to do it."

Max set Christina down on a hay bale while he made arrangements with the groom to have a carriage readied. When he returned, he sat beside her, pulled her close to the warmth of his body, dipped his head and lightly kissed her. "We're off to the Tatton station where a train stops at midnight."

"A train going where?"

"Does it matter?"

She smiled and shook her head.

"Exactly. As long as it's away from here."

"Somewhere no one can find us."

"Minster Hill?"

"That's the first place anyone would look."

"*If* they could get past my gatekeeper."

She grinned. "Privacy."

"*Absolute* privacy."

She nodded. "Very well, I agree."

He laughed. "Good, because I sent Danny a message to bring our luggage there tomorrow."

"We're going to have to discuss this propensity of yours for taking charge," she sportively said.

"Anytime, darling. I'm putty in your hands."

She briefly glanced at his crotch. "I certainly hope not."

"Merely a figure of speech, darling. If I'm anywhere near you, I have a hard-on."

"And we're having a coachman drive us to the station. How perfectly lovely," she purred.

"No," he sternly declared. "There isn't time, and you'll freeze in this weather—on second thought, probably not," he sardonically noted, recalling her heated passions, "but it's too short a distance, so *no*," he briskly repeated. "You're going to have to wait."

"I've been waiting twelve years . . . ," she murmured, pouting prettily.

"And that's the problem." He grinned. "Actually not a problem so much as a gift from God, but darling," he gently cajoled, "be patient. I promise, I'll make it up to you."

"How long do I have to wait?" Part dramatic lament, part genuine disappointment, she made a small moue.

Quickly calculating the distance to his country home against her impatience, he realized an alternative was required. "If we can't procure a private compartment on the train, we'll stay in Tatton tonight." He smiled. "So you don't have to wait."

"You're ever so nice, my lord." Her voice was throaty with laughter.

His brows arched in roguish response. "Do I have a choice?"

"Of course you have a choice."

"Other than making love to you in the carriage?"

"Would that be a hardship?"

He rolled his eyes. "I'm not eighteen anymore."

"Then, I'll compromise on Tatton."

"You're so kind," he mockingly replied. "But *I'd* prefer Minster Hill."

"So I won't be having my way?"

Beneath her teasing tone was a small poignancy that reminded him of the oppressive constraints of her life when his had none. "Since it's getting late," he kindly said, "Tatton probably makes more sense."

Her eyes filled with tears. "Thank you."

"My pleasure," he whispered, kissing away the tears spilling over and running down her cheeks. "And don't cry . . . I don't care where we stay."

"I'll try not to," she whispered, sniffling, "but everything suddenly seemed—"

"We'll be fine anywhere," he soothed, thinking the Prince of Zeiss should be taught a lesson in manners. But he said, instead, his voice sportive and low, "Now what can I do to stop those tears? Gifts are always good, I've found, or—"

"Tatton will be . . . gift enough," she quavered, offering him a tentative smile.

He grinned. "You're easy. No diamonds or rubies or cigarette cases from Faberge?"

She managed a real smile. "That comes later—when I have you caught in my net."

"Too late, darling. I'm already caught, landed and not even fighting anymore."

"When you usually do?"

"When none of the above have ever remotely touched my life."

A quiet joy shone in her eyes. "Then, I'm the first."

He nodded. "And that's the problem," he gruffly said.

"We still have two weeks."

"Starting with Tatton," he lightly noted, because he had sense enough to understand the futility in begrudging her marriage.

"Because you're sweet."

"Because I'm probably crazy not insisting we get farther from Bertie's reach."

"But nice crazy."

Chapter 10

Max had the coachman drop them off at the Tatton station, hoping to put any possible pursuit off the scent. Not that he expected to be followed, but it didn't hurt to be cautious. He had scribbled a note of apology to Bertie and Shelagh at the stables, and while Shelagh would be accommodating, Bertie was unpredictable in his demands. Like his mother, the queen, he was accustomed to having his way.

The moon was bright as they walked down the street toward the lights of the village square; the illuminated facade of the inn, clearly visible; the bright red sign out front, conspicuous.

"A unicorn," Max noted, regarding the armorial pose of a white animal on a red-painted ground. "Could that be considered significant?"

"Fantastical, you mean?"

"Like our meeting."

"Definitely the stuff of dreams, for me," Christina murmured.

He glanced down at her and smiled. "I had no intention of asking you to go riding. It almost makes one believe in fate."

"Or lucky circumstances," she said, thinking if Hans hadn't been indifferent to her feelings, if he had been in bed in the morning, perhaps she would never have gone to the stables.

"Now, if we can find a room tonight, I'll consider myself the luckiest of men once again," Max observed, aware of how close he had come to refusing her.

"Oh, dear, I never thought. Do you suppose they have a room?"

"They'll probably have something, but I can't guarantee any splendor."

"You'll provide the splendor." She twined her fingers in his.

"And you the beauty." He squeezed her hand. "Come, my darling wife, let's see what they have available."

She smiled up at him. "I'm getting used to this."

When Max asked for a room, the thin, tight-lipped woman behind the counter looked them over with a bold scrutiny and said, "At this hour?"

"Yes, at this hour," Max returned, his voice chill. "And if you can't help me, I'll find someone who can."

"No one here but me. And I don't see any luggage," the middle-aged woman disdainfully added.

"I'm the Marquis of Vale. Kindly do as you're told."

If not his arrogance and title, the contentious look in his eyes curtailed the woman's rudeness. "I beg your pardon, my lord"—a sycophantic note crept into her voice—"but we have young bucks coming in here at all hours of the night—particular in hunting season now—with, er . . . women of a certain—"

"I'm not interested in your village tales." Max cut her short. "A room, if you please and posthaste."

The proprietress quickly surveyed Christina again and decided the jewels visible beneath the marquis's coat were as real as those on her wrists and fingers. A king's ransom all told, she didn't doubt, and tart or not, the woman was obviously wealthy. And a nobleman who spoke in that tone of voice couldn't be gainsaid regardless of the questionable circumstances. But her moral righteousness prompted her to say, "I will require payment first, my lord."

"*First,* show me the room," Max ordered. Turning to Christina, he murmured, "If you'll wait here, dear, I'll see if the accommodations are adequate."

"Hmpf." The landlady's mouth set into a thin line. "I'll have you know, we have gentry stay here all the time, and we've never had any complaints."

"I'll be the judge of that." Max indicated with a nod of his head that she precede him. As she flounced off through the small lobby, Max winked at Christina. "I'll be right back."

He selected the largest of the two chambers shown him, grateful they had found accommodations with the hunting season in full swing. "We *are* lucky, darling," he said as he ushered Christina into the room a few minutes later. "Apparently these quarters are available only because of a cancellation by Lord Picard's secretary."

"We must send the man a note of thanks." She smiled. "Anonymously, of course."

"I'll have my secretary see to it the moment we reach Minster Hill."

"In the meantime . . . I have you all alone."

His brows rose, amusement in his eyes. "Should I be alarmed?"

"I'd prefer compliant," she replied in a sultry whisper.

He laughed. "I think we've been through that before. Available and eager, even easily persuaded, but compliant"—his grin was wicked—"I can't guarantee that."

"Never mind, darling. In my impatience, I'm quite willing to accede anything to you—power, authority, dominance—as long as I come in the next few minutes."

He looked back from turning the key in the lock to see she had discarded his jacket and was swiftly pulling the pins from her hair. "And now we're back on frenzied track?" he teased, leaning back against the door.

"We are." She smiled. "You have to admit I was patient on the ride over here."

"If you call me fighting you off for five miles, 'patient.' "

She made a small moue. "Perhaps some of the hunting gentlemen here at the inn wouldn't find my eagerness so disconcerting . . ."

"If you could manage to get past me and out the door, you might have the opportunity to see," he lazily drawled.

Her sudden smile was coquettish. "I love when you're jealous."

His dark brows rose fractionally. "Take a step toward the door and you'll find out exactly how jealous I am."

"Ummm," she purred, kicking off her satin evening slippers. "How deliciously forceful. Are you forceful in other ways, my lord?"

"It depends . . ."

"On?"

"What you want."

"So you have certain reservations."

"Not reservations so much as partialities. I don't do animals." Her eyes widened in such astonishment, he laughed, and pushing away from the door, he murmured, "So you're looking for brute force with your sex . . ."

"No, no—actually, no . . . ," she protested, moving away, mildly alarmed after his comments. "You misunderstood. I didn't mean—" A moment later she was backed into a table, and he was towering over her, the heat in his eyes unnerving.

"You're no longer impatient?" A low, deep, teasing rang in his voice.

"No, actually yes, but no to, well—whatever you were alluding to . . ."

"You're so far out of your league, darling, you have no idea what I was alluding to," he whispered, reaching out to slip the velvet strap of her gown down her shoulder. "I could be dangerous."

"I know you're not," she breathed, but a tremulous note underscored her words.

"You don't know anything about me except I can bring you to orgasm as many times as you want." His voice was silky. "Not sufficient vetting to bring me home for supper. And now you want rough sex."

"I don't—not really . . ."

He slipped the second strap down. "Maybe *I* do."

"Max!" A small, breathy protest.

"You might like it," he whispered, tracing his finger lightly over the curve of her breasts mounded above the corseted bodice of her gown. "You might like me to rip this dress off you and make you service me." He ran his finger under the edge of her low décolletage, the grape-colored chiffon, ornamented with elaborate silver beading and black velvet ribbons, figure-hugging and fashionably provocative. "You could pass for a tart in this purple dress—a very high class tart," he murmured, sliding his finger down her cleavage. "And if you were for sale tonight, I could make you do whatever I wanted."

"No . . . Max—don't . . ." But she could feel the pulsing between her legs intensify at his heated suggestion, at the riveting pressure of his finger between her breasts, and shamed at her sudden yearning, she tried to push away.

"Sorry . . . ," he murmured, grasping her arms firmly, pulling her back. "You're not going anywhere."

She should insist he unhand her, but her body had responded to the pitch of his voice on the most primitive level, to the blunt sexuality implied in his decree, to the hard, thrusting imprint of his erection pressing into her stomach. Awash with naked desire, she wondered with a tantalizing shiver what he could make her do. "What if I were for sale?" she breathed, feeling herself open in readiness even as she spoke, shocked at both her query and the rush of heat rippling through her vagina.

His dark eyes held a sudden glint of amusement and the unmistakable promise of pleasure she had come to recognize. "Tell me your name," he drawled, "and I'll tell you if I'm interested in buying."

She hesitated, the obscure notion of playing the courtesan exploitive, terrifyingly wicked. But he was breathtakingly beautiful, his dark hair ruffled where the wind had gotten to it, a wildness in his gaze, his shoulders massive like his tautly honed body, a sexual pirate in silk shirt and hand-tailored evening clothes and so irrepressibly exciting, she heard herself say, "My name's Lola. And I hope you like me because I'm excessively attracted to you."

"You want my money, you mean," he said with a roguish smile.

"No, not at all . . . that is—I suppose I should but I don't."

"A whore with a heart of gold. Is your cunt as benevolent?"

"Welcoming certainly, my lord. Its benevolence would be for you to decide."

"Do you follow orders?"

Her hesitation was brief, and a modicum of apprehension shone in her eyes when she spoke. "I think I could, sir."

"I would insist on that."

Drawing in a small breath, she said, "Very well."

"Then, we have only to decide on a price for your"—his smile was gently mocking—"submission."

"I really wouldn't know . . ."

His brows rose in feigned surprise. "Come, darling, you don't have the look of a novice. There's no need to bargain."

"I beg your pardon." Genuine resentment rang in her words.

"No need to take offense, Lola. I'm not interested in innocence anyway."

"I see." A snappish, tart response.

"If you'd rather not participate," he lazily murmured, "I could always find someone else to entertain me."

He played the game better than she.

"Damn you."

"Just a word of advice, darling," he genially noted. "You're more apt to please your clients if you don't swear at them. Now take off your dress so I can see your delectable body and I'll overlook your temper."

"How kind of you, my lord, but we haven't agreed on a price yet."

This time his surprise was genuine, but he said, "Five hundred," with a casualness that implied familiarity with the trade.

"A thousand."

"You'd better be good."

"I've been told I am."

Temper flared in his eyes, regardless of the fiction. "Really."

She lifted her chin slightly and squarely met his gaze. "Really."

"I imagine you want it up front." Plunging his hand into his trouser pocket, he pulled out a wad of bills, quickly peeled off two, returned the money to his pocket and stuffed her payment down her cleavage. "I'm ready whenever you are," he curtly said.

"I've heard you're always ready."

"You've heard right. Now take off that dress. I want to see what I bought tonight."

"I can't reach the hooks." Turning around, she presented her back to him.

Whether it was her imperious tone or the pale beauty of her flesh or more pertinently, the lush rounded curve of her bottom in the tight-fitting gown, he decided he could wait for her disrobing. Lifting up her skirt with one hand, he pressed her facedown on the table with the other, and ignoring her struggles, he swiftly stripped her drawers away, spread her legs and, unbuttoning his trousers, moved between her legs with single-minded purpose.

"I thought you had more finesse," she sputtered.

"Finesse isn't a requirement in dealing with ladies of the night. Only my pleasure matters. Lift that sweet cunt, darling, and let me in." Putting action to words, he slid his hand under her stomach and raised her bottom high. "You might be worth a thousand after all," he murmured. "Your cunt's so wet, it looks as though you could last all night."

"Let's hope you can," she said with acid sweetness.

"Should we compare records?" He slid the swollen crest of his erection over the slippery tissue of her labia. "Although I wouldn't suggest you bet on the outcome."

"I suppose we can't all be raging libertines." But she caught her breath at the last and softly moaned because he was slowly invading her and a wildfire of scorching sensation took precedence in her brain.

"Finished bitching?" he unnecessarily murmured, when she was already moving backward to draw him in more deeply. But his voice was as silken as his hands on her hips, and as she eased back, he dragged her closer, his hard, rigid length stretching her, filling her. When he had reached the plunging limit, he held her impaled, immobile, and listening to the erratic rhythm of her breathing, her soft moans, he was gratified beyond the superficial vanity of his acquired skills that he was giving her pleasure.

She was softly sobbing, and bending low, he tenderly kissed her nape, whispering against her scented flesh, "I'm going to fuck you all night . . ."

He could feel himself swell inside her at the lascivious possibilities, and she gasped as her distended tissue absorbed the added dimension of his engorged penis.

"I hope you don't mind . . . but then it doesn't matter if you do, does it?" he significantly added.

When she didn't reply, he said, brusque and low, "Answer me."

She tried, and if he had not pressed deeper that precise moment, she might have found the breath to speak. But he did, and the orgasm hovering on the boundaries of her senses broke in a great crashing spasm that shuddered up her vagina, fluttered through her throbbing clitoris, jolted clear down to her toes, and she screamed and screamed and screamed.

An answer of sorts, no doubt.

His climax was over brief seconds after hers, and quickly wiping away his semen from the small of her back with her petticoat, he left her prostrate on the table. Pulling up a chair, he dropped into it with a small sigh and stretched out in a sprawl. "When you're rested, we'll try it again."

She minutely turned her head so he came into view.

"Perhaps something less precipitous next time." His voice was pleasant, neutral, like a chance acquaintance.

"There won't be a next time," she huffily declared. "I'm done." Standing upright, she briskly brushed down her skirts and turned to face him, her vexation plain in the aftermath of orgasmic rapture.

"But I'm not."

"Max . . . I'm not interested in this game."

"But I'm still horny as hell." Sliding lower in the chair so the entire length of his erection was obvious, he gazed at her from under his lashes. "All I need is a minimum degree of participation." His voice still held the same faint detachment.

Leaning back against the table, she found herself mildly disconcerted by his bland gaze. "Perhaps later."

"Now *and* later," he softly corrected. Grasping his rampant penis, he ran his hand down the rigid length, temporarily smoothing out the dilated, pulsing veins, flexing his spine slightly at the strumming pleasure. "I won't need you long this time."

"Maybe you don't need me at all."

He smiled faintly. "I like a sense of humor in a woman, but I prefer compliance right now. So bring your luscious body a little closer and we'll both be satisfied."

"And if I do?"

"Then maybe I'll let you come again."

She took issue with his blunt coercion, with his nonchalance, and forcing herself to ignore the tantalizing sight of his thrusting erection, she said, "Sorry. You're too annoying."

His brows rose faintly. "You'd never make a living in the demimonde, sweetheart."

"I certainly wouldn't if all the men were as uncivil as you."

"Most of them are worse."

And much less beautiful, she suspected, feeling a moment of jealousy, not only for all the ladies in his past, but for the pleasure he had given them. "I don't want to do this anymore," she said, pettish and pouty. "I want you to make love to me, and help me off with this dress and stop sounding disinterested."

"And I want to know if you'd consider sleeping with one of the hunting gentlemen at the inn tonight," he coolly replied.

"If anyone should be green-eyed with jealousy, it should be me," she protested.

"This isn't a debate. Answer the question."

She had never been the recipient of his chill, seething anger, and she was struck by the suppressed violence in his eyes. "How can you even think it? Max, stop looking at me like that!"

"You're sure, now."

"Of course I'm sure! Good God, Max, what's come over you?"

His glowering scowl lifted so he no longer seemed a stranger, and quickly buttoning his trousers, he came to his feet. "You're a spoiled little bitch," he said, his mouth curving into his familiar teasing smile as he walked toward her, "but you're *my* spoiled little bitch."

She wrinkled her nose. "And you're an arrogant man too used to having your way."

"Who's having her way now?"

"I thought we'd take turns."

He laughed. "Let me know when it's my turn."

"It's your turn to unhook my dress."

"In contrast to the maid's turn?"

"Very funny." Turning in a swish of chiffon, she presented her back to him.

"You're pressing your luck," he murmured, the sense of déjà vu intense. It would have taken a man of more principle than he to resist so tempting a lure, and succumbing to impulse, he swiftly lifted the filmy fabric of her skirt and slipped two fingers into her heated cleft. Her knees went weak. She whispered,

"Oh, God," and then softly groaned as he forced a third finger up her pulsing vagina. She was drenching wet, pearly liquid oozing over his fingers as he jammed his fingers upward to the base of his palm, and he wanted her like he always did, like he had from the first time he saw her. Rock-hard with the scent of her cunt in his nostrils, he wasn't inclined to wait, or play lady's maid or politely take some god damned turn as though this were a civilized teatime dance.

God knew she was ready with her juices running down his wrist.

When he withdrew his fingers, she whimpered, "Please no . . . Max . . ."

He twisted her around, his hands almost encircling her narrow waist. "I've got something better," he murmured, taking her hand, curling her fingers around his thrusting erection. "And you still haven't earned your thousand pounds."

"Tell me what I have to do . . ." Breathless, fevered, all she could think of was feeling him inside, of coming, of finding surcease for her trembling lust, and she pulled on his penis, trying to draw him near.

It required significant strength to unclasp her fingers, and holding her hands hard at her sides, he bent his head slightly so their eyes were on a level. "For starters, you'll have to say yes when I want you to say yes."

"Whatever you say . . ." Her voice was a wisp of sound, her eyes half-shut, her thighs clenched tightly together.

"If you're here to service me tonight, my wishes are paramount. Do you understand?"

Gently rocking in rhythm to the throbbing ache between her legs, she vaguely nodded.

Catching her chin between his thumb and forefinger, Max lifted her face. "Tell me what I said."

"Lord, Max, you're torturing me. I have no idea what you said. Make love to me, please . . ."

"And what are you going to do for me?"

"Whatever you want . . . whatever you want . . . just please . . . don't make me wait . . ." Reaching down, she jerked up the beaded skirt, ignoring the rending sound of tearing fabric, bunching it around her waist. "Please, Max . . . I'll do anything you want if you give me . . . that." She tried to touch him, but he brushed her hand aside.

"Anything?" Driven by frustrations he wasn't ready to acknowledge, he persisted in his torment.

"I want you to make love to me. I want to lie in bed with you and have sex with you every day of my life. I want to run away with you somewhere no one can ever find us—I want to have your child—"

He put his hand over her mouth.

And a second later, he lifted her up on the table and immediately plunged inside her like a man possessed.

He didn't want to think.

He just wanted to fuck.

He thrust in savagely, fiercely, intent on forgetting everything but hot-blooded lust.

"Don't move," she breathlessly whispered, ecstasy bombarding her brain as he lay buried to the hilt.

"Yes, ma'am," he murmured and pushed deeper.

She screamed, a high-pitched, wild sound.

He shuddered at the raw shock to his senses.

How could it be this fucking good, he thought, holding himself hard against her womb, when he had done this a thousand times before?

How could she need him so desperately, she wondered, when sex had always been commonplace?

And then he slid his hands under her bottom and lifted her so his next downstroke penetrated more profoundly, and she caught her breath and, trembling, wrapped her arms around his shoulders, her legs around his hips, and met his hard-driving rhythm with a selfish violence that seemed immune to reason.

It was a night removed from temperance or restraint.

It was a night of untamed passion, carried-away sex and orgasmic delight.

It was dissipation at its very best.

Chapter 11

Looking up from his breakfast the next morning, Max gazed across the table at Christina, attired in his shirt-cum-dressing gown, and smiled the smile of a deeply contented man. "We should see if we can find you some clothes for traveling."

Christina regarded him over the rim of her teacup, her gaze as besotted as his. "Will you wave your magic wand?"

He tipped his head toward the windows. "Perhaps toward that dressmaker's shop across the street."

Christina swiveled around in her chair, but when she faced him again, she shook her head. "I couldn't. Can you imagine the dressmaker's look when we walk in wearing ruined evening clothes? And it's not just a matter of staring someone down for a few minutes while we wait for a room. A fitting takes time, and all of this"—she half lifted her hand in his direction—"is too new for me, flaunting my—"

"Lover?"

She colored. "Yes."

"I can see I'm going to have to manage the dressmaker myself," he pleasantly noted. "I'm long ago immune to looks of censure, and you're going to need a coat or cloak at least. Your gown—"

"Was in the way last night." Christina smiled.

He winked. "You're too damned hot, darling. We'll have your gown repaired at Minster Hill."

"And have every servant look at me a certain way? Thank you, no, that rip is—"

"Suggestive of haste?" he lazily queried, one brow faintly arched.

"It's all your fault. I take no responsibility. If you weren't so tempting, like now . . . all naked brawn and virility and conveniently within reach," she said, her voice low and teasing, "I wouldn't want you so, and I wouldn't be making selfish demands of you—all the time and too often and I should probably apologize for being so—"

"No and never and don't even think of apologizing," he replied, reaching across the table and touching her hand. "I'm besotted and more than willing." He gently turned over her hand and ran his finger down her palm. "And when I get you to Minster Hill, I'm seriously thinking of keeping you there."

"And if dreams were possible, I'd seriously think of staying." She shut her eyes as a shimmering heat rushed downward.

"On second thought"—he glanced at the clock—"maybe there's no immediate need to leave on the first train this morning."

Her lashes lifted. "I'd like that." She took a shallow breath, feeling insatiable, the light pressure of his finger on her palm overpowering. "Are you finished eating?"

He glanced at the food on his plate, his hesitation minute, and then he nodded. "I'm finished." Releasing her hand, he picked up a portion of his buttered crumpet and came to his feet.

She held out her hands so he could see the tremor. "Look what you do to me. I feel like an addict . . . wanting you every second, never having enough of you, taking you from your breakfast . . ."

Swallowing the morsel of crumpet, he took her hands in his

and pulled her to her feet. "I can eat anytime. Right now, let's see what we can do to satisfy your addiction."

She took a step closer and gazed at him from under her lashes, his confidence as tantalizing as his beauty, his sexual allure so powerful she understood the legions of women at his feet. "You're always so—inexhaustible . . ." A perverse frisson raced through her senses; the fact that she was one of many, curiously provocative; his sexual prowess, lurid enticement. "Have you ever refused a lady?"

"Certainly not you," he said, charming and evasive.

"And how do you decide, my lord," she asked with a seductive purr, "which one to pick?"

His smile formed slowly. "Does it matter?"

"Am I not allowed to ask?"

"You're allowed anything, darling."

"So tell me what appeals—most to you . . ."

He had caught the undertone of excitement in her voice. "You're thinking of coming out to play again this morning?"

"And if I did?"

Placing his hands on either side of her face, he bent low and held her gaze. "Then, I'd have to fuck you," he whispered, "like I always do with ladies who come out to play."

"On the other hand"—her voice took on a sultry intonation—"I'm not sure whether I want to just yet." She had never played before, even as a child, her mother considering fantasy inappropriate, and she was enjoying the sweet whimsy now.

He softly laughed and stood upright, his hands falling away from her face. "Don't you remember, Miss Grey?" he murmured, lightly brushing his finger over her bottom lip, deliberately using her maiden name because he preferred the fiction of availability. "*I* decide when and where and *if* you want to."

"Such arrogance, my lord. Do women find that attractive?"

"I think most women are focused on something else."

"And what might that be?"

"Satisfaction," he casually replied.

"Sexual satisfaction."

He shrugged. "Mostly. But then, you know that."

"Is there more?"

"There's lots more, Miss Grey." He smiled. "Would you like some lessons on satisfaction?"

"Would it take long?"

"That depends on what you're looking for."

Her gaze traveled down his muscled chest and abdomen and lower to his blatant erection. "That, of course."

"Somehow I thought you'd be wanting cock," he murmured. "How much do you want it?"

"Very, very much. Too much"—her mouth curved in a seductive smile—"actually not too much at the moment."

He grinned at her evasive language. "Say the word for me, darling, or don't young ladies like you say 'cock'?"

"I beg your pardon."

A modicum of reproof colored her voice, and whether it was real or feigned wasn't apparent. Curious, Max thought he would find out. "You have to say it"—his dark gaze was roguish—"or you won't get it."

She took a small breath and shook her head. "I couldn't." But she shifted faintly in her stance as she spoke, the salacious challenge inciting a liquid response in the heated core of her body.

He took note of her slight movement with a connoisseur's eye, understood, as well, how little she was disposed to wait. "All you have to do is say the word, Miss Grey, and I'll slide this big, long cock all the way in. And you can come as many times as you like."

"Why don't we see what *you* like," she whispered, intent on her own extortion. Reaching out, she ran her fingers up the distended veins of his erection and gently circled the swollen head.

More experienced than she at sexual pacing, he lifted her hand away. "You're not going to win on this, darling," he murmured, and gripping his penis, he slid his fingers downward so the gleaming crimson crest reared higher, the length and breadth swelling before her fascinated gaze. "So why don't you ask for it?"

"Please, Max . . ."

He faintly shook his head. "Not good enough."

Her gaze was on his enormous erection, and for a dizzying moment the focus of the world was finite, irrepressibly carnal. She shivered faintly, helpless against her longing. "Please, I want . . . that"—his brows rose in rebuke—"your . . . cock," she whispered, her voice barely audible.

Compassionate in victory, he drew her close. "You were very good, Miss Grey." His deep voice was a caress. "You deserve a reward."

With a small whimper, she melted into his body, the throbbing deep inside her a frantic drumbeat of desire. "I've never felt like this before—insatiable . . . craving sex—wanting you inside me every second . . ."

He went rigid for a moment at her oblique allusion to her husband. But quickly regaining his equanimity, he reminded himself that amorous play was distinct from personal histories, from husbands. "Hush, darling, I'm here," he murmured, and needing what she needed, as aware as she of irrepressible craving, he abruptly lifted her with effortless strength and, holding her bottom with one palm, adjusted her legs around his waist. Clinging to his shoulders, she was panting as he raised her enough to guide her throbbing cleft over the crest of his erection. And as he gently eased her downward, she sighed, his hard length filling her in a slow, sleek friction, pleasure inundating every pulsing nerve like molten bliss. Controlling her descent, he languidly invaded her, wanting to experience by deliberate degrees the exquisite yielding of her flesh, and at the point of ultimate penetration, when he was completely absorbed, when any further advance was impossible, a moment of suspended animation prevailed.

Then he moved.

Her suffocated gasp matched his, the world reeled, killing pleasure hammered their senses.

When he managed to drag air into his lungs once again, when his consciousness was restored enough to marginally withdraw and ease the sensual buffeting, he muttered, "We're never going to get out of here."

"I don't care," she panted.

"Don't say that," he growled, not sure he could be reasonable for them both.

"I don't care, I don't care, I don't care . . . ," she recklessly whispered, and releasing her hold on his shoulders, she propelled herself downward toward the ecstasy she craved.

Cerebral concerns gave way to more riveting sensations, and he tightened his grip on her bottom, as though she had given him broad license with her words, and holding her hard against his violent upthrust, he said with unabashed insolence, "Then, I'm keeping you."

He drove in savagely.

And delirium pounded their bodies.

There was no time after that for politic wisdom as he settled into a hard, driving rhythm, seething rapture overwhelming reason, frantic need muting all but rapacious desire.

Inflamed, overwrought, she abruptly bit his neck.

Grunting in pain, he tamped down his impulse to bite her back only with supreme effort.

Instantly contrite, she cried, "Oh, God, I'm sorry," the taste of blood strong in her mouth. "I'm so sorry . . ."

"Aren't we both," he growled, resentful at a number of levels, not least, the inherent disaster in wanting her as much as he did. Moving to the wall in three swift strides, he braced her against the oak paneling, put the entire weight of his body into his next driving thrust and rammed upward as though sheer force might assuage the raging tumult in his brain.

Susceptible to the same wild madness, she sobbed in fevered

appeal, wanting more, wanting all of him, wanting the ultimate glory and splendor she found only in his arms.

It turned into a brutal mating—excessive . . . out of control.

Audacious, shameless in its greed.

Fantastic, impossibly fine.

And when he climaxed, like a man on a rampage, he poured into her unprotected body with savage unconcern.

In the hushed aftermath, disaster and ruin took on a palpable presence.

Leaning his head against the wall, Max softly swore.

Christina wanted to say, "don't worry," but couldn't bring herself to be so cavalier when she was rigid with fear.

"We'll have to take care of that," he murmured.

"*We?*" She couldn't keep the umbrage from her tone.

"*I'll* take care of it," he corrected. And with a small frown he stood upright, lifted her away and carried her to the bed. "There must be a chemist in town," he added, laying her down.

"Max!" Appalled, she stared up at him. Her whole life was turning into a public spectacle.

"Don't look at me like that. We need something to wash away the sperm."

"You'd better say you're sorry, dammit." She was furious at him, at herself, at the total folly of their actions.

"I'm sorry. I've never done anything like that before, although that's hardly an excuse. But I'm really sorry."

"I should hope so." Righteous indignation rang through her words.

He was reaching for his trousers, and he spun around, temper in his dark gaze. "Excuse me," he said with stinging sarcasm, "but I don't recall you saying no at any point."

"So it's my fault?"

After a small pause, he had the good grace to look contrite. "No, it's not your fault."

"Thank you."

He scowled, then blew out his breath. "You can be fucking annoying."

"And you can be stupid."

A dead silence greeted her remark.

Sullen and moody, he buttoned his trousers, and then looking up, his frown lifted and he slowly smiled. "I'd like to smack you right now and kiss you, too, and most incredibly make you pregnant, and I'm obviously crazy; but then, that's been pretty plain from the first time I saw you. I don't like virtuous women, by the way."

She smiled because he had precisely defined her own lunacy. "At least virtue is no longer a problem."

"Since replaced by more traumatic problems." His fleeting grimace was replaced by a speculative look. "I can't say I relish the thought of my child being raised in Germany."

"There's not going to be a child."

"Thank you for your confidence. Does that mean I don't have to run to the chemist's?"

"It never hurts to have insurance," she returned, a trace of apology in her voice. "Although I hope you know what to ask for because I don't."

"Nor do I. But I'll find out." He wasn't in the habit of bedding innocents; the ladies in his life were sophisticated enough to take care of their own contraception. But in the interests of harmony, he prudently refrained from mentioning that fact.

Chapter 12

When Max strode into the chemist's shop, the proprietor and a female clerk stared at him with such patent shock, he assumed they had never seen anyone in evening dress in the daytime. Or perhaps, rumpled evening dress was the problem, he satirically thought, his attire lacking the crispness of first use.

"I need two items of a personal nature," Max said into the stunned silence.

The woman seemed to start, her mouth opened, quickly shut again, and the elderly man dismissed her with a nod. "I'll take care of this, Clare."

After she had exited the room, Max briefly explained his needs.

It wasn't difficult for Max to choose the item. A village the size of Tatton apparently had little call for the particular device he required, and after pulling out a dusty box and blowing off the residue of years of poor housekeeping, the chemist shoved it across the counter toward Max. "As for the condoms, we get more call for those. What kind would you like?"

"I'll take what you have."

"All of them?"

"Yes, please." Ignoring the chemist's astonishment, Max decided their departure from The Unicorn might turn out to be equivocal in terms of time, and he preferred not shocking these people again if he could avoid it.

"I have a considerable number, sir."

"Fine. Wrap them up. Quickly if you please."

The chemist began wrapping the first of four boxes of condoms, his gaze over his wire-rimmed spectacles examining. "You're staying at the inn, I see."

"Yes." Max glanced at his watch.

"From around these parts, are you?"

"No."

"Visiting in our area?"

Max repressed a sigh. "No. Give me some paper. I'll help with that."

The man handed Max paper and string. "Are you just passing through, then?" he inquired, seeking a clue to his mysterious customer.

"More or less," Max gruffly replied, not in the mood to discuss his life with a curious stranger when his sperm were on the move. He surveyed the man with a cool gaze. "I'm in a distinct hurry, if you don't mind."

Intimidated by Max's warning-off tone, the subtle menace in the brute power beneath the evening dress additional threat, the chemist gulped and fell silent.

There was a further moment of awkwardness when Max paid for his purchases with a large bill. The man fumbled in his change drawer so long, Max took pity on him. "Why don't we call it even."

"I could mail you the change, sir. Or I could run to the bank and leave it at the inn desk."

"That won't be necessary." His purchases in hand, Max was already halfway to the door.

"Thank *you*, sir! You're most gracious, sir. Have a pleasant visit, sir!"

But the chemist's final words were cut short by the slam of the door, and an instant later, his clerk burst into the shop from the back room, her eyes wide. "Well, I never," she blurted out, racing to the front door as fast as her plump form would allow. "I heard every word. He must be right rich, that one, to leave you so large a tip!" Watching Max walk across the street, she breathlessly added, "And I'd sure like to see the little filly he's got hisself when he wants *four* boxes of you-know-what and has those teeth marks on his neck! He never even tried to hide them. Wait, he's goin' into Masie's shop! What do you suppose he's gettin' there!"

"We'll know soon enough," the chemist drily replied. "Masie's the biggest gossip in town."

"He's ever so handsome . . ."

The elderly man glanced at his helper in surprise. Widow Clare was as near a misanthrope as a God-fearing Christian woman could be.

"I mean you can't help but notice," she said, quickly recovering her righteousness, "there's God's hand in the making of that one."

"And apparently the devil's hand in his vices," the chemist observed.

Now, Masie Carter didn't have a righteous bone in her body, and when Max walked through her door, she was hoping she had died and gone to heaven and he was going to be her reward for a lifetime of bowing and scraping to rude, ill-tempered gentry who had a habit of not paying their bills.

"Good morning, sir," she purred, smoothing a hand over her dyed blond locks and wishing she had worn her best gown that morning.

Max knew that tone, could recognize it in the dark in a raging gale, and surveying the woman before him with a swift glance, he replied, "Good morning," in a courteous but guarded tone.

"Call me Masie," the dressmaker brightly declared. "Everybody does. And what might your name be?" *My fine stud*, she was thinking. "My lord," she more diplomatically murmured instead.

"I'm the Marquis of Vale," Max answered, knowing deception was useless in a village this size, "and much in need of your services this morning." He smiled because he had learned long ago how effective that small gesture. "I'm in a bit of a hurry, too. I hope you can help me."

"You can count on it, my lord."

His smile broadened. "Good." Surveying the shop, Max's gaze fell on a spectacular sable wrap spread out on the counter. "I need something like that," he said, and with his hands occupied with packages, he indicated the cloak with a nod of his head. "It's perfect."

While Masie was hoping the handsome young lord's comments might have been of a more personal nature, she was experienced enough to know better. But she couldn't help but wish, and taking a deep breath so her considerable bosom was shown to advantage, she gently shook her head. "I'm sorry, sir, but it's spoken for. The Countess Temple's footman is comin' to pick it up today."

"The countess is a good friend. She won't mind doing me a favor."

Nor would *any* woman, Masie didn't doubt; but the countess *did* give her considerable business, and she was expecting her sable wrap today.

"I'd be willing to pay a premium for your understanding," Max offered.

"You're not from around here, are you?" Her eyes narrowed slightly. "You sound like an American."

"I am, partly."

"Not the Vale part."

"No."

She looked him up and down. "So you are a friend of the countess?"

"And the Prince of Wales if that helps," he mentioned, practical about the sycophantic nature of society. "I really *do* need that fur and a gown as well."

"And you'll pay me extra?"

"Whatever you like."

She laughed. "You sure aren't from around here. Most o' them bargain for every penny."

"I promise not to bargain at all. Name your price."

"So you're a *rich* American." She surveyed the cut of his evening clothes, his hand-made shoes, the diamond studs on his shirtfront.

"Moderately." He smiled faintly at the blatant appraisal he was undergoing. "I hope I don't need a note from my banker."

"You have enough cash for a sable coat? Looks like you left wherever you were in a hurry."

"I have enough." When one anticipated playing cards with the Prince of Wales, a considerable sum of money was required because the prince not only played high, but he liked to win. "And I'd appreciate it if you could find a gown quickly."

"Came from the chemists, I see." A woman of the world, she recognized the shape of some of the boxes he carried.

"Yes, is that all right?"

She grinned. "Cheeky devil, aren't you? Although with your looks, no one minds, I expect."

"Masie, dear," he softly said. "I'm in a damned hurry."

"She must be a beauty."

A tenderness eclipsed the urgency in his expression. "She is . . . and more."

Masie's soft heart further melted at such obvious affection. "A man with that look in his eyes deserves to get that sable coat."

"Thank you. And a gown?" he gently prodded.

"Because your lady left in her evening dress."

He nodded. "Because of that."

"What size? Although I don't have ready-made, I have one or two things waiting to be picked up."

"She's the same size as the Countess Temple."

"Then, she can have her walking suit—a nice Harris tweed in green. We do sporting clothes here in the country. And my brother Ben might have a riding jacket that would fit you. His shop is just down the street. Although with your size . . . I'm not sure."

"I don't have time right now."

"Later, then. I'll have him find something for you. Maybe a scarf to cover your neck might be a good idea, too," she said with a wink.

"He didn't even blink an eyelash," she later said, when she was relating the details of her encounter with the handsome marquis to her friends. "A regular Don Juan, that one." She sighed. "And plenty of money to boot."

Chapter 13

"It's too late, it's too late," Christina wailed as Max walked into the room. "What took so long?" In the brief time Max was gone, she had worked herself into a frenzy, every conceivable disaster having entered her mind. She had blamed him and herself and even her husband, although she knew moral responsibility was a personal issue and ultimately no one's fault but her own. "Show me what you have." Moving toward him, she waved away the clothes he carried in a muslin cover over his arm. "I mean the things from the chemist's."

"You'll like the clothes more," he noted with a grin, tossing the garments on a chair.

"I'm not capable of appreciating humor right now," she tartly said.

"Sorry. But I moved as fast as I could, and it's not too late." Placing his purchases on the table, he moved toward her. "I'll fix everything," he promised, taking her in his arms. "Don't worry."

"Easy for you to say."

"I'm really sorry, darling, and you may chastize me to your heart's content—once we've taken care of this." Lifting her face, he gently kissed her. "Now, come see what I've purchased at the chemist's."

She was in turn horrified and pleased, interested and shocked, and once they had managed to make the douche function effectively—not without some moments of humor in the hands of two tyros—she was relieved and once again composed.

Lying on the bed, she lazily stretched and smiled at Max. "When you can even make that enjoyable," she teased, "I'm yours forever . . ."

"Wait until you see the wrap I found for you in this rural backwater," Max noted, in the process of disposing of the recently used apparatus. "You'll be even more pleased." After shutting the cabinet doors under the washstand, he wiped his hands and, taking the muslin-wrapped garment from the chair, pulled it out and tossed it at her. "I told the dressmaker I needed it more than Lady Cavendish."

"It's Shelagh's?"

"Not anymore."

"Oh, dear. Do you think you should have?"

"There's no should, darling. I already did."

"It's absolutely lovely, Max." She stroked the rare, golden-hued fur. "But good God, sable. Much as I love it, I couldn't take something so outrageously expensive."

"Of course you can. Don't be ridiculous." Returning to the bed, he arranged the cloak over her like a blanket before sitting down beside her. "And if any of your notions of propriety need assuaging, why not consider I bought this for myself. It's going to be damned soft to fuck you on."

Her brows rose, a niggling resentment surfacing at his cavalier disregard for her feelings. "Do you ever think of anything else? And I'm not keeping it."

"Please, I'm a master of constraint next to you, and I'll keep it if you don't."

She shouldn't take issue when he was the kindest of men in so many ways, but her newfound need for independence was keen. "So I have nothing to say about this. And are you *complaining* about my lack of restraint?"

"Not as long as I have breath in my body," he silkily replied, "and let's not fight over this wrap that Shelagh doesn't need. Don't look at me like that—you know she has a dozen fur coats."

"That's not the point."

"So we're arguing about . . . ?" He grinned. "Tell me, because you lost me somewhere."

"You can't always have your own way. That's what we're arguing about."

"At the risk of escalating this senseless argument, may I politely point out that I do everything you want, whenever you want—*it*," he softly emphasized, "and if you'd like me to be more specific, I'll gladly—"

"Never mind," she quickly interposed, reminded of her continual sexual demands—and his willing compliance. "I suppose you're right. And don't you dare gloat."

"I won't, and thank you," he said with an impudent gleam in his eyes. "And now that you've acceded to my superior courtesy, might I diplomatically mention we *really* need to move on to Minster Hill. Just a suggestion, of course—but a very strong one after my recent incursion into the village. Gossip is rife, I'm sure, in light of the particular items purchased." He gently touched her fingers. "So . . . what do you think?"

"We have to, I suppose," she said with obvious reluctance.

"It might be wise. In terms of discretion, et cetera, et cetera . . ."

"Always your first consideration." She arched her brows and smiled.

"Not even my hundredth, normally, but with you, I'm more prudent. Because—"

"I don't want any problems."

"Exactly. So much as I'd like to stay in this warm bed with you for endless time, especially now that we have sable to lie on," he said, grinning, "I'm going to leave you briefly again and find myself a jacket and trousers, and when I return, you're going to be dressed. *Aren't* you, darling," he softly urged.

"And if I am?" She regarded him with an coy look.

He grinned. "You'll be suitably rewarded once we reach Minster Hill."

"Do I need that in writing?"

"Not likely with my libido in ramming speed." His smile was affectionate. "I'm sure we can offer a degree of satisfaction my lady will find gratifying. Now, darling," he added, "we have an hour before the next train. Can you manage that?"

She nodded. He kissed her and came to his feet with a briskness of purpose. The sooner they reached his country home, the sooner they would be guaranteed privacy.

When Max returned, he had the train tickets in hand along with his new clothes. "Our luck is holding," he remarked, holding up the tickets. "We have a private compartment."

"You are eminently resourceful." Dressed and ready, with the exception of her silk evening pumps only partially visible beneath the folds of the sable cloak, she looked fashionably attired.

"The concept of a well-greased palm is alive and well in Tatton. The village solicitor will find himself riding coach today. But he's a young man, I'm told, so he won't suffer unduly."

Christina smiled. "Then, I needn't feel too guilty."

"You needn't feel guilty at all. You are but a party to my selfishness, for which I take full responsibility. I wanted to hold you, and now I can."

And so he did on the train ride south, although Christina dozed off almost immediately after they left the station. Less used to sleepless nights than he and unfamiliar with the energy expended in a night of sex, she was exhausted.

He had time while she slept to fully appreciate the rare wonder of his feelings for her and reflect, as well, on the hampered nature of their relationship. Having such intense feelings for a woman was a novel sensation for a man who never stayed anywhere long. And while he knew to a nicety how to exit gracefully and say goodbye with charm, he couldn't so easily come to terms with the powerful emotions Christina evoked—or the impact of her leaving.

A fortnight passed quickly.

Smiling, he considered how unique the thought of spending two weeks with a woman. Such a prospect in the past would have generated panic, and now he was looking forward to it without alarm, not only anticipating the pleasure of her company, but lamenting the brevity of their time together.

He softly chuckled. Ironic justice, perhaps, for a man who had left so many women behind.

But realistic to the marrow, he had no intention of bemoaning the hand of fate. He would have Christina to himself at Minster Hill for a fortnight. And with that he would be content.

As for the future. . . .

He shrugged away the unknown.

The telegram Max had sent from Tatton that morning had specified their arrival time, so a carriage was waiting for them at the Emery station. With the sun brilliant in the sky and the autumn foliage at the height of its beauty, his driver took them home along the scenic river road. Hardy was proud of the estate his family had served on for twenty generations.

The full array of staff were lined up on the drive when the carriage came to a stop, and Max and Christina were welcomed by Wilder, the butler, and the housekeeper, Mrs. Drummond.

"My goodness," Christina murmured, sotto voce. "I've never seen so many people. You must live in royal splendor."

Max glanced down the line of servants that seemed longer than he recalled and wondered if his butler had decided a princess required additional homage. "I think they brought in people from the neighboring villages in your honor," he whispered. "I hope you're suitably impressed."

"Without a doubt. Are you very rich?" she teased. "Because Lulu is always telling me I should have the good sense to find a man with money when I take a lover."

"Like she does." His voice had turned cool.

"I'm sorry. I was only teasing."

He looked grim for a moment and then took her hand and walked down the long line of retainers, accepting their greetings with a smile or brief word. "By the way," he murmured, as they moved past the servants to Minster Hill's imposing entrance, "you won't be taking any other lovers."

"Yes, sir . . . whatever you say, my lord. Consider me your servant in all things. Would you like your shoes polished as well? I can't actually offer to polish them." She smiled faintly. "A defect in my upbringing, I'm afraid, but I know how to give directions to servants, if that would be satisfactory to you, my lord."

"Don't fuck with me," he grumbled. But an instant later, conscious of his limited role in her life, he said, "Forgive me. I was out of line. And *my* education *does* include shoe polishing"—his grin crinkled the corners of his eyes—"should you ever require that of me."

"Be assured, my lord Vale, I have more important requests of you."

He raised one brow. "Demands, you mean."

"I was trying to be diplomatic after that display of sullenness, but definitely demands, I agree."

"At least we agree on something," he drolly said.

"On a most important something, my lord. And I promise to never take a lover; not to please you, but to please myself." She stuck out her tongue. "So there."

For a moment he was inclined to offer her the same promise, but realistic about his past and their future, he couldn't so blatantly lie. "And I promise," he said instead, "to control my jealousy in future."

The double doors opened before them with a dramatic sweep, and additional servants greeted them, curtailing their conversation. As he led her across the imposing entrance hall to the bank of marble stairs, Max pointed out a number of portraits of his ancestors in the innocuous tone of a guide. She responded in kind on their ascent to the main floor, admiring the artists, commenting on the luxury of the interior, speaking while they were near servants as would any well-mannered guest.

But as they followed a footman down what seemed an endless corridor, she finally whispered, "How much farther?"

"Too damned far," he whispered back, and then in a conversational tone asked her opinion of a tulip vase on display in a wall niche.

"Sixteenth century?" she queried.

"Yes, it's one of the earliest, I'm told."

"How nice."

"I'm glad you like it."

She giggled.

Max said with a sigh, "The servants are just going to have to get used to looking the other way. If I want to kiss you outside my rooms, I'm going to. If you don't mind, of course." He was never sure about her erratic notions of propriety.

"It's not as though this is a visit between platonic friends."

"Thank God, no. I'd be taking a lot of cold shower baths if it were."

"You mean you could actually restrain your desires."

He looked at her for a brief moment. "Probably not."

"Even with cold baths?"

"Even if an Arctic blizzard descended on us."

"How sweet."

"I'm glad you feel that way."

"How glad? "

"Say, in-about-five-minutes glad?"

"That long?"

"Hell, no." And scooping her up into his arms, he strode down the corridor past the footman at top speed, servants be damned.

Their precipitate lovemaking that first afternoon at Minster Hill was the beginning of a fortnight of unprecedented happiness for them both. They did nothing and they did everything, depending on their mood—some days not leaving bed, others walking or riding the estate for hours on end, like tourists taking in the sights, like lovers content only in each other's company.

One evening, they dressed for dinner and played lord and lady of the manor as though children at play, relishing the pretense, making believe they lived in this ancestral pile as husband and wife. They even spoke of children, of how they would someday have a girl and a boy of their own, of the names they favored and the schools their children would attend.

The mummery eventually brought tears to Christina's eyes. Quickly rising, Max came to her down the length of the enormous table where they had been playing their silly game, and lifting her into his arms, he carried her upstairs past all the servants and made love to her with exquisite tenderness. So she would forget her sadness, so he would forget the diminishing number of days left to them, so only pleasure filled their hearts and minds and heated bodies.

And tomorrows didn't matter.

The tomorrows were all gone in time, and the lovers precious idyll came to an end.

When Christina woke in Max's arms the morning they were to leave for London, she was instantly assailed by melancholy. It took a moment to gather her sensibilities, to remind herself that lovers' rendezvous were by nature impermanent, and while she couldn't have Max in her life, she would always have the memory of the great happiness they had shared.

"I ordered a sunny day for you," Max whispered.

Christina looked up into his sweet smile and wondered how she would live without him. "I'm not going to cry," she murmured as tears welled in her eyes.

"I promise not to either." While his tone was playful, the thought of her leaving him was intolerable.

Christina's smile was shaky. "That's a comfort."

He firmed his mouth in comic parody. "I shall aspire to the British stiff upper lip."

She giggled. "You don't look one bit British."

"Now, that's a comfort," he said in mockery of her previous comment, pleased he had made her laugh.

"Will you write to me?"

"As often as you like," he replied, when he didn't know if he could, if he would want to, if he could stand the thought of her living with another man.

"Every minute would be nice."

"That's what I love about you. You're not in the least demanding."

Did he mean it, she wondered, when he had said he loved her?

He was wondering the same, but not for long because he wasn't prone to futile musing, and when he kissed her, he thought instead of how he could please her one last time.

He offered her only unalloyed pleasure that morning and sweet kisses, young boy kisses that surprised and delighted her. "I wish I would have known you when you were young," she murmured, as she lay atop him sometime later, the afterglow of orgasm still pinking her cheeks.

He grinned. "I'm better now."

"But not so sweet, I expect."

"I didn't realize you were looking for sweetness," he teased, although he knew full well what she meant.

"And now you're being cynical when I'm still basking in the glow of those innocent young kisses."

"I'm glad you liked them, ma'am . . . ," he drawled, his western twang pronounced. It was going to be difficult enough having her leave. He had no intention of sinking into maudlin reverie this morning. "I've plenty more if you're in the mood."

"I'm always in the mood." But her eyes filled with tears as she spoke.

"Don't cry, darling. I'll write, you'll write, I'll have a telegraph operator installed in my home," he playfully declared. "And when all else fails, we'll make plans to meet somewhere."

She hiccupped and nodded.

"And I'll kiss you all the way to London."

But she did cry, and he almost wept with her when they drove away from Minster Hill. As he held her close and kissed away her tears, he wondered what he was going to do with the rest of his life.

Chapter 14

When they entered the foyer of Christina's London home late that afternoon, the servants wouldn't meet their eyes, and the butler's voice lacked its usual haughtiness as he greeted them. Unfamiliar with the establishment, Max didn't immediately respond, but Christina instantly felt the fear. Before she could question her majordomo, the library doors flew open, and Hans stood framed in the doorway, his face white with rage.

"Where the bloody hell have you been?—and *you!*" he bellowed, jabbing his finger at Max. "Get out of my house!" Striding forward, he seized Christina's arm in a viselike grip. "Slut," he hissed, shoving her toward the stairs. "I'll deal with you later."

"Let her go." Peremptory and brusque, Max swiftly moved toward Christina.

Quickly turning back, she put her hand out to stop him. "Please, Max, don't." Her gaze was imploring. "Just go."

"You heard her," the prince growled. "Get the hell out of here!"

Max hesitated, reluctant to leave Christina to face her husband's wrath alone. But she mouthed the word, "please," and turning away, she began to ascend the stairway.

"You see?" Spiteful and triumphant, Hans smiled. "She knows what's good for her."

Glancing at Christina, already midway up the stairs, Max felt a rankling helplessness, his power and authority useless in the face of her wishes. He swung back to the prince, his expression grim. "Don't you dare lay a hand on her."

"She's my wife, Vale. Surely you understand the legalities better than anyone with your propensity for fucking married ladies."

"Screw the legalities," Max muttered. "If you hurt her, I'll come for you."

Hans's lip curled into a sneer. "Is that a threat?"

"It's a threat and a lethal promise and a guarantee."

"But then, you don't live in Silesia."

"The world's getting damned small."

"So gallant, Vale. You don't seem the type."

"I've changed." His voice was curt and chill.

"I'm sure your next conquest will appreciate your newfound gallantry," Hans derisively noted. "But, as you know, I can do anything I want to my wife." His pale blue eyes narrowed. "Now get out of my house." And turning, he followed Christina up the stairs.

Frustrated and provoked, worried for Christina, Max watched Hans until he disappeared from sight at the top of the stairs, and even then he debated going to Christina's defense. But when she had asked him to leave, did he have any right to interfere? The answer, of course, was unpalatable—a brutal reminder of the prodigal life he led, of what happened when he dallied with other men's wives.

Max surveyed the cluster of servants in the entrance hall, who appeared uncertain of their role with no direct orders from the prince. "I don't suppose it would do any good to say notify me if the princess is in danger," he brusquely said. Receiving no answer—as expected—he softly swore.

An overwhelming need to punch something washed over him,

but aware of how little a violent scene would help Christina, he walked to the door, instead, and let himself out.

Standing on the porch, he was assailed with misgivings.

Should he should stay or go?

On entering Christina's sitting room, Hans regarded his wife with an icy gaze.

Standing at the window, still dressed in her outerwear, she didn't acknowledge his presence. If only he would leave her alone, she thought, if only she had choices in her life . . . if only a thousand futile wishes would come true.

"He's gone, and he won't be back," Hans said into the heavy silence. "I hope you didn't expect him to rescue you like some romantic knight in shining armor?"

"Living with you, I've learned not to expect anything."

Ignoring her comment, he lazily drawled, "I hope your rich American bought you that expensive sable, because I'm not about to pay for it."

She turned to face her husband, the swish of her cape on the carpet a whisper of sound. "What do you want, Hans? I'm not in the mood to trade insults with you."

"How forlorn you sound, my sweet."

"Your company is distasteful. Is this conversation necessary?" She took a small breath, intent on maintaining her poise against his mocking scorn. "I'm here. That should be enough."

"I hope you didn't think he was in love with you—good God, you did! You stupid cow, he's bedded half of England since he arrived in August. Although, what he saw in a cold bitch like you is amazing. Novelty, no doubt."

Her temper rising at his vulgar insult, at the fretful possibility he spoke the truth about Max, she snapped, "Was Gina novelty enough for you?"

"Certainly not for two bloody weeks. I've been home and back again since Shelagh's."

"You're welcome to return to Silesia—the sooner the better."

"But this time, my *darling wife*," he murmured, his endearment pronounced with cutting sarcasm, "you'll be accompanying me. We leave for home in the morning."

I am home, she wished to say, but her boys were in Silesia. "And if I don't wish to leave at your command?" she testily replied.

"Then, I'll escort you under guard," he said, his voice cold and flat. "You're my property, bought and paid for—although perhaps not with such American largesse," he churlishly added, gesturing at her cape.

Her gaze was unutterably chill. "Are we through?"

How poised she was—her spine ramrod stiff, her pale beauty radiant—the English rose he had selected as the mother for his children all those years ago, unaltered by time. But he didn't share his wife . . . and he resented her damnable poise and cool beauty. Once he had her home again, he would see her bent to his will. "The train leaves at ten," he growled. "See that you're ready."

A moment later, as the door closed on him, Christina found herself trembling. Dropping into a chair before her legs collapsed, she experienced a terror she had never felt before. But then, she had never stepped outside the limits of a docile wife before, or indulged in a blissful, carpe diem existence for a fortnight. Or understood the great gulf between duty and ecstasy.

Any remnant of bliss had disappeared at the sight of Hans in the entrance hall. Instead, remorse and alarm inundated her mind, and self-pity, too, as she contemplated her future. The price she would pay for her brief moments of joy would be grim and unrelenting. She could be a prisoner if Hans chose to exert his rights . . . locked away on one of his remote estates where the civilized world didn't intrude. Her imprudent behavior could have an impact on her relationship with her sons as well. Hans systematically used them as leverage against her, and there was no knowing if he would condemn her before her children.

She had made a terrible mistake. She should never have succumbed to temptation, never gone on that morning ride, never sent Dieter away. . . .

And suddenly, recall of the happiness she had found in that small room at Digby filled her senses, the sweet, pervasive memories vanquishing the worst of her fears, reminding her that there was goodness and glorious bliss in the world. Their time at Minster Hill had only drawn her more deeply into the enchanting world of love, and she found herself reliving the beauty of those carefree days together, as if turning the pages on a picture album one by one. Pleasure had piled upon pleasure, and even now, apprehensive and wretched at the thought of her future, those unforgettable memories warmed her soul.

And beyond her own selfish interests, there was genuine delight in being with her boys once again, her love for them unconditional. They were coming home for the holidays, and with Christmas always a time of excitement for her children, their joy in the season would serve as balm to her self-pity.

She would see that the contentment of motherhood would be sufficient happiness in the future.

But she had once sojourned in paradise, had she not? And that bewitching holiday of the senses would always be hers.

From a shadowed portico across the street, Max surveyed Christina's London town house. Unwilling to desert her, perhaps for reasons that had nothing to do with her husband's anger, he stood silent sentry.

When she had appeared at a window briefly, he had taken note of the location, wondering if it was her room or—worse—Hans's. It took a moment or two to restore his reason after that unhappy speculation, and hunched against the cold, he wondered if his vigil outside her house in the dark meant he had lost his mind completely. Turning up his coat collar against the chill wind, he was forced to admit to something more than his usual casual feelings of amour. No other explanation accounted for his irrational need to linger outside her home in some benighted hope of seeing her again.

As he strove to make some sense of his oppressive gloom, the servants began closing the drapes. Each darkened window further disheartened him, making him feel as though he were being shut out of her life forever, and in the advancing darkness, he pondered the tumultuous disarray of emotions bombarding his brain. Was this indeed love? Or simply an intense infatuation? Or could it be no more than an outrageous degree of lust? Unsure, when to date he had never experienced such feelings, when lust alone had always impelled his amorous adventures, he tried to deal with his susceptibilities and ardor. Perhaps a degree of love at least had to be acknowledged, for he had never before stood outside a lover's house like some pitiful, moonstruck fool.

At his small epiphany, the last curtain was drawn, and frowning, he gazed at the shuttered, darkened facade.

So what the hell was he going to do now?

Stand here all night?

Break down the door and thrash Hans bloody?

Carry Christina away like some marauding barbarian?

The last possibility held the most appeal, but even in his deranged state—for what he was doing was surely bereft of reason—he understood Christina's sons were a serious impediment to such a plan.

At that instant of indecision and seeming checkmate, the front door suddenly opened, and the Prince of Zeiss appeared, dressed for the evening. Stopping on the porch, he slid on his gloves and, descending to the pavement, turned left and strolled away.

Any further equivocation, any ambiguity of feeling, was swept away by impulse, and waiting only long enough for Hans to reach the end of the block, Max stepped from hiding and walked toward the house.

He knocked on the door a few moments later. Before the footman had an opportunity to fully see him, he pushed his way in. Disregarding the servants' protests, he forcefully brushed them aside, strode across the entrance hall and took the stairs at a run. Reaching the main floor, he sprinted down the hall, mentally counting doors, in search of the room where he had earlier glimpsed Christina.

Three, four . . . five, bingo. Dashing into the room, his gaze swept the lamp-lit interior, landing on the sable cape. A split second later he had turned the key in the lock.

In relative safety, he took note of the half-opened door into an adjoining room, caught the familiar scent of lilies of the valley in the air. Moving across the pale yellow carpet, he pushed open the door. At the sight of her lying on the bed, her arms above her head like a child in sleep, his heart filled with tenderness.

A sudden pounding on the sitting room door abruptly checked any further benevolent emotions, as Christina sat upright in a flash. When her fearful gaze fell on him, Max smiled. "Don't worry. They can't get in."

"Oh, God, no!" Half whisper, half alarm, she began scrambling from the bed.

"It's fine," he soothed, walking toward her. "The door's locked."

"But, Hans!"

She was clearly panicked. "He left and"—Max tipped his head toward the continuing drumming noise—"that door's solid."

Leaning back against the bed, she visibly relaxed. "You're mad," she whispered, the faintest of smiles appearing.

"No argument there." He grinned. "I missed you." He stopped just short of her, not wishing to cause further alarm now that he was where he most wanted to be.

"They may send someone to bring Hans home."

Max tipped his head fractionally. "May?"

"He isn't well liked."

"And you are, I expect. In that case, I'd suggest you go and tell your servants that your visitor won't be staying long enough to endanger any of their jobs."

She gazed at him for a speculative moment.

"I may be mad but not stupid. I have no intention of putting you in jeopardy. Tell them I'll be gone soon."

She softly exhaled. "Thank you."

Stepping aside, he gracefully bowed and waved her by. But he couldn't resist pulling her into his arms as she passed, no more than she could resist lifting her face for a kiss. "I think I'm in love," he whispered as his mouth touched hers.

She shook her head, but his gloved hands came up and tangled in her hair, curtailing any further dissent. "And you can't stop me . . ." His kiss was gentle and swift, a teasing touch of paradise, and then he released her and pushed her toward the door. "Tell them not to bother us for ten minutes."

He stayed out of sight while she spoke to her servants. Once she had sent them away, he stripped off his gloves. As she locked the door, Max quickly shed his coat, and when she turned to him, he strode toward her, smiling.

"You can't stay long."

"I know." He hauled her close.

"He could be back anytime."

Max doubted it, considering Hans's propensity for night life, but he respected her concern. "A few minutes . . . that's all. I need to talk to you." He drew in a small breath. "And say a proper goodbye or hello or God knows what . . ."

"It has to be goodbye." Christina softly sighed. "We're leaving in the morning."

"And your boys are waiting for you."

She nodded, her throat choking with tears.

"Let me come and visit you at least."

"Lord, no! If he knew you were in Silesia . . ." She bit her lip and shook her head. "I couldn't take the chance."

"What if he didn't know." Max was willing to bargain with the devil if need be to see her again. "Surely you have some freedom of movement."

She shut her eyes against her great longing; to have him come to her would be heaven. And when her lashes lifted, her eyes were wet with tears. "I wish I could say yes; I wish for so many things, darling Max, and I'd almost be willing to do anything to have you near me. Except—"

"Endanger your relationship with your children."

"Except that," she quietly agreed. "If it were only me, I'd be without compunction. I'd go with you to the ends of the earth . . . to the moon and beyond." Her smile was rueful. "You see how much I want you—how I'm without pride in my need for you."

"Then, I'll see that we're together." Plain words, plainly spoken.

"No . . . no," she fearfully protested. "Don't even think it. It's impossible. You know what marriage contracts entail, each part and parcel, each pound of flesh minutely defined. You know how poorly women fare in the courts against a man of influence."

He faintly shrugged. "Given time and money and the occasional word from other men of influence, nothing's impossible."

"Max . . . please . . . you're being ridiculous. You don't even know if you love me. I don't know if what I'm feeling is—"

"It *is,*" he firmly said, suddenly sure. "We *are.* You don't love your husband. That's certain at least," he growled.

She shivered in his arms. "I despise him."

He gently touched her cheek. "If I could see that you didn't lose your sons . . ."

"Don't you understand? You can't. My oldest son is heir to the principality. I can't take him away . . . and you won't be living down the road or even on the same continent."

"Maybe you're right," he calmly replied.

"You *know* I am," she declared with a quiet vehemence.

"Only about your sons," he qualified, the mildness of his voice antithetical to hers. "We'll have to deal with that."

"You're not listening!" she cried. "There's nothing to deal with. There's nothing you or I can do. I *won't* leave my sons, and they can't leave their home."

"And you'll be miserable for the rest of your life."

"I'm not the only woman in an unhappy marriage."

"But you're the only one I love," he gently said.

She shook her head. "You can't know that. Not after only two weeks."

"So you want to just say goodbye and never see each other again?"

"I don't have a choice."

His arms dropped from her waist. "I see."

"Don't be angry . . . please, Max . . ."

"Too late."

"Tell me you understand at least."

"If you tell me you'll leave him if I find a way for you to keep your sons."

"Very well." He couldn't, not in a million years.

Pleased, his smile was suddenly all boyish warmth. "Word of honor?"

She nodded.

"Say it." He was on the cusp of enormous life changes, and he wanted assurance.

"Word of honor," she easily answered, because her marriage settlement precluded any advantage to her in terms of her children. As did the law.

Enfolding her in his arms once again, Max gently stroked her back. "In that case, I'll just say *adieu.*"

She cautioned him, "I won't have my sons put in jeopardy."

"I understand." He just needed the smallest window of opportunity; that was all he asked.

"And don't come to Silesia."

"If I do, no one will see me."

"That's not a reassuring response."

"I won't lie to you. I won't say I'll never see you again. In fact, I think I'll stay in England for a time. Do you know when you might be back?"

"I have no idea." She dared not say she might be locked away, nor could she, in good conscience, offer him undue hope.

He grinned. "Not a complete negative at least. I'll light candles in church for your safe return," he waggishly offered.

"You attend church?" Somehow the concept seemed unlikely.

"I will now."

She softly laughed.

"That's better. I dislike sad goodbyes. Or in your case, any goodbye at all."

"Max!"

"I know, I know. Marriage contracts, shackled wives, heirs to the throne. This is beginning to sound like a damned fairy tale."

She sighed. "I wish it were and I could shut my eyes and it would all disappear."

"Never fear. I intend to save the damsel in distress," he teased.

A soft knock on the door was followed by a murmured, "Ten minutes have passed, my lady."

"And if I don't leave now, my coach will turn into a pumpkin," Max lightly said. But a second later, his expression sobered, and when he spoke, the levity was gone from his voice. "I need a kiss before I go—to last me . . ."

Or a last kiss, Christina sadly thought. But she refused to give in to the tears threatening to spill over, and focusing on her sons as talismans to her despair, she lifted her face. "You've given me my only glimpse of paradise . . . and I'll always be grateful."

"You'll be seeing me again, darling. Don't cry." He kissed away the tear that had slipped down her cheek, and then lowering his mouth to hers, he kissed her softly, gently . . . and held her close and gave her comfort in her sadness.

At the second sharp knock on the door, they hugged each other one last time, and then Max stepped away.

"Don't forget me," he whispered.

"Not likely," she murmured, managing a smile even while she recognized she might never see him again. He was beautiful as sin, dark as Lucifer, tall and strong, yet capable of the most exquisite gentleness—and he had been hers for a few glorious days.

Halfway to the door, he turned back and, taking her hand, drew her with him into the sitting room. "A few seconds more," he murmured, squeezing her fingers.

She wanted time to stop.

He picked up his coat and gloves and kissed her when he reached the outer door, on her eyelids and cheeks, on the perfect bridge of her nose, on her trembling lips. "I'll be back," he whispered, the words a flutter on her mouth, a small ray of hope in her heart, and she tried to answer with some casual politesse when she despaired of ever seeing him again. But only tears came and a great wave of hopelessness, and she found herself sobbing uncontrollably.

"Hey, hey . . . ," he whispered, wiping away her tears with his shirt cuff. "You don't know what I can do. I can move mountains—literally . . ." He grinned. "We took down four thousand feet of quartzite to get at the gold in our Montana mine, so don't think I can't save one damsel in distress."

"My problems . . . are a . . . very large mountain," she sobbed.

"Not for me." Upon digging out his handkerchief, he mopped her cheeks and offered her a reassuring smile. "Give me a couple weeks to sort out everything."

His confidence bolstered her sagging spirits, and taking a deep breath, she forced back her tears. "I'm fine . . . now—really," she added with a gulping hiccup.

"Stiff upper lip till you hear from me?" he gently cajoled.

She nodded.

"Perfect." His grin was a tantalizing flash of sensuality. "I'm very good, you know."

She couldn't help but smile. "I know."

"Besides that," he murmured, his wink roguish. "I mean in moving mountains."

Having regained her composure, her tone was lightly arch. "In that case, I shall await your arrival on your snow-white steed."

"Good," he simply said, and with a last kiss, he left.

But as she stood at the window and watched him walk away under the dim glow of the street lamps, her feelings of despair returned. Despite Max's bravado, she knew the obstacles he would encounter, knew better than he the doctrinaire infallibility of her marriage contract. Understood the utter ruthlessness of her husband. And feeling desperately alone, she railed against the injustice of her world.

Chapter 15

A sense of desperation gripped Max as well, but his was predicated by limited opportunity. He had to find a way to free Christina from her marriage without harming her sons' future . . . and quickly, for his peace of mind. He wasn't naive about her uncertainty, nor would he attempt to impose his wishes on her, but within that narrow framework, he wanted to offer her some choices.

Finding a hackney on the next corner, he had the driver take him to a disreputable part of town—for a sizeable added fee—although the man refused to wait regardless of the price. And shortly after, Max was walking into a rough bar near the waterfront. The room immediately went quiet, his fine dress setting him apart from the clientele, his size and muscled form also giving them pause. Under ordinary circumstances such obvious wealth would have intrigued those of a more unsavory nature, but when a man's head skimmed the ceiling beams, gain had to be weighed against possible physical injury.

That equation quickly calculated, the patrons of the waterfront bar chose discretion over valor, and Max made his way through the crowded room unmolested. Familiar with frontier culture and that of the oil fields, he had no qualms entering a world of violence. And when he reached the bar and spoke to the barkeep, his voice was calm. "I'm looking for Burt Davis."

The man's gaze narrowed."Why?"

Max met the man's look with boldness. "Are you his agent?"

"Might be." The man crossed his arms across his dirty shirtfront. "Depends."

Max's smile held no warmth. "Then, tell him I have a well-paying job for him. My man, Danny, can vouch for me."

"Danny Gill?"

Max nodded.

A gap-toothed grin appeared. "Why didn't you say so. So you're his rich American."

This time Max smiled in genuine amusement. "I guess so."

"Killed some men in your day, I hear."

"I'm sure you heard wrong."

"Yes, sir. My hearin' ain't what it used to be and that's a fact." The fine cove's tone gave indication the man had spoken out of turn, and in way of apology, the barkeep quickly added, "Burt's due in anytime, gov'ner. Effen you don't mind waitin'."

"Give me a whiskey while I wait."

"Yes, sir. I've a right fine one, I keeps for myself. Pure Irish from County Wexford," he proudly noted, reaching under the bar to pull out his personal cache. He set the bottle on the greasy bar with a flourish and began wiping out a glass with his dirty shirttail.

Having drunk in mining camps and oil fields around the world, Max wasn't overly fastidious, but he considered himself fortunate that alcohol would serve as antiseptic to the dirt being rubbed around his glass. The whiskey, however, turned out to be first-class, and after buying the bartender several drinks in the course of his wait, he found he had made himself a new friend. Apparently Burt Davis had worked for the London police before being dismissed for some questionable, but unproven, activities having to do with shipments coming in from China.

Opium, Max suspected, although the barkeep didn't specify,

nor did Max ask. Hopefully, Burt had been only a middleman of some kind and not a user. An opium addict would be of little use to him—although he doubted Danny would describe the man as a "crackerjack facilitator" without good reason.

Burt's wife and son had died a year ago in a diphtheria epidemic, and he hadn't dealt well with the loss.

"Is he drinking?"

"Nah . . . although it might be better if he did. He's tighter than a spring, if you know what I mean. Work, work, work, that's all he does."

Several whiskeys later, the man Max had been waiting for was pointed out to him as he entered the bar. A second later, the barkeep, Fitch—they were on a first name basis now—shouted across the room, "Hey, Burt, Max here wants a word with you!"

Burt commanded respect, as evidenced by the caps doffed in his direction as he made his way to the bar. He was middle-aged, middle-height, trim, his hair of a nondescript color, neatly combed, his clothes pressed and clean. Clearly, an oddity in the motley crew filling the room.

Max took note of his eyes, having learned at a very young age to be conscious of a man's gaze. And Burt met Max's assessing look calmly.

He was an anomaly in this hell hole, Max thought—perfect to handle a commission that required more than stealth. And whether it was the half bottle of whiskey he had drunk or the look of the man, Max felt a sense of relief.

Step one, perhaps, was accomplished.

"My man, Danny, recommended you highly," Max said, holding out his hand. "I'm Max Falconer."

"The marquis." The much smaller man slanted his gaze upward and surveyed Max as they shook hands. "You're a long way from Mayfair."

"I'm a bit pressed for time or I would have sent for you tomorrow."

"Something can't wait?"

"Something important to me. Could we go elsewhere to discuss it?"

"Elsewhere?" There was a touch of suspicion in his voice.

"My house if you like."

The man was wary, with reason, no doubt, if his business took place in public houses such as this.

Max shrugged. "A place of your choosing if you prefer."

Burt nodded his head in the direction of the door. "Outside—in the open." He waved his hand. "You first."

The man was cautious. Good. Max preceded him out into the night.

After indicating they walk down the street, Burt bluntly said, "I'm listening."

Max spoke with equal directness. "I have a job for you. Something that would require you leave London in the morning."

"And if I hadn't come into Paddy's tonight?"

"I would have found you."

Burt cast a glance at the man walking beside him. "London's a big place."

"Money makes a town smaller."

"I don't take kindly to arrogant nobles."

"I rarely use my title. And you misunderstood. I'm just intent on accomplishing a mission with all speed."

"This trip out of town."

"That. You wouldn't happen to know German, would you?"

"I might."

"Well?"

"Well enough to navigate the waterfront of Hamburg."

Max felt a small rush of pleasure for the first time since they had walked into Christina's house and confronted Hans. "I need you for a surveillance situation—abroad. You can name your price."

"You don't bargain."

"In this case I don't. Danny said you're the best. I need the best."

"This surveillance is in Germany?"

"Silesia."

"On the prince or the princess?"

Max came to a standstill, his brows drawn together in a frown. "What do you know about that?"

"I know that you've been at Minster Hill for two weeks with the princess. Gossip like that spreads fast, my lord." He smiled for the first time. "Everyone's interested in your love life. The likes of you hasn't hit London in a long time. Has the cuckolded husband taken offense?"

"Jesus," Max murmured. "This is a fucking small country."

"I suppose you can romance the ladies with more immunity in the sprawling colonies."

He had come uncomfortably close to the truth, but Max hadn't searched him out to discuss his love life, or at least not in general. Or at least not his previous love life that had suddenly become insignificant and forgettable. "No doubt," Max muttered, beginning to move forward once again. "Would you mind coming to my house? Or more to the point, would you accept my commission?"

"After I hear what you want . . . maybe."

Max felt like hugging the man, but restrained himself. "We'll find a hackney," he said instead with apparent calm.

A short time later, the two men sat opposite each other in Max's study, a brandy in Max's hand and a tea tray beside Burt. The door had just closed on the butler, and Max came straight to the point.

"I need the princess watched." He scowled faintly. "Mainly for her protection. Her husband's a first-class bastard, and I don't trust him."

Burt looked up, a sugar spoon poised over his teacup. "How long do you want her watched and to what purpose. I'm not interested in spending the rest of my life in Silesia."

"Frankly?"

Burt stirred his tea. "If you don't know, say so. But I'm not in the business of playing detective for jealous lovers."

"After speaking with you, I intend to track down my barrister and see what I have to do to marry the princess."

"Ah," Burt said, the shock of the marquis's statement concealed behind the soft exclamation. "Then, you're serious."

The brandy glass Max held had gone undrunk, and he set it down now and leaned forward. "I've never been so serious in my life."

"She won't just leave him? Surely, she has cause enough with a man like him."

"Not without her sons. The princess is hostage to their future. The oldest, of course, is heir to the principality. And apparently, the marriage settlement allows her husband full custody."

"A not unusual stipulation," Burt remarked, lifting the cup to his mouth. "Women generally have to give up their children if they divorce. You're aware of that, I suspect." He drank a deep draft.

"Naturally. But I'm not concerned with "generally"; I'm concerned with finding a way the princess can keep her children."

"And while you pursue these avenues with your solicitor, I'm to see that she remains safe."

"I would be very grateful."

Burt drank the remainder of his tea and carefully placed the cup on the tray. "How long do you realistically expect the legal proceedings to take? I have business interests here that can be put on hold, but not indefinitely."

"If I had my way, tomorrow would be too long, and I intend to push Lawson and whomever he recruits in Silesia mercilessly. But realistically?" Max shrugged. "Six weeks."

"And if you fail? German courts won't be sympathetic to your cause."

"It would depend on the princess, of course, but I know what I'd like to do."

"Take her away?"

"To the States. It won't happen, though. Not with her sons' lives in the balance."

"I should probably find a position in the prince's household."

"You'll do it, then?"

"The Prince of Zeiss reported me to my superior one night when the police were cordoning off a theater for a rare appearance of the queen and I didn't move out of his way fast enough. He called me an anarchist agitator and insisted I be punished." It had been the beginning of a series of events that ultimately cost him his job. "He made problems for me," Burt mildly said.

"He makes problems for everyone," Max murmured, wondering if Burt Davis was involved in the new socialist politics. Not that he cared.

"I wouldn't mind turning the tables on him this time," Burt said. "I'll agree to put in six weeks over there."

Relieved and gratified, Max held out his hand. "Thank you. I'll sleep better knowing someone is with her. And with luck," he added, leaning back in his chair, "we'll have some resolution soon. Let me know how you wish to be paid. I'll see that you have sufficient money for travel and expenses before you leave tonight, of course. How will we handle communication?"

"When I hear anything of interest, I'll send you a telegram. I have a simple cipher I use."

"Excellent. I'll alert my staff so I'll receive your messages with all speed. And I may be over from time to time as well, so if you could find me lodgings that would offer secure cover, I'd appreciate it. And now at the risk of appearing rude, I'm anxious to find Lawson yet this evening."

"I understand." Burt rose to his feet.

Max followed suit, indicating the door with a wave of his hand. "We'll find my secretary, and he'll handle all the details. Tell him what you want and need. And if you'd like Danny to accompany you, just say the word."

Burt shook his head. "I work alone."

"Certainly. And thank you again—*very much*. The thought of leaving Christina unprotected was disquieting."

A few moments later, Max introduced Burt Davis to his secretary, Nigel Cummings, and after delivering his instructions, and apologizing once again for his abrupt departure, he took his leave.

Tom Lawson's maid helpfully gave Max her employer's direction a short time later, and before long, Max was being ushered into Judge Advocate Ralston's home. The guests were still at dinner, he was told by the judge's butler, the majordomo's tone infinitely polite despite Max's lack of evening dress. Aristocrats rarely crossed the thresholds of judges' homes.

"If you'd be so kind as to give Mr. Lawson a message," Max declared. "It's a matter of some importance."

After being shown into a small drawing room, he commenced pacing. When the butler came in to offer him refreshments, Max refused so curtly, he immediately apologized for his abruptness. And with such courtesy, the butler related to the footmen, that there was much to be said for the democracy in the colonies.

Seated opposite her husband at the dining table, Margaret Lawson frowned as he listened to the message a servant was whispering in his ear, her scowl deepening as he gave his apologies to their host. She so hated his unnecessary attention to his clients when everyone knew the means of rising in the world had nothing to do with clients and everything to do with making the right contacts. She coughed as he rose from the table, intent on warning him not to offend Judge Ralston, but he ignored her and hurried from the room.

"My husband is so dedicated to his profession," she said with a dramatic sigh, offering her dinner companions a rueful smile. "Sometimes, I worry for his health. But then, such devotion to duty is to be applauded, no doubt," she added with what she hoped was a becoming expression of virtue.

"My apologies, Tom, for interrupting your dinner," Max observed as his barrister walked through the drawing room doorway. "But I'm in a damned state of panic and need your counsel."

The barrister shrugged his brawny shoulders. "Margaret loves the politics of social climbing, while I find it incredibly boring. Consider, you saved me from certain misery."

"In that case, you won't mind me asking you to leave."

Interest flared in the lawyer's eyes. "What the hell's going on?"

"I'm getting married."

Tom grinned. "Tonight?"

"Cute."

"Sorry, I couldn't resist. If I didn't know better, I'd ask who she was, but since I do, let me give you a word of advice. It's not going to happen."

"But that's why I need you. You're going to make it happen."

"Not in Germany, I'm not."

Max was momentarily confounded. "Does everyone know my business?"

"When you take the beautiful Christina Grey away to your country home for a fortnight, the world takes notice. Or at least the world attuned to the amusements of society. She's been watched with great fascination since she blossomed into a beauty in her teens. When she married a handsome prince, every female in Britain sighed with envy. Her picture's in the papers more than any of the ugly daughters of the queen. What the hell did you think you were doing? Taking some pretty chambermaid to bed?"

"Her husband took offense," Max calmly noted. "He's taking her back to Silesia in the morning."

"And your heart's breaking. Pardon me if I challenge the constancy of your affections. Your reputation isn't the best."

"Have you ever been in love?"

"With my wife?"

"I don't care—with anyone. If you have, you know how I feel. If you haven't, I feel sorry for you."

"The fanaticism of the newly converted," Tom murmured.

"Mock if you wish. I'm not asking you to believe me. I'm only asking you to put your considerable legal skills to use. And if you leave with me right now, I'll add another five thousand to your fee."

Tom grinned and waved toward the door. "After you, my dear marquis."

Max laughed. "That's better. I don't need a lecture. I'm bloody near out of my mind with worry for her. Her husband's fucking evil, and I don't use the word loosely."

Max had his carriage outside, and on the way to Tom's office, he outlined his wishes. "First, I'd like you to get your hands on a copy of Christina's marriage settlement. Then research the particulars on the inheritance of the Zeiss princely title from father to son. Can Hans interfere with the transfer in any way? Also, I need the complete protocol on mothers' rights to their children in Silesia. Put whatever people you need on the case. Hire more if necessary. I'm in a damned hurry."

"Relax," Tom suggested. "There's nothing open at this hour of the night."

"Surely you can talk to some people yet this evening. You understand, she's *leaving* London in the morning."

The barrister was familiar with panic in his clients. And he was more than willing to help. Not only did Max pay well, but he was without the pretensions assumed by so many of the aristocracy. A likeable trait to a man from a working-class background who had succeeded in the world through talent and hard work. "I know a young underconsul in the German embassy," Tom kindly said. "He might be available."

"I'd appreciate whatever you could do. I want a divorce for Christina, and I want her children safe."

"And you want it tomorrow," Tom said with a smile.

Max relaxed marginally against the leather seat. "You read my mind."

"I'll know a few things by late tomorrow, but this is going to take time. You're not unrealistic about that, I hope."

"Use my money where need be to expedite things."

"That's a given."

"Do you happen to know any judges in Silesia?"

"I will in a week or so."

"Perfect."

"Don't have your wedding suit fitted yet, though," Tom cautioned. "Those young boys are going to be our greatest obstacle. Mothers don't get their children in divorces. You know that."

"She has to."

"You're sure of her affections, now? This wasn't just some lighthearted holiday for her—away from the cares of her luxurious world?"

"I don't think so."

"I hope like hell you're slightly more sure than that before you spend a fortune on this damned-near-impossible venture."

He hadn't said impossible, and that subtlety didn't go unnoticed by the marquis. That valiant intrepidity was, in fact, the difference between Tom and the great bulk of his fellow barristers. "I'm sure enough," Max softly said. "And you may spend my money with my blessing."

"I wish I had gold mines and oil wells."

"I wish I had a wife."

"Take mine," Tom offered waggishly.

Max gently shook his head. "I'm already spoken for."

"As is the princess, in case you didn't notice."

"Not for long, if you're as good as they say."

Tom grinned. "Fuck yes."

Max's smile flashed white in the dim light of the carriage lamps. "That's what I wanted to hear."

Chapter 16

Christina didn't sleep that night, nor did Max, the meeting with the German underconsul lengthy. Nor, for that matter, did Hans, involved as he was in his usual amorous entertainments.

The next morning, fatigued from his excesses, the prince was brusque and curt on the way to the station, and Christina sat as far away from him as possible within the confines of the carriage.

He seemed not to take notice of her, half dozing in the corner of the opposite seat, and when they arrived at the train depot, she quickly stepped down from the carriage. Without waiting, she moved down the platform toward the train, wishing to avoid any contact with her husband, hoping their journey passed quickly. Two men followed her—apparently Hans was taking no chances she might bolt. As if she would with her children in Silesia.

A young flower girl called to her halfway down the platform. "Flowers for you, my lady? Ten pence for violets today!"

She turned to her with a smile, the child's toothy grin, despite her ragged dress, touching. And when the girl thrust a small bouquet in her hand, Christina dropped a guinea in the child's palm.

"I don't have no change, ma'am."

"It's yours to keep, child." Lifting the bouquet to her nose, Christina inhaled the delicate fragrance.

"Look at the wrapping," the young girl whispered and then, turning away, shouted, "Ten pence for violets! Fresh today!"

Christina's heart began racing, and she quickly moved away, not wishing to draw attention to herself or the child. Glancing about in the remaining distance to their private railcar, nothing untoward caught her eye, but he was *here*, she thought, joy filling her heart. And she felt gloriously cheered after her long, sleepless night. He may have touched the violets she clutched in her hand, she reflected, and smiling, she brushed the velvety blossoms against her cheek.

Watching her, Max felt an answering imprint on his own cheek and found his weariness lifting.

Soon, he vowed, he would have her back.

Hans went immediately to his bedroom when he entered the private car, and with relief, Christina entered her bedroom and locked the door. Only then did she untie the white ribbon that held the small twist of paper around the flower stems. Spreading the crumpled sheet flat, she read the bold, penciled script.

"I'll bring my Christmas present in person. Love and kisses till then, Max."

He shouldn't. She should warn him off. Such boldness and daring was incredibly reckless. But the thought of seeing him again brought her such pleasure, she felt only deliriously elated.

If she saw him at Christmas, the season would be truly joyful.

If she saw him at Christmas, she would indeed believe in miracles.

Christina's boys had just arrived from school when she and Hans finally reached Zeiss Schloss that evening, and as she hugged them and listened to their excited tale of the wolf they had seen on their sleigh ride from the station, she knew where she belonged. Her sons needed her, and she them, their bond deep and strong—more so, perhaps, than other boys whose fathers' loved them. And at nine and eleven, they were still young enough to want her hugs and kisses.

She sat up late with them that night, drinking cocoa and listening to their tales of school—of their friendships and play, the teachers they enjoyed and those they didn't, their favorite subjects that had shifted this year to fencing and science, a poignant reminder, perhaps, of how fleeting their youth.

"I don't want to see you come home with scars on your faces," she teased.

"Not till university, Mama, when we join the dueling clubs."

"Please, Fritz—not even then."

"But, Mama, one has to," Hans junior, known as Johnnie to his family, seriously noted. "A scar is a badge of honor. Even the emperor approves."

Christina sighed. "He shouldn't, of course." Two years ago, the emperor had undone years of efforts to prohibit dueling in Germany by praising the dueling clubs as "providing the best education which a young man can get for his future life."

"Mama, it's only a scar. Nobody ever dies," Fritz said in an effort to console his mother. "And Johnnie is ever so good already. And Herr Anders says if I learn to use my wrist better, I'll be just as good in two years."

There was no holding back time, she reflected, listening to her sons compare fencing techniques and sword makers. In only a few years they would be at university, and she would be drinking cocoa alone on winter evenings. Morbid thought. God knew where Hans would be. Even tonight on their first night home, when he had not seen his sons for weeks, he had only criticized their boisterousness before going on to his own suite of rooms.

"Tell me what you most want for Christmas," she interjected, wanting to keep her sons young for a few more years—not wishing to think of her solitary life once they were gone. "I hope you're not too old for toys yet."

"Not me!" Fritz retorted. "I want some new cars for my train and a bigger microscope and a chemistry set that has real things that will blow up!"

"Only with supervision, darling," Christina said with a smile. Last summer, Fritz had set the garden shed on fire with one of his experiments. "Have you passed the stage for toys, Johnnie?" she asked, turning to her older boy. "Or are there still some things you'd like?"

He thought for a moment. "I'd like a new fishing rod for salmon fishing in Scotland. Auntie Charlotte says we can spend a whole month at their fishing lodge next summer. And Charles and Edward have the best rods from Osborn's."

Christina had already purchased the fishing gear, but she said with feigned seriousness, "I'm not sure we can find you one like your cousins' on such short notice."

"It's not important, Mama. Your presents are always the best." Her eldest son spoke with such a grave courtesy it always saddened her. As if he were on his best behavior. And she wondered if his childhood might have been different without the trauma of her marriage. Luckily, Fritz seemed immune to the undercurrents of hostility in their household, but as her firstborn, Johnnie had always been too aware.

"Did you enjoy your holiday in England?"

The abruptness of his question surprised her, and a multitude of possibilities raced through her mind. Had Johnnie heard something at school or from the servants? Had Hans spoken to the boys without her knowing?

"I know you always like to visit with Auntie Charlotte."

"I do," she quickly replied, relieved by the innocuousness of his query. "My visit was great fun," she added in the understatement of the century. "Maybe after the holidays we could take a flying trip to London before your classes begin. Osborn's could make you a custom rod," she said, smiling at her eldest son before turning to her youngest. "And I know who has the best toy trains in the city."

"Yippee! And cook can pack me the sandwiches I like with plum jelly, and maybe I can sit with the train engineer!"

"I can guarantee the sandwiches," Christina replied, grinning. "And if we arrive early enough, perhaps the engineer won't mind if you pester him for a few minutes."

"Charles and Edward don't go back to Eton till mid-January," Johnnie said. "Charles wrote me."

"Then, we'll have to make plans. I'll send Auntie Charlotte a note."

And if all the fates were properly aligned, if her husband's watchdogs could be eluded, if Hans went skiing as he often did after the holidays, she might even snatch a moment to see Max, she winsomely thought.

In the meantime, Tom Lawson was concentrating his efforts on gaining a sympathetic ear in the judiciary of Zielona Góra. Without much luck. A great deal of saber rattling had overtaken German foreign policy with the advent of Bismarck's chancellorship, not to mention the young emperor's propensity for bluster, and the target for much of their chauvinistic ill will had been Britain. An English wife unhappy with her German husband wasn't likely to find advocates in German courts.

"I wish I had better news for you," Tom said, gazing across his desk at Max, who was regarding him with a grim look. "Von Thaler seemed as though he'd cooperate, but apparently he changed his mind. As you already know, the marriage settlement is ironclad. Hans has sole custody of the children should they divorce, and even a divorce is questionable. Women can't petition for divorce in that jurisdiction, and even if Hans beat her, the courts rule very conservatively on that issue. The prince would have to be proved grossly abusive. And I don't mean a split lip or a bruise."

"Jesus Christ," Max muttered. "It sounds like medieval bondage."

"In some ways it is. Particularly in a case like this, where influence and wealth are so unequal. And while your money could possibly expedite a divorce, custody is another matter. When another man—you for instance—is involved with the wife, even without a marriage settlement, the courts view the mother's behavior with prejudice."

"So there is no hope."

Tom grimaced faintly. "There *is* another possibility."

"Tell me and make the news encouraging because I haven't seen Christina for ten days. Do you know how long that is when you're dying of privation? It's eight hundred sixty-four thousand seconds in case you were wondering."

The lawyer's brows rose in mild incredulity at the shocking change in the marquis who only weeks ago would have scoffed at the notion of love. "I have a detective on his way to Silesia," he said, "although I'm reluctant to promise anything."

"I know," Max murmured, sighing faintly. "But tell me anyway. I'm currently in a clutching-at-straws mode."

"This might be a modicum better than that. Do you remember when Burt sent us that little tidbit of information about Hans's cousin, Marlena?"

"The one Hans had an affair with years ago? How the hell is that going to help? He's had a thousand more affairs since then."

"I'm having my man check on some church records in Legnica. The cousin still lives there, it seems."

"And?"

"That's all we know so far. But according to Burt, Hans visits her on a regular basis."

"What the hell kind of hold does she have over him? From all accounts, he hasn't been faithful to anyone his entire life."

"We don't know. But it's an avenue we can't afford to overlook."

"Considering we're basically without hope at the moment," Max muttered, slumping lower in his chair.

"As a last resort, you could consider making Hans an offer for partial custody rights."

"Give him marks for his children, you mean."

"If that's what it takes."

Max shoved himself upright and gazed at Tom from under his dark brows. "If that's what it takes, then, that's what we'll do."

"Have you had any contact with the princess since she left London? Do you have any indication she still feels the same way?" The barrister pursed his lips, moved the pen on his desk, his unease apparent. "What I'm trying to say is"—he pursed his mouth—"do you think she may have changed her mind?"

Max smiled for the first time that day. "She's not allowed to change her mind."

Tom chuckled. "We'll charge ahead, then."

"Damn right. I intend to win this one," Max maintained, coming to his feet in a surge of power. "I don't care what the obstacles or legalities." He suddenly smiled. "I don't lose."

As he left the sprawling law offices, Max understood he was facing very long odds, and walking down Piccadilly, unmindful of the cold, he cast and recast the available data in his mind, struggling to find a way out of the impasse of marriage settlements and intractable divorce law.

He had telegraphed his family the day Christina left London, giving them a brief explanation for his decision to stay in England. And in the days since then, he had written more fully of his affairs and received letters and telegrams in return. "If you love her, we'll love her," his mother had written. "And if you need our help, Celia, Ted and I will come to England. We'll miss you at Christmas," she had said in her last telegram, and the next day, a dozen packages had been delivered to his home. They were sitting on the floor of his study now. Not in the holiday spirit, he hadn't had the heart to put up a tree. He was planning on being in Silesia for Christmas anyway. But Tom's news today had been particularly disheartening. They had been under the impression one of the local judges might have looked kindly on their cause. And now the man had reneged.

A tug on his sleeve broke into his musing, and looking down, Max saw a small, dirty urchin gazing at him with plaintive eyes. "Need your shoes polished, sir. Two pence is all and I'm right good." The young boy was shivering from the cold, his coat threadbare, his shoes tied on with rags.

"How old are you?" Max gently asked, touched by the youngster's poverty, reminded of Christina's sons as he looked into the boy's face. They were of an age, he suspected, although eons apart in fortune.

"I'm not underage or nuthin', sir. I'm old enough to be workin'."

He could see the fear in the boy's eyes. "Come out of the wind." Deliberately keeping his voice calm, Max pointed at a church door a few yards down the street. "You can polish my shoes there."

The heavily carved doorjambs offered protection from the wind, and once they were removed from the buffeting gusts, Max said in the way of putting the boy at ease, "How's business today?"

"Why do you want to know?" The youngster backed off a step, his expression wary.

"I'm not going to harm you."

"Business is good 'nuff, I suppose," the boy reluctantly noted.

Johnnie was eleven, Christina had said; Fritz was nine and according to his mother full of fun. He doubted this child had much time for fun. "Do you have a family?" he asked.

"Why?"

Max shrugged. "No reason." Touched by melancholy as he was, perhaps he empathized more with the plight of those less fortunate.

The boy hesitated, debating the liabilities in revealing his background, and then struck by the kindness in Max's eyes, he said, "My ma's home with the younger kids."

"Do you have a father?" Would he ever be one himself? Max wondered, a novel reflection for a man who had previously regarded fatherhood with alarm.

"Ain't seen him for years. An' just as well. I can take care of my ma and the kids better'n him," the boy said defensively.

"I bet you can."

Suddenly tears welled in the boy's eyes, and he looked away.

"I was feeling sorry for myself," Max remarked, tugging his handkerchief from his pocket and handing it to the boy. "I know how you feel."

"A swell cove like you ain't got no reason to feel sad," the boy murmured, leaving dirty streaks on his cheeks as he wiped away his tears.

From the mouths of babes, Max thought. "You're right, I don't."

"You ready to have your shoes polished now?" The boy spoke briskly, ashamed of his tears.

"Ready," Max replied, and placed his foot on the small box the boy had set on the pavement. The youngster worked quickly, his thin arms stronger than they appeared, and when he had finished, he drew himself up to his full height and said, "That'll be two pence."

As Max handed the boy a guinea, a gust of wind swirled around them, the boy visibly shivered and Max thought of his large, heated home, of Christmas drawing near, of the desperation of this young boy's life. "Would you like a job working for me?" he abruptly asked.

"Whadda you have in mind?" That wariness again.

"I could use someone to help my valet with my shoes. Five pounds a week and room and board for your family."

"Yer jokin', right?" It was an unheard-of sum.

Max shook his head. "I'm serious. My valet, Danny, was younger than you when he came to work for me. There's an apartment over the stables that should be big enough for your family. How many brothers and sisters do you have?"

"Six." But the boy hung back, distrustful of such largesse. "Nobody gives you sumpin' for nuthin'."

"I'm not giving it to you. You'd have to work for your wages."

"Ain't afraid o' work." But the suspicion remained in his eyes.

"Good. Then, come with me and I'll introduce you to Danny and my staff."

"My ma expects me home right soon." A warning that he would be missed if Max had nefarious designs on him.

"I don't live far from here, and I'm offering you a job, that's all."

"I suppose I could look . . ." His apprehension was plain; miracles didn't happen in his world.

But the Christmas season was a time of miracles, and after Danny took young Ned under his wing, after he was fed by the cook until he couldn't eat another morsel, after Max and Danny had gone with him to the dark cellar room that was home to his family of eight, and after the weeping, grateful Owenses had been transported in Max's carriage to the apartment over the stables, even Ned believed in miracles.

Much later, when the newly situated Owens family was finally settled for the night, Max sat before the fire in his study, drinking, thinking of Christina—his normal nighttime occupation since her departure. Unable to sleep as usual, he went for a walk near midnight, finding himself after a time before the church where he and Ned had met. Pushing open the door, he stepped inside.

Standing in the main aisle, he was struck by a sudden sense of peace, as though the shadowed house of God offered instant salvation to the torment of his soul, and he beheld with wonder the calm that had descended on him. Tall, soaring arches stretched heavenward; great banks of stained-glass windows glowed luminous in the moonlight, the gothic design elements mystical and unearthly in the half light. Immemorial time potent in the air.

In the distance, a tiny flicker of flame caught his eye, and he moved toward the glow, lured by the small radiance. As he drew near, he saw a single flame guttering low in a bank of votive candles.

The vital flame almost extinguished.

Like his hope.

He didn't know what prompted him, maybe it was his facetious promise to light candles for Christina's return or maybe it was his desperate need for renewed hope, but beginning at one row of candles, he systematically lit them, moving left to right and upward in a slow, steady circuit until the rack of tapers was ablaze. The resplendent glow illuminated the surrounding area, revealing the pieta above the altar. He gazed at the melancholy figures of mother and son, reminded of Christina's love for her children, of the suffering she was willing to endure for them, of the pain she would feel if she lost them, and he offered up a small prayer for their happiness. Then emptying his pockets of money, he stuffed the bills into the donation box and gazed once more at the blaze of flickering candles, his spirits lighter, his confidence restored.

While not overlooking Christina's fears and reservations, he would do whatever was legally possible apropos of her divorce, but if the legal options failed, as it appeared they might, he was prepared to see that Hans understood the merits and advantages of shared custody.

Turning from the altar, he moved back down the aisle, his feelings and methodology resolved.

Perhaps he should go to church more often, he cheerfully thought, pushing open the outside door.

There were effective measures that could be taken beyond those of his lawyers, and if all else failed. . . .

He felt encouraged as he stood on the darkened steps.

Day after tomorrow, he was leaving for Silesia.

He had a Christmas Eve engagement he didn't want to miss.

Chapter 17

The Christmas holiday would be a round of entertaining with Hans's entire family scheduled to be in residence at the palace. His mother had already arrived, her presence always daunting, for the dowager Princess of Zeiss still regarded the palace as hers. She ordered the staff about without thought for Christina's wishes or the servants' feelings. "Like mother, like son," Christina's lady's maid whispered as the dowager exited Christina's boudoir early one morning after having berated her daughter-in-law for not remembering that the Neopolitan creche was always placed in the blue drawing room, not in the main hall.

"It shows so much better in the hallway," Lise said in consolation.

"So I thought," Christina said with a smile, lazily stretching in bed. Nothing could dampen her spirits with the prospect of seeing Max inching closer by the day. Not even her mother-in-law's razor-sharp tongue at seven in the morning.

"Cook says one of these days she's going to put arsenic in the old lady's tea."

"Hush, Lise. Someone might hear," Christina warned, but she smiled and added, "Her cook at Wether House says the same."

The two women giggled.

"We're terrible," Christina ruefully noted.

"Not half as terrible as that old witch, my lady."

Finding it impossible to refute the truth, Christina inquired, instead, if her boys were up yet.

"No. I asked the footman before I brought your chocolate."

"They're bound to wake soon, though, so I wish to dress quickly. We're going skating this morning at the pond."

"The rest of the relatives are coming on the noon train," her maid reminded her.

"In case I'm not back by then," Christina replied, feeling newly liberated since her glorious days with Max when she realized happiness was given to those unafraid to embrace it, "the housekeeper knows what rooms are assigned to each of Hans's brothers and their families. The boys like to skate, as do I, and there's plenty of time to listen to my sisters-in-law complain when I return."

"Cook will serve tea if you're not back."

"And Hans's mother will preside as usual anyway. I doubt I'll be missed." Throwing back the covers, she slid from the bed. "Do you realize there's only two more days until Christmas."

Lise glanced at her mistress, the elation in her voice unmistakable, as had been her good spirits since she had returned from London. "Yes, ma'am."

"And all the presents are under the tree?"

"Every last one." Except the one locked in her desk, she thought.

"Perfect. Everything is absolutely perfect," Christina gaily noted, twirling in a open-armed pirouette, her smile dazzling. "I just adore Christmas."

A footman accompanied them to the skating pond, but Hans had dispensed with her watchdogs once they had reached Zeiss Schloss. For which she was grateful. In the event Max actually appeared in Silesia, she wished as little surveillance as possible.

She and the boys raced to see who could lace up their skates first, and Johnnie won. Gliding out on the shiny ice, he shouted, "Try and catch me!"

She and Fritz soon set off in pursuit, chasing Johnnie until Fritz caught the sleeve of his brother's jacket, and then he was chased in turn. The pond narrowed to a strip of river to the east, the groundskeepers having swept it clean, and after playing tag until they were all red-cheeked and winded, they leisurely skated down the river to the village and had hot cider at the inn. Sitting in their stocking feet in the window seat that faced the square, they drank cider and ate apple fritters dusted in cinnamon sugar and talked about the presents they were giving to their cousins and relatives.

"Look, Mama, look!" Rising to his knees to gain a better view, Fritz pressed his nose against the windowpane. "See that splendid red sleigh!"

"The driver's coming in too fast," Johnnie murmured, a warning note in his voice. "But those are prime blacks he's driving."

"Arabs," Fritz noted.

"Barbs. They're better carriage horses," his brother corrected. "Look at those noses. You can tell they're not Arabians."

"You're not always right!" the younger boy retorted.

"I am this time."

"Are not!"

"Am too."

"Are not!"

And then Christina gasped, and both boys looked at her.

"I choked on some cider," she dissembled, her face ashen.

"He's going to run his horses right into the inn!" Fritz cried, the boys attentions refocused on the team of blacks racing straight at them.

"The driver's standing up! He's not going to stop them in time! He's going to crash!" Johnnie said, not frightened so much as fascinated by the drama outside their window.

"That's enough, boys." Christina motioned them down, her heart beating like a drum.

Ignoring her, eyes wide, Fritz shouted, "He's hauling them to a stop!"

"He did it, smooth as silk," Johnnie softly said, awe in his voice.

"Come now," Christina coaxed. "It's all over. Sit down and finish your cider."

"I want to see those horses." Fritz was already scrambling down from the window seat.

"No! Fritz, no!" But her protest fell on deaf ears, her youngest son bounding toward the door in his stocking feet.

"Could I see them, too, Mama? I've never seen such prime mounts."

How could she refuse when Fritz was already out the door. "Don't be long," she murmured. Glancing around the small parlor, she took note of the lack of patrons and hoped the boys would soon return. With luck, Max would take his mounts to the stables, and she could escape before encountering him in so public a venue.

But prudent wishes fared poorly against boyish enthusiasm, and only moments later, her sons walked into the inn parlor with Max in tow.

"Mama! He said he'd tell us about his horses!" Fritz cried, his hand in Max's, his smile spreading from ear to ear.

Startled, she took note of her eldest boy holding Max's other hand. Johnnie didn't make friends like Fritz did, but he, too, looked transported.

Seconds later, the trio was standing before her.

"Mama, Mr. Weir. Bill, this is our mother," Johnnie said, well-mannered and courteous.

"Good morning." Max bowed faintly and smiled.

"He bought his horses in Algeria, Mama! Tell her how far out in the desert you went for them!" Fritz spoke in tones of wonder.

"Is it all right if he joins us, Mama?" Johnnie asked, recognizing his mother's reserve.

"If it's inconvenient," Max politely remarked. "Although it seems quite deserted in here at the moment."

He was right, of course, and she wanted to throw herself into his arms at any rate. "Please, join us," she offered with a casualness she was far from feeling.

The boys literally hopped about while Max unbuttoned his bearskin coat. When Fritz cried, "I'll take it, I'll take it!" and held out his hands, Max gently lowered the garment into his outstretched arms.

The young boy staggered under the weight of the ankle-length coat, but manfully struggled to a nearby table and heaved it up onto the polished top.

Waiting to seat himself until after the boys had taken their places, Max pulled up a chair across from Christina.

"Tell us about Algeria. Everything!" Fritz commanded, leaning his elbows on the table and his chin on his hands, looking as though he were ready to listen for hours.

Max smiled. "There's not time to tell you everything."

"We've plenty of time, haven't we, Mama?" Johnnie interposed. "We don't have to be back until teatime, and even then you said cook could serve tea if we weren't back."

Max held her gaze for a moment, amusement in his eyes. "It's up to you," he gently said. "I'm not in a hurry."

"The villagers might be coming in for lunch soon." She hoped her message was clear.

"Should I bespeak a private room. Then we wouldn't be disturbed." His voice was mild, as was his expression, and for all the emotion he displayed, they could have been the chance acquaintances they appeared.

"Say yes, Mama!" Fritz literally bounced on the window seat cushion.

"We don't have to be back until dark," Johnnie quietly reminded her, his wishes plain.

A small silence ensued while she tried to say no.

"Since I just arrived, perhaps during lunch the boys could tell me where I might do some hunting," Max suggested, not about to relinquish her so quickly.

"Mama!" More volatile, Fritz plucked at his mother's sleeve.

"Let me see whether a private dining room is available." Already rising to his feet, Max surveyed the room, looking for an attendant.

She could stop him. She should. It was madness to be sequestered in a private room with Max and her sons. If someone she knew saw her, Hans might be told. But paradise was so near, her sons were pink with excitement, and Max was already talking to a servant near the kitchen door. She couldn't bring herself to refuse.

Returning a moment later, Max said, "We're all set. They have a private dining room."

The boys were tumbling from the window seat, and as Max held her gaze above their heads, he mouthed the words *I love you.*

She flushed cherry red.

He grinned, raised his brows in a flicker of acknowledgment and offered her his hand.

She laid her fingers on his open palm because she couldn't refuse without drawing attention.

But neither was prepared for the shock to their senses.

She visibly trembled.

It required a deep, constrained breath before Max could close his fingers over hers and another before he was able to speak. "Are you hungry?" he murmured, meaning upon meaning in the brief phrase.

"I am," Fritz cheerfully replied, swinging his skates on his arm. "Can we have some more fritters, Mama?"

She nodded, unable to speak with Max's fingers burning into her flesh and she wondered how she would survive luncheon.

"Let me get your skates," Max suggested, releasing her hand, understanding if she didn't, that any further physical contact was out of the question.

"Thank you." She managed to speak in a near normal tone. She even smiled faintly like one would when responding to a courtesy. What she couldn't do, however, was contain the urgency of her desires. And against that ravenous physicality, she could only steel herself.

Max deliberately took a seat distant from hers when they sat down at the table in the private parlor. And during the meal, he scarcely dared look at her. For a man familiar with casual attachments, he was hard-pressed to maintain his calm. But he did because he had to, because he wasn't about to jeopardize future meetings with her, because he had every intention of sleeping with her tonight.

He conversed mainly with the boys, answering their numerous questions, asking some of his own concerning the local hunting. Eating because he didn't want to appear disconcerted. Refusing the local beer because he couldn't trust himself with even the slightest amount of liquor in such close proximity to Christina.

He took leave of them immediately after the meal, making an excuse about meeting a local guide, unable to stay a moment longer and not take Christina in his arms. He rose so abruptly, he knocked over his chair, apologized, and in response to Fritz's request to see him again, gazed at him blankly for a moment. "Perhaps after the holidays," he finally said.

The boys' faces fell. "We're going to London after the holidays," Johnnie noted.

Max quickly glanced at Christina.

"It depends on circumstances," she said.

"If Auntie Charlotte is home and Father goes skiing," Fritz offered, hopeful of seeing Max instead.

"I see." Max bowed faintly. "Thank you for a pleasant lunch."

"Tell us where you're staying." Fritz demanded, ignoring his mother's frown.

"I don't know yet," Max replied, picking up his coat. "I'm sure we'll meet again," he politely added and took his leave.

"Do you think we'll see him again?" Johnnie asked, clearly having enjoyed Max's company.

"Perhaps," Christina evasively replied.

"We could come here again; he might be here," Fritz proposed.

"We're going to be busy entertaining." Christina offered a small rueful smile.

"Maybe our company won't stay long." Hope echoed in Johnnie's voice.

"Perhaps we might steal away some morning," Christina suggested, her son's expressions so mournful.

"Yippee!"

"I'd like that."

Both boys were smiling again.

"So we'd better go back and be pleasant to everyone now."

They all groaned in unison.

"I'm buying horses like those blacks when I grow up," Fritz declared, coming to his feet as his mother rose from the table.

Maybe you could have Max's, Christina whimsically thought, allowing herself a blissful fantasy in exchange for the stultifying evening to come.

"And I'm going to ask that new gatekeeper, Burt, if he can find out where Bill is staying," Johnnie said. "He knows everything."

Chapter 18

"Where the hell have you been?" Hans growled, keeping his voice low as Christina and the boys trooped into the entrance hall. The dowager was descending the staircase, and he didn't wish to be heard. "Everyone's here and you're going to be late for tea."

"Cook has instructions to serve without me."

"And I'm telling you, you'd better be back downstairs in ten minutes or I'll—"

"Hans! Give me your arm!"

The dowager princess's commanding voice curtailed Hans's harangue, but he scowled and muttered, "Ten minutes, you hear," before turning to his mother.

The boys had stopped half-hidden behind Christina at the sight of their father's grim expression, and only after he walked away did they dare move.

They both touched their mother's hands.

"Go up to your rooms now," Christina quietly said. "I'll come to see you after tea."

"We only went skating."

At Johnnie's guarded tone, Christina offered him a reassuring smile. "I doubt your father will ask, darling." The boys had learned long ago to tell Hans very little. His reactions were generally negative, his temper unreliable. "Why don't I have some cakes sent upstairs for you."

"May we go skating tomorrow?" Fritz's voice held a plea.

"We'll try to get away early in the morning," she offered, wishing their lives were less fettered.

"I'll wake up whenever you say," her youngest promised.

"Me, too," Johnnie agreed.

"We'll talk about it after tea, darlings. Come, I'll race you upstairs."

When Christina walked into the drawing room a short time later, she felt as though she were entering an enemy camp, everyone's piercing gaze suddenly focused on her. Even after twelve years of marriage, she remained an outsider—"that English wife"—although, long ago, she had ceased caring what any of them thought of her.

Hans's brothers, as younger sons, had been obliged to marry for money, and consequently their wives were famous for their dowries rather than their looks. The daughters of rich burghers, they were bourgeois in temperament and outlook and deeply resented Christina's aristocratic antecedents. They viewed not only her nobility but her beauty with implacable rancor.

Hans's brothers, like he, subscribed to the male prerogatives of their class that allowed them to overlook their wives' feelings and indulge in extramarital affairs. Had she only known . . . Christina had often lamented. But at the moment, she had to get through an incredibly dull teatime. It was all a matter of timing, she had discovered in the course of her sojourn in the Zeiss family. If she mentally calculated each diminishing minute of an occasion, or in this case, a visit, it was possible to envision the ultimate end of the tedium.

However, now that Max was near, she had more to look forward to than the end of a dull house party. She could contemplate the glorious pleasure of possibly seeing him again. And with that lovely thought in mind, her attention drifted away from the hum of conversation, and she became unaware of the sniping and malicious gossip. Even her tea went cold unnoticed.

Suddenly, she became conscious of her sisters-in-law rising from their chairs in a rustle of the taffeta they favored when something less glossy would have been more becoming to their plump forms. Relieved another ordeal was over, she came to her feet. "Dinner is served at nine," she blandly murmured. "Until then." And with a graceful dip of her head, she walked away.

"She didn't say one word," her eldest sister-in-law said with a scowl.

"She was tipsy." Another pursed her lips and nodded knowingly.

"She looked happy," a third resentfully observed.

And they exchanged malevolent looks like evil harpies.

Hans glanced at his brothers and rolled his eyes. "There's time for a drink before dressing. Anyone for billiards?" The family gatherings were a trial for him as well, since he found his sisters-in-law odious and having to be at his mother's beck and call wearisome.

"Your wife isn't with child, is she?" The dowager princess cast a sharply skeptical look at her son.

"God, no." And then a loathsome thought struck his senses, and Hans's expression turned grim. "If you'll excuse me, I'll join you in the billiard room shortly."

Racing up the stairs, Hans then stalked down the corridor and stormed into Christina's sitting room like a rampaging bull. Finding it empty, he strode across the broad expanse of carpet and shoved open the door to her bedroom.

Still in her tea gown, she lay on a chaise, her eyes closed.

"You'd better not be pregnant, you bitch!"

The explosive cry shattered her blissful dream, and Christina's eyes flew open. "Not in front of the servants," she snapped, scrambling into a seated position. "Lise will hear." Her maid was readying her dinner gown in the adjacent dressing room.

"I don't give a damn about the servants," Hans snarled. "I want a fucking answer! Are you pregnant?"

"Kindly leave." He didn't deserve an answer, not with his record of infidelities and indifference.

His fists clenched. "Answer me, dammit!"

"No. Now get out of my sight." Rising in a whisper of white chiffon, she began walking away.

"Just a bloody minute," her husband growled, stepping into her path, reaching out for her.

"If you touch me," she said, low and chill, "I'll scream so loudly, your mother will hear me downstairs or in the next parish or wherever the old harridan's fat bottom is planted."

His hands dropped to his sides, his mother still a force in the administration of the principality. She also had staunch views on keeping up appearances. "I'm not finished with you," he whispered.

"But I'm finished with you." At least as long as her mother-in-law was at the palace.

"If you're pregnant, I'll kill you . . . after she leaves," he softly added.

The malevolence in his pale eyes was chilling, and only sheer will kept her from showing fear. "Fortunately, that won't be necessary," she murmured, and stepping around him, she moved toward her dressing room.

"I own you," he growled, looking daggers at her as she walked away. "Don't forget it . . ."

When she entered her dressing room, she sent Lise on an errand, needing a few moments alone to deal with Hans's shocking threat. What had initiated his furious question? Was she in real danger or were his words only an angry outburst? Would he reinstate her guards if he was concerned with her virtue? Now that Max was in the village, she dearly hoped not. But at base, she was frightened of her husband's violence, and Max's presence had suddenly become a terrifying liability.

At dinner that evening, Christina played her role of hostess to perfection, smiling with feigned sincerity, replying to questions with exquisite politesse, laughing at her brother-in-laws' clumsy humor, seeing that the meal was served smoothly and efficiently. She drank very little, uncertain of her control should she imbibe more than the smallest measure, surreptitiously glancing at the clock from time to time, wondering briefly if the timepiece had broken when the boredom grew too heavy. But the minute hand finally moved, and she inwardly sighed, outwardly forced a smile and signaled a footman to refill her brother-in-law's wineglass.

The men sat at table with their port after the meal. The ladies retired to the drawing room for tea, and Christina memorized the placement of the roses on the skirts of the Meissen shepherdesses atop the mantel while her guests dissected the current gossip at court.

Finally, the men reappeared; more wine was consumed.

And finally, finally . . . the clock struck eleven, and Christina could say with good grace, "It's getting late. If you'll excuse me."

Christina felt like a child let out of school, and gratified and relieved, she looked forward to the peace and quiet of her apartment. Lise met her at the door to her sitting room, but after the long, irksome evening of unwanted company and forced conversation, Christina wished the solitude of her own thoughts. "I can undress myself, Lise," she said, smiling with genuine cheer now that she had escaped purgatory. "I'll see you in the morning. Wake me at five. The boys and I have plans to skate before breakfast."

Where she would have to warn off Max.

"Yes, ma'am," her maid replied, bobbing a small curtsy. "Let me help you with your pearls before I go."

Christina waved her away with a smile. "I'm fine, really. Good night."

Chapter 19

"Let me help you with those pearls."

The voice was deep and low, achingly familiar, and she spun around, her heart beating like a drum. "How did you get in?" Shock and fear vibrated in her voice; irresistible joy infused her soul.

"No one saw me. Was dinner scintillating?" Max stood near the windows, dressed casually in a white sweater, twill trousers and hunting boots, his voice equally casual as though he weren't in peril. As though she weren't.

"Max! You can't be here! You have to go!"

"Hans has been leaving the palace at night, I hear. Later than usual, though, now that his mother is in residence. So we won't be bothered, if that's what's worrying you."

She couldn't mention Hans's latest threat or Max would demand she leave—when she couldn't. When she would never leave her boys. And all good intentions aside, Max wasn't capable of overcoming the obstacles of her marriage contract. "It's too dangerous for you to be here. The boys and I are going skating early in the morning. I'll be able to talk to you for a minute then. Please, now, go . . ."

"He said something to you." Her degree of alarm had escalated since morning.

"No." She nervously twisted her hands. "He didn't say anything. But you can't be found here!"

"You weren't this distressed when I saw you in the village. What happened?"

"Please, Max," she implored. "It doesn't matter. You have to consider my sons . . ."

"If I could assure you of their safety, could I see you later? Your new gatekeeper, Burt, is in my employ. If he were to corroborate the fact that your husband had left the palace tonight—would you agree to talk to me for a few minutes at least? I have to know how you are . . . whether you're safe." How could he leave her undefended when she was so obviously frightened. "And I need to hold you," he softly added.

She nervously fluttered her hand—whether a gesture to go or stay was uncertain—and biting her lip, she glanced toward the draped windows, then the door. "I don't know, Max . . . I want to . . . but—not here—good God!"

Trying to be heedful of her fear and not press her when he wanted desperately to take her in his arms and promise her the moon, he punctiliously kept his distance. "I wouldn't stay long," he offered. "A few minutes once it's safe."

Taking a deep breath, she tried to stem her tears, her emotions in chaos, the love of her life so close and yet so impossibly far. And then a flood tide of longing swept over her, and she whispered, "I've missed you so."

Her wretchedness hit him like a blow, and disregarding her resistance, he closed the distance between them in a few rapid strides and gathered her in his arms. "I'll go or stay," he breathed. "Whatever you want. I'll meet you anywhere; I'll wait for you anywhere. Just tell me . . ."

"I wish I knew. I wish for a thousand things I can't have," she murmured. Lifting her face to his, she couldn't conceal the love in her eyes.

Suddenly sure when he hadn't been before, suddenly undaunted when the world had seemed bleak, he smiled like he had at Digby that first morning, with boyish warmth and unalloyed promise. "Whatever you wish for, I'll give you. Whatever you want, I'll deliver." Then dipping his head low, his lips touched hers, and he kissed her like he had been aching to do for weeks.

The world became mere backdrop to their joy, jubilation sang in their souls, their murmured love words redolent of sweet passion and glorious hope, and for a fleeting moment they forgot the ominous present.

But desperation underlay their fragile happiness, and Christina came to her senses first because the terror of Hans's threat was still brutally fresh. "You can't stay . . . it's too dangerous . . ."

"A minute more," he murmured, the words warm against her mouth.

Footsteps echoed in the hall, and Christina went rigid in his arms. "You *have* to go." She shoved at his chest.

Releasing her, Max whispered, "I'll be back after midnight, after Hans is gone."

"Only if you're absolutely sure it's safe," she hissed, stepping away. "I mean it, Max. I can't take risks."

He wanted to pull her back in his arms, hold her for a thousand years. "I understand," he said.

"If it were only me . . ." She sighed. "I feel as though I have to apologize."

"No." He shook his head. "Not with your sons' future in the balance." Touching his fingers to his mouth, he offered her a kiss in lieu of touching her. "I'll be back." And then he walked to her balcony door and disappeared behind the draperies.

She heard the door open and softly shut.

* * *

Once alone, fear washed over her in suffocating waves, and if she had known where Max had gone, she would have run after him and begged him to leave. But his footprints on the balcony snow had already disappeared in the howling wind, and even had she wished to find him, it was too late.

She quickly locked the door to her apartment, but as quickly unlocked it, not sure which point of entry he would choose on his return. Although, she should lock him out if she were strong enough to renounce all happiness.

If she were . . .

She prayed he wasn't so irresponsible as to use the palace corridors; the building was awash with servants, guests, and holiday help from the village. And then her mind raced with possibilities. He had spoken of the new gatekeeper—was the man the same Burt the boys had mentioned? Did the gatekeeper have access to her rooms? Was Max only minutes away in his cottage? Should she go to him there? Would it be more or less prudent to leave her rooms?

But in the end she waited because Max expected her to be there when he returned, although every sound in the corridor made her start, every noise outside the window caused alarm.

How could he be so reckless and come to her here?

How could he ignore the danger to her boys?

How could he be so rash?

How would she survive if he didn't come back to her?

Christina fluctuated between agitation, alarm, and dizzying elation. She paced and sat and paced some more. Should she have some wine to calm her nerves? But after pouring herself a glass, she looked at it with dismay and set it back down. Would it be better to have the lamps on or off? she wondered next. Which would cause less notice? Should she change from her dinner gown? Should she not?

Taut with nerves, she couldn't make a decision, and wavering and capricious, she did nothing until the balcony door opened shortly after midnight and Max stepped into the room.

Wild longing overcame puny reason, and she flew to him, threw herself into his arms and hugged him with all her might. "I want a miracle," she fiercely whispered. "I want you."

Holding her close, he brushed her ear with his mouth. "I'm your miracle man—but say hello to Burt first . . ."

Embarrassed, color flaring on her cheeks, she broke away.

Less modest, Max casually waved the man in. "Darling, this is Burt Davis. Burt, Princess Christina. Now, tell her who's gone."

Burt politely put his hand to his cap. "The prince left the estate ten minutes ago, ma'am."

She uttered a heartfelt sigh and visibly relaxed. "Thank you for the information. And thank you for helping—us." She ruefully smiled. "Hopefully all will be reconciled someday."

"Yes, ma'am. The marquis here seems hellbent on it."

"I'll be back to the gatehouse soon," Max interposed, nodding at Burt in dismissal. He had more pressing things on his mind—like holding the woman he loved.

"Yes, sir. Watch for the lights from the billiard room when you leave. Those brothers are still drinkin'."

"I'll take care."

As Burt disappeared into the night, Max pulled the balcony door shut and turned back to Christina with a smile. "Now then . . . where were we? Something about miracles," he teased, pulling her back into his arms. "What do you say we rearrange the world to our liking? Do you have a first request?"

She inhaled, trying to calm her nerves. "I can't even think straight. It's too terrifying, having you here."

"No one knows I'm here. Hans is gone." Her husband's name had a jarring sound even to his ear, and he saw the instant terror in her eyes.

"You can't stay long," she whispered. "I'm sorry . . . but—"

"A few minutes. You sit down," he quietly said, leading her to a chair, "and I'll check all the doors and windows. Just to be safe."

He could feel her gaze on him as he circled the room, pulling the drapes shut more completely, checking the latch on the door, listening for any untoward sounds before returning to her. Sitting on the floor beside her chair, he gently touched her hands clenched in her lap. "Tell me what he said."

"Nothing," she murmured, not looking at him. "He was just obnoxious and rude. Nothing different." Then her gaze met his, and she smiled. "Now that I know what happiness is . . . I find him more irritating than usual, that's all."

"He didn't threaten you?"

"He's all loud bluster."

"He did, then."

"No more than he has in the past. Darling, I don't want to talk about him. I don't want to think about him. Ever."

"You looked beautiful this morning in the village, all rosy-cheeked and fresh."

His cooperation was immediate, his smile enchanting.

Her frown disappeared. "And you looked like a dream come true."

"I couldn't stay away."

"I'm glad, even though my heart is beating at triple speed."

"May I sit with you?" He felt like an adolescent, asking, but the situation was awkward, the tension palpable. "The door is locked," he pointed out as she hesitated, "and even if someone tries to break in, I'll be out the balcony door and away before they can enter. They'll find you alone."

She rubbed her fingers together briefly and then said, "Please do," wanting what he wanted, if only for a moment.

He released the breath he had been unconsciously holding and came to his feet in a swift, graceful flow of muscle. Taking her hands, he pulled her up from the chair and led her a few steps to an embroidered settee. Sitting down, he placed her on his lap because he wasn't completely unselfish, but he scrupulously refrained from kissing her.

"Tell me no one can get in," she nervously said, sitting stiffly upright, as though she were being graded on posture.

"You're safe." His voice was gentle.

"And you won't stay long."

"I'll leave whenever you say."

"You're sure? No one can get in?"

"They'd have to break down the door, sweetheart," he said in what he hoped was a reassuring tone.

She slowly exhaled, lightly touching his arm. The warmth of his body penetrated through the sweater, heating her palm, his quiet strength calming her. "I suppose you think I'm—"

"I know why you're frightened, darling. Why wouldn't you be? And if I weren't so madly in love, I wouldn't be here scaring you right now. I apologize. I should go, I know, but"—he faintly shrugged—"I can't."

"And I don't want you to go or I would have pushed you out the door long ago."

He grinned. "So we're both out of our minds."

"Or in love."

"Sometimes, I think it's the same thing. I've never been to Silesia before, nor would I ever have come here, except for you." He lifted his dark brows and smiled. "So there you are—lost to all reason."

She slowly slid her hand up his arm, resting it on his shoulder. "Which accounts for you climbing up to balconies in the snow."

"Exactly," he replied, sitting very still, savoring her touch. "I've never been so inspired before."

"But you love me."

"I do," he whispered.

"Unwisely."

He shook his head. "You don't know what I can accomplish."

"You certainly delivered a glorious bit of heaven tonight," she whispered, sliding her arms around his neck, his love warming her soul, his confidence giving her courage.

"I knew you'd want some."

"You always know what I want."

He drew in a small breath of restraint. "You probably shouldn't say that."

She felt his erection rise against her bottom and gently ruffled his hair. "I missed that, too," she murmured.

He blew out a small breath. "Jesus, Christina, I'm trying to act the gentleman here."

Her green eyes sparkled. "We could hurry."

"Are you sure?" His voice was tight with constraint; he had never been so self-sacrificing.

"*You* seem to be." His erection had instantly swelled at her proposal, and smiling, she moved her bottom against the long, hard length, a rush of desire warming her senses.

"I'm barely in control," he whispered. "Don't do that unless you mean it."

She gently squirmed, pressing down harder. "It's been a long time . . ."

"Too damned long," he said on a suffocated breath.

"Do you need a bed?"

His dark eyes burned into hers. "What do you think?"

"I think you could take me standing up in the middle of the town square at high noon."

"And I think you might let me," he softly growled, abruptly lifting her enough to pull her skirt and petticoat from under her. With her seated across his lap, he easily pushed her thighs apart. Sliding his hand through the split legs of her drawers, he slipped two fingers into her wet slit and whispered against her ear, "Do you really want me to hurry?"

She whimpered, his touch like wildfire to her senses, memory and wanting, precipitous lust washing over her in a torrent. She shook her head, but he didn't notice because he was swiftly opening his trouser buttons with his other hand. A moment later he had swung her around so she was straddling his thighs, and holding her up effortlessly with one hand under her bottom, he guided his erection to her honeyed sweetness.

Poised on the brink, his nostrils flared. "Last chance to stop me."

Her eyes were shut, her body taut with expectation.

His brief concession to conscience dissolved in the heat of passion, and he lowered her down his rigid length.

She engulfed him, welcomed him with a small, rapturous sob, an echo of his own fevered longing.

As her thighs came to rest on his, as blond pubic hair met black, when his erection was sunk deep, deep inside her, he stopped, not because he wanted to, but because he couldn't breathe.

Nor for a mute moment could she. She had forgotten how big he was, how long and flagrantly immense, and spreading her legs wider, she shifted to make room for him.

He drew in a rasping breath at the riveting friction. "Fast or slow?" His voice was rough, insistent; whether he was up to the choice was moot.

"Fast, fast. I can't wait." She ground her hips downward, wanting him with a deep, terrible craving.

He surged upward, ignoring the momentary resistance as her flesh gave way to his spiking inroad.

Gasping, she uttered a small cry and then clung to him as he lifted her, his large hands circling her waist, his withdrawal stroke sliding delectably downward, igniting every centimeter of pulsing, fevered tissue. Too quickly, she felt the first orgasmic ripple. "No . . . ," she wailed, distrait, wanting more.

"No?" he choked out.

She shook her head, not capable of speech. It was already too late, and frenzied, she clawed at his hands, broke his hold, plunged downward and, gorged full, crammed to surfeit, softly panted as her climax washed over her.

When her soft whimpers ceased, he instantly resumed his rhythm; his own urgency after so many celibate weeks, ferociously single-minded. She quickly came again as he drove into her body with hot-spur violence, and moments later, just when his first convulsive spasm began coursing downward, she suddenly cried, "No, no—you can't come in me."

Sooner stop a team of racing horses.

He swore, swept her upward in a galvanic display of muscled strength, and dumped her on the settee beside him, just as his orgasm exploded in a wild, gushing trajectory. A fountain of semen spurted everywhere, on her skirt draped over his legs, on his trousers, the settee, the carpet.

"Thank you," she breathed, lying sprawled against the settee arm.

Panting, he turned to look at her, his eyes slits, his expression a combination of shock and bewilderment. "Jesus fucking Christ," he gasped. "Don't call it—so close next time."

"I thought you knew."

"I thought you'd have a sponge in. You knew—I was coming back."

"I don't have any."

He swore again, then quickly apologized because tears had welled in her eyes. Reaching for her, he suddenly stopped, having brushed his hand over a clot of come on her skirt. Rubbing his palm on his trousers, he muttered, "Sorry about that."

She chuckled. "I can't call the maid, I'm afraid."

"At least I made you smile."

"You looked so disgusted."

"Christ, I feel like a fifteen-year-old." He softly sighed. "I'll wipe it up." He glanced at her skirt. "Although that stain is beyond my capabilities."

"I'll throw the dress in the back of my wardrobe."

A roguish gleam immediately lit his eyes. "You're going to need some help with that gown."

"Taking it off?"

"Yes."

"And you're willing to help."

His voice was silky smooth. "Courtesy is my middle name."

"I thought it was vice."

He grinned. "Don't believe idle gossip."

"At least we're not *both* amateurs."

"For my part, I find your amateur status appealing."

"While I find everything about you appealing."

"Everything?" Without waiting for an answer, he reached behind his neck, gripped his sweater collar, pulled the garment over his head and dropped it beside him.

Did he know how impossible it would be to send him away when he looked like that?

"Your turn now," he said, his voice husky and low, and stretching his arms along the back of the settee, she watched, fascinated, as the powerful muscles of his shoulders and arms flexed and bulged.

An unconscious manifestation of male strength and beauty, she thought, gazing at the taut, honed body sprawled beside her, the curve of his smile boldly teasing, his dark, sensual eyes shameless in their asking.

He glanced downward as if in invitation, and her gaze followed his, drifting over his broad chest and sculpted abdominals to the sweep of dark body hair tapering to a narrow trail below his navel and then lower to his arousal, still gleaming wet from her body, spiking upward from his opened trousers.

He knew she was ravenous for more. He knew.

"Don't look so smug."

"Content, darling, not smug. And in rut as you can see. Now, take something off."

"My shoes?" she archly queried.

"It's a start," he pleasantly said. "I'll take mine off, too." Unlacing his boots, he discarded them, pulled off his wool stockings and then sprawled back again. "Your stockings next, darling," he murmured, "and then I'll unhook your gown for you."

His quiet orders resonated through her body like molten heat, settling with tingling susceptibility in her pulsing cleft. "Why are *you* always the one giving orders?"

"Habit."

"What if I don't like it?"

"Then, you'll just have to wait longer for your next orgasm."

"And you're ready now?"

"You decide," he softly said, his gaze flickering downward, before returning to hers.

"Arrogant man."

He shook his head. "I'm only here to give you what you want. But we should get rid of that soiled gown." He was pleased her fear was gone, that she was fresh and cheeky, taking teasing issue with him again. "Feel free to order me about if you prefer," he offered, intent on keeping her mind off her apprehension.

"As if you'd obey."

"I could try."

She arched one brow. "Like at Tatton."

He smiled. "I *do* apologize."

"How much?"

"How much do you want?"

"Are we talking about the same thing?"

"As soon as you get out of that gown, we will be."

"You're not giving me an order, are you?"

"Consider it the most abject of requests."

"Abject?"

"Abject in the extreme."

"Liar."

His eyes widened. "Are we supposed to be telling the truth?"

She lunged upward and punched his chest.

"Is that the best you can do?" he asked, grinning.

She swung at him again, but he easily caught her fist, his grip light, but firm. "I've a better way for you to release your frustrations, darling," he said, husky and low. "You need cock." And this time, he didn't ask for permission. Lifting her up, he set her on her feet, spun her around so her back was to him and quickly unhooked her dress while she waited with irrepressible longing for what he would give her.

He was fast and sure, competent. This wasn't his first time undressing a woman. The thought was perversely exciting, rather than disturbing, as though she were about the receive the bounty of his much vaunted sexual skills.

"That's better," he murmured, tossing her gown aside, turning her around to face him. His gaze slowly drifted down her corseted form.

She should take issue—with his knowing smile, with his shameless assurance, with his quiet mastery—although she doubted any of his lovers ever did, at least not with his huge erection, irresistible and oh, so close.

"Take off your petticoat and drawers, so I'll have access to your cunt."

She blushed at his bluntness, at the brusque tenor of his voice. At the quickening his words provoked in her throbbing flesh.

"Do you need help?" His voice was velvety, low.

She gazed at him, a skittish heat in her eyes.

"Hurry and I'll give you this." He arched his hips faintly, his turgid arousal lengthened, and impelled by the lush sight, she quickly began to untie her petticoat. Seconds later, she stood before him clad in only her white lace corset.

"Your breasts are huge," he pleasantly said, as though he were complimenting her on her deportment. The tightly laced boning pushed her breasts into high, swelling mounds, the lace cups straining under the abundant weight. "And your pretty blond pussy . . ." His voice had dropped to a heated whisper, his erection stirred, and intensely aware of his readiness, Christina unconsciously licked her lips.

"You can't suck on me yet, darling. You have to wait. I want to ram this into you first." He forced his rigid penis away from his body so she had a better view. "Show me where it goes."

Lust burned through her senses, and indifferent to former issues of submission or command, she instantly complied, sliding her fingers over her silky blond curls.

He crooked his finger. “Bring that closer.” He pointed between his spread legs.

Without hesitation, she moved forward and stood before him trembling.

“You like it when I tell you what to do, don’t you?”

“No.” The sound was barely audible.

“Well, your cunt does. Look. You’re so excited to have my cock, that hot little pussy is dripping wet.” He ran a finger up the warm, pearly fluid running down her inner thigh while she shuddered under his touch. “Look,” he softly ordered.

When she didn’t immediately obey, he reached up, caught her chin between his fingers and forced her head down.

“You’re ready for fucking, aren’t you?” He turned his finger, so the lamplight illuminated the small runnels of liquid.

She nodded.

“Your breasts are flushed pink,” he murmured, sliding his wet finger over the mounded flesh, slipping it under the lace to rub her nipple. “Does that mean you want to be fucked?”

She drew in a small breath at the streaking heat racing downward.

“Your breasts are so damned big,” he whispered, massaging the taut bud of her nipple, “you look like you might be pregnant . . .”

“Don’t say that.” She shuddered.

He saw the sudden fear in her eyes, and slipping his hand free, he pulled her closer. “I’m sorry,” he whispered.

“Just don’t say that,” she breathed. His legs pressed into hers, and his palms were warm on her back, his forbidden presence posing incredible danger.

She tried to step back, but he held her.

“Max, we have to talk about this.” Restless, agitated, her voice quavered. “What are we going to do? I don’t have any sponges, and I want you so; but we can’t do this—or at least not now or at least—”

"We don't *have* to do anything," he gently said.

"But I want to." Part wail, part cry, all petulant need.

He didn't speak for a second. "Then, I just won't come in you," he declared with more calmness than he was feeling because *that* was going to be hell.

"I like it better when you do."

Fuck. Now what? His mind racing, he quickly closed a minimum of buttons on his trousers and rose from the settee, wanting what she wanted, wanting it all. "Surely, you must have some sponges in your bathroom. Say yes," he muttered. "Make me a happy man."

"My God . . . of course." Her smile was instant. "You see what panic does to reason. Although, I wasn't planning on having you stay, so I suppose my brain was focused on one thing."

"Like now."

Her smile broadened. "But this is better."

And there *were* sponges when they went to look—enough in the cabinets for a dozen brothels. Something Max prudently didn't mention.

But when they reached her bed a short time later, their contraceptive dilemma solved, he stopped, a faint scowl creasing his forehead.

"He's never slept in here." She understood.

He turned to her, his gaze shuttered. "Jealousy's a terrible thing."

She took his hand. "But we're together now."

He sighed, discontent, wanting more.

"And I need you." She smiled. "In a great, great, GREAT number of ways . . ."

He laughed. "Do you think I'd forget?"

"I wouldn't have let you."

"Am I on stud service tonight?" His mocking drawl matched the roguish light in his eyes.

"I thought you understood. Was I too discreet?"

"Actually, your wet cunt was a pretty good clue."

"So, what exactly can I expect from a beautifully endowed stud like you?"

"Satisfaction, ma'am, all night long."

"My goodness! All night?"

"If you last that long," he mildly noted, tumbling her back on the bed. He lay atop her, his weight lightly balanced on his elbows, his erection pressing into her stomach, his lower body gently oscillating so she felt the tantalizing hardness slide back and forth. "If you get tired, let me know," he whispered, "and I'll let you rest for a few minutes."

"What if I want to stop?" Her gaze was heated, wanton.

"You can't . . . and you can't call for your maid or cry for help or even scream when you come." He slid his tongue over her upper lip. "How the hell will you climax when you can't scream?"

"How will you climax if I don't let you in?" she playfully murmured, and shoving hard against his chest, she caught him by surprise and rolled away.

For a fleeting second.

He caught her leg, jerked her back and, flipping her over, nimbly covered her again.

Her smile was delicious; a temptress with hot green eyes stared up at him. "You're very fast, my lord," she purred. "And strong like an ox." Her gaze drifted downward, and when her lashes lifted again, a mischievous light shone in her eyes. "Or is it hung like an ox."

"Would you like to find out?"

"I dearly would—if you don't think me—"

"A salacious little tart?"

"You have scruples?" she murmured.

He looked amused. "None."

"Then, what must I do to engage your interest?"

He lifted his body slightly. "Spread your legs."

"That's all?"

"It's the only relevant requirement I've found."

"Libertine."

"Were you looking for personal enlightenment or sex?"

"Like this?" she silkily queried, slowly opening her thighs.

He lowered himself between her legs. "Wider." He grinned. "There are degrees of relevancy."

She squirmed a little, lifting her pelvis, stretching her legs wider. "Is that satisfactory?" She could feel herself open, a sweet ache of wanting spiraling upward.

"Very nice," he murmured, rolling back on his haunches, taking in the delectable view. "A hot little cunt just waiting to be fucked . . ."

"Thanks to your quick thinking."

"And your well-supplied bathroom. Are you ready for me?"

"Oh, yes . . . ever so ready."

"You can't scream," he warned, beginning to unbutton his trousers.

"I'll be very good."

He looked up and smiled. "You always are." His trousers were half-lowered.

"May I touch you?"

"No." He gazed at her from under his lashes. "I can't guarantee my good behavior yet."

"I'm not interested in good behavior."

"Then, I'm in the right place," he whispered, sliding off his trousers and moving between her legs. On first entering her, he suddenly stopped, savoring the lush, throbbing heat, the enveloping rapture. How long had he waited to be here; how far had he come to feel this; more pertinently, how tenuous was his restraint when his senses were wildly impatient?

Christina's hands slid around his waist, then slipped downward to the base of his spine, and lifting her hips, she pressed on his lower back, instantly sheathing him in her hot, covetous body.

So much for restraint.

Too long deprived, she was as impatient and ravenous as he, as immune to moderation and self-denial. She drove the pace that first time, and gentleman that he was, he kept up. Afterward, she said, "Thank you," so sweetly, he made a point of showing his gratitude in her next three orgasms.

She didn't tire that night as he had teasingly suggested, no more than he could subdue his rampant cock. It was insatiable. He was, they were . . . mindless to all but carnal passion and rapacious cravings.

But they were deep in love, too, and impetuously living for the moment. He made love to her and she to him and them together in a glorious, heated reunion night that overlooked strife and caution and the foreboding future.

Because they were blissfully together again.

"You have to go." The clock had struck four, then the quarter hour and now the half hour. "The servants will be up soon."

"I know." He tightened his hold on her.

"I mean it, Max." He shouldn't have stayed so long. She shouldn't have allowed it.

"I know."

"Don't say 'I know' again."

"Yes, dear."

"And don't say 'yes, dear' like that, like you have no intention of moving."

"*Yes, dear*. Is that better?"

"Better, if I weren't in a state of panic."

"He never comes back this early." Max lazily stroked her shoulder.

She pushed away and, resting on her elbow, glared at him. "If you don't get out of my bed this instant, I'll manhandle you out the door myself."

"Mmmm . . . hardly the impetus to bring me to heel—the thought of you manhandling me." His brows rose in a teasing flicker.

"Max," she said in that utterly quiet voice he had often heard his mother use, the one that made it clear playtime was over.

Quickly kissing her, he muttered, "I'm gone, I'm gone . . . ," and leaped out of bed. "But I'll be waiting at the inn," he said, pulling his sweater over his head.

"If we can get away." Her wanting overcame her fear.

"I'll be there anyway. Otherwise, I'll be waiting at Burt's cottage late tonight."

In short moments, Max was dressed, and bending over the bed, he kissed her with delicious tenderness. "So you don't forget me," he whispered as he stood to leave.

"I never could in ten lifetimes," she murmured, glowing with happiness.

Christina and the boys' skating was ruined that morning by the arrival of Hans's brother, who insisted on accompanying them to the inn. Max stayed out of sight, hoping Christina might rid herself of her company, but the youngest Zeiss brother did his solicitous best to charm his sister-in-law. While Christina did her polite best to keep her distance. Very soon after their arrival, she realized it was useless to think that she might have a fleeting chance to see Max, that her boys could speak with the Mr. Weir they had so enjoyed yesterday; so she conveniently recalled a commitment at the palace, and they all returned.

The boys were disappointed they had missed an opportunity to visit with Bill, but Christina devoted the rest of the day to her sons, coming down from their apartments only for lunch and tea. And even the boys were included at the dinner table that festive evening. Once the last course had been served, the men forewent their port, and everyone trooped into the drawing room where the enormous tree and presents were on display. Christina and her sons had exchanged some of their gifts that afternoon because those under the tree had to pass the censure of the dowager princess in terms of practicality or edification. Hans's mother didn't believe in frivolity, which squelched the notion of any playful high jinks during the holidays.

The sisters-in-law received jewelry, another piece each year from the Zeiss family vaults, while as wife of the titular head of the family, Christina was given stocks in the mining company the family owned—as were the boys. Not that any of them had access to the funds; it was merely a token. The dowager always received several Meissen figures especially made for her collection, and Hans and his brothers exchanged custom-made firearms of various types. This year, apparently, a tiger hunt was on the schedule, for each man received a shotgun of sufficient caliber to take down a tiger.

The dowager then read several passages from the Bible as always, and the festivities were over.

It was nearing midnight when Christina returned to the main floor after tucking her sons into bed. If she hoped to leave the palace, it was necessary to take a head count of her guests' locations. The dowager, it seemed, had gone to bed along with the sisters-in-law. Hans had left the house, the hall porter replied in answer to her question. Why was she surprised? Christmas was no different from any other day for her philandering husband. But she was also deeply relieved. He would be gone till morning. The brothers were drinking brandy in the library, and she bid them good night from the doorway, politely refusing their offer of a drink. As she pulled the library door shut, she could feel her heart thumping in her chest, and as she walked up the stairs to her rooms, she had to put her hand over her mouth to cover her smile.

Even though she shouldn't . . .

Soon, she would be with Max.

Chapter 20

His scent still lingered on her sable wrap, the fragrance in her nostrils with the collar lifted high against the cold, triggering sweet memory. She flew over the crisply packed snow toward the lights of the gatekeeper's cottage, her green suede boots peaking out from under the long-skirted fur as she ran, her cheeks pinked by the cold and excitement.

Suddenly, a tall, shadowed form stepped into her path, and with a muffled cry, she stumbled backward.

Strong hands righted her, instant familiarity flooded her brain, and fear gave way to pleasure.

"I thought you'd never come," Max murmured, opening the front of his bearskin coat, pulling her into his warmth, closing the coat around her.

"And I thought the house would never quiet," she murmured, smiling up at him, feeling a rapturous sense of homecoming. "Have you been waiting long?"

"No," he lied, when he had been standing watch for hours. "But now that you're here, Merry Christmas . . ."

"The very, very merriest," she whispered, snuggling close.

"It gets better," he teased.

She tilted her chin slightly, taking in the roguish light in his eyes. "I suppose you say that to all the ladies," she murmured, feeling joyfully alive.

"All the ladies about to fall into my bed this Christmas Eve," he drawled.

She fluttered her lashes at him. "That would be me."

"Good, then, I caught the right lady outside my den tonight."

"Are you the big, bad wolf?"

He shook his head and swept her up into his arms. "I'm the very, very good—"

"Angel in my life," she whispered, tipping her head to kiss his cheek.

"Some might disagree," he murmured, striding toward the cottage. "But thank you. And in the spirit of the season, might I offer the lady—"

"Everything . . ."

He came to a halt at the raw beauty of the whispered word, and when he gazed down at her, his dark eyes held a piercing witchery. "If only I could . . ."

"You can—tonight the world is ours." Her gaze lifted to the sky. "The brilliant stars and the black sweep of the heavens and—"

"A gatekeeper's cottage with our name on it."

"What name?" It was fantasy, but she hungered for it.

He knew. "The Marquis and Marchioness of Vale."

"And where are our children?"

"Sleeping, dreaming of sugar plums. I put them to bed myself."

"Next time, I'll help."

"Yes, I know." He kissed her very gently under the sparkling stars and vast dark sky. "Don't wake them," he whispered against her mouth, "when we go inside."

She had tears in her eyes when he set her down in the small parlor, and he said, "Don't cry or I will," and screwed up his face to make her laugh.

She did, and he felt better, too, because it would be hard enough to send her back to the palace without dwelling on cold, stark reality.

He helped her off with her cape and took off his coat, then unlooped the small reticule at her wrist and set it aside, like a mother might for a child. "Are you tired?" he gently asked, because she hadn't moved.

Swinging her head the merest distance, she smiled at him. "I'm basking in the beauty of this very special Christmas Eve. Thank you for coming."

"I counted the days."

"Me, too."

A small silence fell, the ticking of the mantel clock suddenly loud.

"What would you like?"

She shivered in the heat of the small fire-lit parlor, notorious temptation in the query.

"What I meant to say is, would you like a glass of wine or brandy. I was trying to be polite."

She shook her head.

"Would you like to sit before the fire?"

She seemed not to hear him, and glancing around, she asked, "Where's my purse?"

Reaching over the small distance, he plucked it from the side table and handed it to her.

"I brought you a present," she said, quickly glancing up at him and then back at her small embroidered reticule, adding in a low rush of words, "I hope you don't think it presumptuous or ill-conceived"—she took a breath—"or scandalously forward." She was fumbling with the tiny gold clasp. "I bought it on impulse, and then thought maybe I'd overstepped—"

He stopped her agitated discourse with a light finger on her mouth and, taking the purse from her hands, easily unfastened the clasp. "Whatever you give me will be perfect," he murmured, handing her the pocketbook.

"Good—I hope—that is . . . you may think—" Biting her lip, she reached inside the purse, pulled out a small red leather box and shoved it at him.

Her brows were drawn together in a faint frown as he opened the lid.

"A ring," he softly said, lifting a gold band from its velvet bed.

"You see," she muttered, watching his unreadable expression. "I shouldn't have . . . I knew I shouldn't." He could have a hundred lovers giving him gifts.

Max's smile appeared. "It's wonderful . . . beautiful . . ." He turned it in his fingers, the wide band without ornament except for a small square-cut ruby.

"I knew ruby was your birth stone; there's something engraved inside," she pointed out.

"You didn't buy it here, I take it."

She shook her head. "I went incognito to a small shop in Berlin. But the young jeweler who engraved it must have known. He said, 'I envy your lover, Princess,' when I came back for the ring."

"And I'm the lucky man he envies," Max said with a smile, lifting the ring to the light. "To the Love of My Life," he read and then chuckled. "You don't know how perfect this is."

She didn't know whether to be relieved or disgruntled at his laughter.

"Come into the bedroom," he proposed. "See what I have for you."

"If we're going into the bedroom, I know what you have for me."

"You might be surprised." He held out his hand.

She hesitated at his broad smile. "How surprised?"

His grin widened."Good surprised, Your Wariness."

When he led her to the bedroom at the back of a short hall and opened the door, she gasped. "Where did you get violets in December?" A score of small crystal vases sat on the dresser and chair, and on the bedside table.

"I think the lady said Italy. But that's not what I want to show you. Come in. Sit down."

"And where would you like me to sit?"

"On my bed." He grinned. "If you don't think me too forward."

Her smile was flirtatious. "I do believe that's one of your sterling qualities."

"Then, we'll get along just fine, ma'am," he murmured, waving her in with a graceful bow.

When she sat down and began to take off her boots, he said, "Let me," and dropping to his knees, he slipped off one then the other. As she lifted her legs to move onto the bed, he stopped her. "Just a minute," he murmured, placing her feet back on the floor. "I've something for you."

His voice had changed, the teasing casualness stripped away, and she felt a flutter of nerves.

Pulling something from his trouser pocket, he opened his fist and let a small ring slide down into the cup of his fingers. "This was my grandmother's and then my mother's and then mine," he said, his voice soft with memory. "I wore it on my little finger until it no longer fit." He looked up and smiled. "I want you to have it. It brings luck."

"I could use some."

"*We* could use some. And there's more." He handed it to her. "I had an inscription done as well." A flashing smile lit up his eyes. "You see why I chuckled. Two ruby rings, two inscriptions, you needn't have worried about your impulse. We're meant to be together."

"If only the gods would agree," she murmured, glancing inside the ring. "Digby forever." Joy warmed her heart. "Where we first made love."

"Where we *fell* in love." Taking the ring from her, his voice turned husky. "As long as I'm here on my knees . . ."

Her heart skipped a beat.

"I've been waiting to do this for weeks . . ." His dark gaze held hers. "Would you do me the great honor—"

"Max," she softly protested, trying to pull him up. "No . . . don't . . ."

Taking her hands and placing them back in her lap, he said, soft and low, "You can't stop me."

"I won't listen."

"Then, don't."

"Max, please be practical . . ."

His smile was indulgent. "I'm not a practical man as you may have noticed."

"As the whole world has noticed. But, darling . . ." She shut her eyes against the awesome wonder of his unstated words.

"Don't listen. Close your eyes if you wish," he murmured, "but I'm saying what I'm saying anyway because I've never felt this way before and I have no intention of giving you up and every intention of moving every damned mountain in the world if that's what it takes. I've loved you from the first moment I saw you, and on numerous occasions I've made my feelings clear. And if you don't think me too immodest, I was under the impression those feelings were returned." He grinned. "It might have been your screams or perhaps the inexhaustible nature of your—shall we say—interest in me." Encouraged by her small smile, regardless that her eyes were still tightly shut, he went on. "And need I remind you, you owe me. I've ignored my business and family, given up all my social activities, and traveled a great distance to see you in this remote location."

Her eyes snapped open. "I didn't ask you to come."

"But you wanted me to."

How could she lie?

"And I had the distinct impression our reunion last night was satisfactory," he drawled, amusement in his gaze.

"Do you want compliments?" He could always make her smile, make the world seem a better place.

"I want more than compliments, darling. I want to sleep again at night. I want to enjoy a sunrise, a ride through the countryside, a brandy without fear of my melancholy deepening. I want happiness back in my life. Marry me, darling." He grinned. "There's only one acceptable answer."

"Yes," she heard herself say, as though rational thought had suddenly taken a holiday, as though she could so simply agree.

"Then I'll take you to see the roses in Montana next summer," he promised, receiving her answer without curiosity or surprise, never questioning his ability to alter the world. Lifting her left hand, he slid his grandmother's ring on her ring finger, ignoring the band she already wore.

"And I'll show you my cottage on the ocean near Brighton," she whispered, overlooking everything but the great, immense love in her heart.

Tumbling her back on the bed, he covered her and, bending his head, murmured low, "We'll have everything—you and I . . ."

"Tonight . . ."

"Tonight and always . . ."

She seemed more fragile here in Silesia, buffeted and unsure, and he held her close and didn't speak again of the future. It was enough to have her with him this Christmas Eve, his own small miracle, and he kissed her, tenderly, lightly, with gentleman kisses that wouldn't offend. Until she whispered, breathy and flushed, "Give me more than just kisses."

"We're not even married yet and you're issuing orders," he teased.

"But I can't wait. I don't want to. I thought about you a thousand times today, about seeing you again, about last night, about . . . now—"

"Then, I have your permission?" Half-serious, half-playful, he had been cautious with the specter of fear tempering her mood.

"Not only my permission, but my most fervent invitation," she replied, a small heat in the words. "I'm not breakable, you know."

"I know," he lied, when she was so different from their time in England.

"You don't have to treat me like a china doll."

"Then, I shall pillage and plunder to my heart's content," he said with a roguish grin, coming to a seated position and beginning to undress.

"Ah . . . my hero—when I'd begun to despair. Should I undress or are you going to rip off my clothes?"

He shot her an amused glance. "You might not like to wreck that cashmere gown."

"What if I'm in a desperately passionate mood?" Her smile was dramatically seductive.

"Then, we'll have to see what we can do about it." Shirtless and barefoot, he winked at her.

"I'm getting what I want for Christmas," she sang in a cheery, light refrain. "I'm getting what I want for Christmas . . ."

"How the hell can I pillage and plunder when you're so eager?"

"I've changed my fantasy."

He laughed. "Then, you'd better give me a clue before I start."

"I'm riding a unicorn through a sun-dappled forest—"

"And a prince with a big hard-on—"

"A pirate, darling . . . please, this is my fantasy, although definitely a well-endowed pirate."

His clothes disposed of, he turned to her. Pushing the soft green cashmere of her skirt up over her thighs, he reached for her garters. A look of surprise crossed his face, and he swiftly shoved the skirt waist high. "You're going to be damned easy to plunder," he drawled. "Where the hell is your underwear?"

"Did I forget to put on my under things?" Arch, honeyed words.

"It sure as hell looks that way."

She offered him a flirtatious glance. "I must have been thinking of you."

"Well, thank you, ma'am," he silkily murmured, sliding his middle finger down her cleft, stroking up and down. "You must have been thinking of me a lot. You're damned wet."

"I confess, you did come into my thoughts once or twice today. And maybe you thought of me once or twice, too, or are you always hard like that?"

"Only for you. You're the only woman I stay hard as a rock for. Word of God."

"When you talk like that—all flattery and charm—I don't even mind that you're not a pirate."

"Maybe I am," he said, slipping her garters and stockings down her legs. "Maybe I'm going to take you away and chain you in my cabin and make you service me from morning to night."

"Umm . . . morning till night—how wonderful . . . what kind of boat do you have?"

He laughed. "They're not boats, Miss Captive Maiden, they're vessels, and mine's a yacht as if it matters when you're as wet as you are." Rolling her over, he unbuttoned the small amber buttons at the back of her neck.

"I have my standards," she replied, her voice partly muffled by the quilt pressing into her face.

"When I thought all you needed was a hard cock and plenty of time." He flipped her back over. "Lift your arms."

"I think my pirate would speak in more romantic terms," she muttered through the folds of cashmere sliding over her face.

"How about endless, boundless time and that hard cock tied in a red silk bow, seeing how it's Christmas." Pulling the dress away, her face appeared, her smile, the joy in her eyes.

"I was just missing that red ribbon," she purred. "How ever did you know?"

"I know everything about you," he whispered, settling in a sprawl beside her, trailing a fingertip down her throat. "I know how deep you like it and how often; I know you like your nipples sucked hard so you feel it clear down to your toes. I know you scream when you come, and I know how long I can make you scream. And I know that if you really wanted a red bow, I'd find one for you. But what I know most is I love you with all my heart and I've never had a better Christmas in my life . . ."

"Oh, Max . . ." Her eyes filled with tears, and she threw her arms around him.

He kissed away her tears, and then kissed her like she wanted to be kissed. But not for long, because he knew what she really wanted, and he wanted it, too.

And when he entered her, when he slid inside her bewitching warmth, it wasn't about skill or technique or expertise, or about pirates or fantasy, or even about passion or desire; it was about two people in love who needed to feel, if only for a time, that the world belonged to them. That they belonged together. That their love would survive.

Much later when the most potent lust had been sated in both sweet and hot-blooded play, when they lay in the shambles of the bed, when the scent of violets and sex permeated the room, Max rolled over on his side and, lightly kissing her rosy cheek, said, "Look under your pillow."

She smiled up at him. "Why?"

"Because I want you to."

"Hmmm . . ."

"Do it, troublesome wench."

"Will I like it?"

He grinned. "Damn right."

Half-drowsy from excess, almost too lazy to move, she slid her hand under the pillow and felt blindly. Touching a smooth metal object, she pulled it out and held a gold cameo locket up to the light. "How lovely." Turning the small oval in her fingers, she examined the pendant. "Does it open?"

"If you know how."

"Tell me."

"Slide the cameo to the right."

She did, and a hidden spring latch opened, revealing a small compartment inside.

"Lift the small door."

Inside were portraits of them. "Where did you get my picture?"

"From one of the hundreds of shops that sell photos of the reigning beauties, my naive darling. I had the image made smaller."

"And now you'll always be with me," she murmured, touching the small portrait of Max.

"Until better times," he replied, taking the locket from her hands and sliding the gold chain over her head. "There now, that's where I want to be," he playfully noted, arranging the locket between her breasts. But his gaze turned serious, and he added, "I couldn't buy you anything big, hence the jewelry. You can take that back with you . . . and think of me."

"As if I don't every moment. How long can you stay, although I shouldn't ask when you have a busy life of your own."

"For a while," he replied, his business affairs at a stage where they would soon require attention. And not long-distance attention.

"How positively blissful to think of you so near. Tell Burt he may have to take to sleeping away on a regular basis."

"I think he already understands. He made himself comfortable quarters over the small stable in the yard outside."

"Will you wear my ring? I know it's childish and immature, but I adore the fantasy."

"Only a temporary fantasy, darling. You don't know me if you think I'll settle for hidden moments like this for long. And of course I'll wear your ring." He held up his hand and showed her. "I'll always wear it. You're my adorable wife."

Her happiness fairly glowed. "You make me feel as though anything is possible."

"Absolutely certain, darling—my word on it. Tom is busy seeing to that. He promises me news very soon."

She half rose on her elbows. "Is there really some possibility—some way to deal with this?"

Not wishing to mention Hans's earlier marriage should the lead turn out to be false, he said instead, "Tom's extremely optimistic, that's all I know. But he's the best, so I'm depending on him."

"While I find I depend on you completely. You alone bring me love, happiness, comfort. I don't know what I'd do if I couldn't see you—" Her voice broke.

"Darling, don't cry," he soothed, pulling her close. "The next few weeks will see you free. I promise." It was a promise he meant to keep—with or without Tom. "Now, sweetheart, it's Christmas Eve, and there are better things to do than worry. For instance," he whispered, "you haven't come in the last five minutes . . ."

Her body responded with a rush of desire as it always did to the temptation he offered. "You do know how to take a girl's mind off her troubles, Lord Vale," she murmured.

His grin was impudent. "We try to be amenable, ma'am."

"A mild word for your talents, my lord."

"Thank you, ma'am," he silkily replied. "Now, there's one last bit of jewelry you might like . . ." Rolling over, he pulled open the drawer on the bedside table and took out an object. Swiveling back, he held it out to her.

"What is it?" She turned the translucent jade in her fingers, the large ring exquisitely carved, the violet hue exotic and rare.

"A toy."

"For me or for you?"

"For you."

Her eyes widened briefly. "Where does it go?"

"I'll show you," he murmured, plucking the ring from her fingers.

"What will it do?"

"Make your orgasms better."

"Better?" she said in wonder, her senses on instant alert. "Better than before?"

He smiled and nodded as he slipped the carved jade ring down his erection, a slight pressure required to slide it completely down to the base of the shaft.

She could feel a liquid heat materialize in her vagina at the sight of his rigid length swelling larger at the forceful pressure. And reaching out, she touched the velvety flesh, moving her fingers from the base upward over the pulsing veins, closing them delicately to circle the swollen red crest. "Does the ring hurt?" she whispered, bending to kiss the object of her delight.

With a low, throaty sound, he slid his fingers through her hair, held her head in place for a moment, and eased the taut head of his erection past her lips, into her mouth. "No more than that hurts you," he softly said.

Opening her mouth wider, she swallowed as much as she could, and as the tip rested against the back of her throat, she closed her mouth midpoint down the splendid length. Her mouth was crammed full, the width and breadth enormous, and she moved her hips in anticipation, a ripple of desire fluttering through her vagina. She softly moaned, greedy, insatiable, her swollen labia slippery, slick with need, the delectable friction raising her carnal passions to fever pitch. She wanted sex, sex and more sex. . . .

Her desire was evident with her bottom raised high, her hips softly gyrating as she suckled him, her pinked breasts hanging like lush ripe fruit, the pressure of her mouth and tongue frenzied, ravenous.

His lust well primed, but disciplined after years of fucking, he leisurely fondled the succulent plumpness of her breasts, lightly pulled on her nipples, his fingers in turn gentle and ungentle. "Such a hot little puss," he murmured. "You really like my cock in your mouth, don't you?" He bounced the heavy globes of her breasts on his palms. "And all this is mine . . ." He tightened his fingers over her breasts, shock waves of rapture streaked downward to her heated core, and she whimpered in longing.

"Do you need cock?" he whispered, sliding his hand down her back, over her bottom, slipping two fingers into the liquid warmth of her cleft. "Maybe we should take my cock out of your mouth and put it here . . ."

After countless orgasms and heated sex, she was in thrall to the lust coiling deep in her belly, abandoned to all but fevered sensation, and she resisted his attempt to pull back. Driven by immediate gratification, she wouldn't let him go, holding him captive with her teeth.

His breath in abeyance, he forced his fingers into her mouth and lifted her away. "I know best, darling," he firmly said, holding her face between his hands. "You haven't tried your new toy yet. And I have this really hard cock. Look, darling, how big it is from your sucking."

She looked, shivered, clenched her hands against the spiking lust as she knelt beside him.

"You don't want this to go to waste, do you, when your cunt is running wet?"

"But I liked what I was doing." A fevered small whisper.

"Afterward, darling, you can suck on me all night."

She was trembling. "How can you be so calm?"

"I've had more practice," he remarked, her ravenous carnal appetite generating the smallest discontent.

"I should say no."

"You can't."

"And you can."

"If I wanted to. But I don't. Now, come." At some inexplicable, subterranean male level, he needed to tame that tantalizing, shameless abandon.

"And I must obey?"

"You must." Sitting up, he slid back against the pillows and headboard.

She could no more resist than she could stop breathing, and

she went to him as he knew she would and took the hand he offered her and lowered herself over him as he wished, shutting her eyes against the sublime pleasure.

He shouldn't have said it; twice he stopped himself. The third time he didn't. "Tell me you can't live without my cock."

As she sat astride him, her eyes were level with his, half-closed in ecstasy, the green like glowing cat's eyes in the lamplight, and she half smiled because she suddenly understood the extent of her power. "I can't. I need your cock—here and there and anywhere," she purred. "Anytime at all . . ."

"Then, here first," he growled, "and *now*." His hands closed hard on her hips, shoving her downward.

The warm, smooth jade was an immediate, recognizable rapture against her throbbing labia. Then he forced her hips lower while he violently thrust upward, and the carved protuberances on the penis ring came into shocking contact with her clitoris.

She screamed.

He heaved his hips upward again, and she screamed a second time, a high, piercing, half-breathless cry that brought a smile to his lips. "How do you like it?" he unnecessarily murmured, holding her firmly against the carved jade ring. Holding her in a vicelike grip that sent wave after wave of delirium coursing through her body, the assault on her senses lasting and lasting in a sustained rampage of frenzied, fanatical, violent orgasms.

"Tell me how much you need it," he fiercely whispered, needing to equalize the balance of power, ramming into her over and over again.

She couldn't speak, could scarcely breathe, powerless against the staggering ravishment, buffeted by climax after climax until finally, she gasped, "No more."

"Just one more," he muttered, beginning to ejaculate, and he poured his white hot seed into her as she fainted away.

Moments later, she rested in his arms, the jade ring discarded, her voluptuous warmth soft against him, the flutter of her lashes giving evidence of her waking. When her eyes fully opened, he whispered, "I'm sorry . . . ," when he never apologized except with her, when he had never needed to before, when he had never cared enough for his feelings to be in disarray. "Take your revenge. Do with me what you will . . ."

"It *is* ten times better," she whispered, her faint smile redolent of pleasure. "But you still have to pay."

"Willingly," he quickly replied, contrite, filled with self-reproach.

Her eyes gleamed with mischief. "You said I could suck on you all night—afterward . . ."

His brows rose. "Not exactly punishment . . ."

"But I'm having my way."

He grinned. "We both are, I'd say."

She patted him gently on the cheek. "Soon, we will. Lie down."

He did, although the minute reserve that came over his features at her command made her smile. "You're not obedient by nature, are you?" she observed, sitting beside him, her expression sunny.

He laced his hands behind his head, lifted one shoulder in the faintest of shrugs and debated his answer when only moments ago he had been eager to atone. "I'll certainly try," he diplomatically replied.

"This shouldn't be unbearable."

She was clearly enjoying herself. "I'm sure it won't be."

"But . . . I definitely sense a 'but' in there."

"You're damned troublesome"—he grinned—"in a loveable way, of course."

"And you're damned self-willed, although your splendid sexual talents make amends for your generalissimo tendencies. And this beautiful erection you seem to keep in a state of unbridled, champing readiness more than makes up for your autocratic temperament." She gently weighed his pendulous testicles in her palm. "Do you have anything left in there?"

"You'll soon find out."

"Should I swallow it?"

His erection lengthened before her eyes.

"You'd like that . . . it seems," she murmured, stroking the hanging pouches, gently squeezing the large spheres within.

He flexed his spine the merest distance, stifled his low groan.

"And you promised to be good," she whispered, stretching the supple, velvety sacs. "So I can play with you as long as I want."

His throaty growl was audible that time; his penis twitched against his stomach as he surveyed her through half-closed, heated eyes. "Maybe not too long."

"You promised," she playfully intoned.

"I must have lied." His voice was a low rasp.

"Perhaps I should hurry."

But he allowed her her game, clench-fisted and tense, when all the time he wished to bury himself inside her with a mindless desperation he had never experienced before. He decided, between the provocative rise and fall of her head and his increasing lust, that their long separation and the uncertainty of their future precipitated his impetuous feelings. And he tried, he really did, to leave her unhampered.

But at one hundred twelve—he was counting to distract himself from his urge to take charge—he capitulated or rather didn't, and Christina found herself flat on her back, her legs spread and chock-full of the erection she had brought to the brink of orgasm.

"Sorry," he whispered, driving in with the strength of considerable frustration. "Sorry . . . sorry . . . sorry . . ." Each word of his apology marked by another powerful thrust of his lower body.

"Next time," she murmured, not really caring, more selfish in her pleasure than in her authority, only wanting to feel him next to her or in her, or always within reach.

And she told him so when they lay together in the shimmering aftermath.

"I'll always be with you," he said. "Always and ever."

His words warmed her heart, and even if it was only a dream, she allowed herself the fantasy. "And we'll have our own Christmas someday . . ."

He leaned over and kissed her temple as she lay in his arms. "This is only our first of many, my adorable wife." He held his ring to the light. "For now and always . . ."

She touched the ring he had given her to his, wishing like a child at play that life would allow such whimsical fancies. "For now and always," she whispered.

Chapter 21

Christina slipped through a basement door and climbed the worn stone steps to the kitchen hallway. It was still dark, the servants not yet awake on Christmas morning, and taking care to tiptoe up the back stairs, she reached the safety of her rooms just as the clock was striking five.

Softly closing the door, she pulled off her sable cape and tossed it on a chair.

"Out for an early walk?"

She froze at the sound of her husband's voice.

"I couldn't sleep," she said, trying to speak calmly.

"I noticed. Your bed hasn't been used."

A shiver went up her spine at the measured cadence of his tone, at the cool indifference in his voice. "Do you want something?"

"I want my wife to keep her cunt at home."

"You're hardly the man to make demands. Where were you last night?"

He rose from a chair, and she saw him for the first time in the shadows of the room, his height and strength more daunting in the half light. "None of your damned business. Now tell me where you were."

"None of your damned business."

"Poor church-mouse wives like you can't afford to be rebellious. Be sensible, my dear."

"I don't have to be sensible," she calmly said. "Your mother's still here."

His smile was reptilian. "She left during the night. She became ill and preferred being home."

Feeling as though she had been punched in the stomach, Christina fought to keep terror at bay. Her trump card was gone.

"Unfortunately you weren't available to bid her goodbye," Hans said with soft malice, "but I offered her your good wishes. Now, about this morning walk," he silkily said. "Who is he?"

"There's no one. I went for a walk. That's all."

"You smell of sex."

"You're hallucinating," she said, refusing to show fear. "Or maybe the scent of your last bed partner is still in your nostrils."

"My last bed partner prefers jasmine. Not your favorite fragrance as I recall."

"This is all unnecessary. I went for a walk; I'm back. I'm sorry you had to waste your time."

"How sweetly naive you are, my dear. But then, you always have been. Now, as for your future—"

"My future is my own."

"Hardly. Your future is whatever I decide it is, and I very much hope you enjoyed yourself tonight because that's the last time you'll ever have sex. I'm putting you under house arrest, as it were, to guard your"—he smiled tightly—"virtue. And my reputation," he coolly added.

"Your reputation's a joke. And you can't keep me prisoner without everyone knowing." But she was bluffing because just last year a young, wayward wife in the community had mysteriously died without her death causing a ripple.

"Actually, I can. I've already talked to Dr. Koetcher, and he's sympathetic to the manifestations of female hysteria. Apparently an overactive social schedule can cause such a precarious state of health. He's already signed the papers." Her husband's gaze was utterly pitiless. "It's very much a man's world, my dear. A shame you didn't realize that sooner."

With a small bow, he moved toward the door, and she desperately hoped he might be leaving, that this had been just a terrifying ruse. But instead, he pulled the door open and beckoned three footmen forward.

"My wife is to have no visitors," Hans gruffly said. "If she does, I'll have you whipped to a bloody pulp."

And brief moments later, she was alone—or almost alone. Two men stood guard outside in the corridor; the third sat on a chair inside the sitting room door. There was no other entrance to her rooms; even the balcony doors opened on the sitting room.

Walking into her bedroom, she closed the door and leaned back against the gilded panel, tears stinging her eyes. What had she ever done to deserve such a fate? *Why me,* she silently wailed, and sliding down the door, she crumpled to the floor and cried in a flood of tears.

She never should have gone out tonight, of course. In hindsight, it was a hideous mistake. Although her biggest mistake had been marrying Hans. Not that she was capable of changing the past, but there was a certain comfort in speculating on what might have been . . . of the possibilities for happiness in the world. For tonight had been heaven, nirvana, the Elysium fields and all the other paradises conceived by man rolled into one. She touched the ruby ring Max had given her, brought it to her lips and kissed it, hoping upon hope that even a small bit of his grandmother's luck would fall on her.

She had no illusions about Hans's brutality. He was capable of anything. But if he thought to break her, he would find it difficult.

She had champions. Max was here, and Burt Davis was a man of accomplishments. Surely there would be questions asked when she remained locked in her rooms. Surely there would be servants' gossip. She rubbed the tears from her eyes and took a deep, calming breath.

There was no reason to panic.

Chapter 22

Early Christmas morning, Johnnie and Fritz were shocked to see their father walk into their room. He had never been on the third floor before, and such unusual behavior caused immediate alarm.

After dismissing the servants, Hans snapped his fingers and waved his sons forward, indicating where they were to stand with a jab of his hand. As the boys reluctantly obeyed, he frowned. "Stand up straight and look me in the eye," he ordered. "You're not some misfit bourgeoisie. You're sons of a prince."

Straightening their shoulders, they nervously gazed up at their father.

"Your mother has taken ill." The boys turned ashen, and Hans's scowl deepened. "Such mama's boys," the prince mocked. "You're getting too old to behave like babies. And your mother needs rest and quiet, so I'm sending you back to school early. You leave on the morning train."

"May we say goodbye to Mama?" Fritz asked, more impulsive than his brother.

"She's sleeping."

"She won't mind if we wake her." Even in his caution, Johnnie impetuously spoke up.

"That won't be possible. The doctor has ordered she rest."

"Doctor!" Both boys spoke in unison, their eyes filled with apprehension.

"I won't tolerate insubordination!" their father barked. "You will do as I say! Be ready to leave in an hour." And after a fierce sweeping glance, he walked from the room and descended to the main floors. He offered a somewhat altered story to his brothers and their wives, explaining that Christina had become indisposed, perhaps with the same ailment as the dowager. He was curtailing the remainder of the holiday activities.

"Do you think she's really sick?" Fritz's face was white, his mouth pinched with worry.

"Let's ask Lise," Johnnie gently replied, trying to comfort his younger brother. "She'll know."

But when the boys ran downstairs to find their mother's personal maid, they were told by the housekeeper that Lise had gone to visit her mother for Christmas.

"But Lise doesn't have a mother," Johnnie whispered as the boys left the housekeeper's room. "Remember, Mama always felt sorry for her because she was an orphan. Father's lying and so is Mrs. Isling."

"What are we going to do?" Fritz's eyes were wet with tears.

"Right now, we'll go back to our room and think."

"But I can't think when I'm so scared."

"Then, I'll think for both of us," Johnnie decisively said. "Mama might need us. Maybe Josef will help. He doesn't like Father."

"Nobody likes Father," Fritz muttered. "He's so mean."

"But everyone's frightened of him. Come, let's ask Josef to go downstairs and see if he can find out if Mama is sick."

Their tutor was more than willing to help his young charges. A young man himself barely out of university, he genuinely liked the boys, and everyone in the household adored the princess, who not only knew all the servants by name, but took a personal interest in their lives. But when he returned, his news wasn't favorable.

The princess's room was guarded by two footmen, and no one was allowed admittance. When he had attempted to inquire about her health, he had been told in a threatening way not to ask any questions.

"I knew it!" Fritz exclaimed. "She isn't sick at all."

"At least that's good," Johnnie declared with a small sigh.

"But we have to leave within the hour," their tutor reminded them. "And you know your father's word is law."

"Could we slip a note under her door?" Fritz hopefully inquired.

Josef shook his head. "Not with the guards."

"Will he hurt her?" Johnnie's voice was shaky, and he gazed at his tutor with such grief-stricken eyes, Josef tried to be reassuring.

"Of course he won't." But the guards had been frightened, too, and when they had shooed him off, it was to save their own skins.

The boys' early departure didn't go unnoticed by the gatekeeper, of course. Burt was there to open the imposing gate and wish the young lads good voyage as they left. But it seemed strange for them to be going back to school on Christmas day and, stranger yet, for the remainder of the guests to be packed and on the road by noon. In order to discover the cause of such unusual events, when his schedule allowed, Burt found his way to the kitchen and had a cup of tea with the head footman. They had become good friends, often spending their leisure hours at the local tavern, drinking and exchanging hunting stories. Burt's father had been head gamekeeper to the Duke of Buckley; he had enough hunting stories to last two lifetimes. And while he gave the appearance of drinking, he actually consumed very little liquor—an advantage when gleaning information.

He first asked the footman whether he cared to track some

rabbits the next day, and the men compared their schedules. They spoke of their Christmas in a general way, the staff more busy than usual during the holidays, and then when Burt was pouring his second cup of tea, he said, "The young lads went back to school right early today. And then all the rest o' them took off, too."

The head footman's gaze went shuttered. "So it seems."

"Unusual, that," Burt calmly noted, stirring a spoonful of sugar into his cup.

"I can't rightly say." The footman's shrug was overdone, his smile unnatural. "You know the ways of the rich . . ."

"That I do, that I do . . ." Burt murmured, lifting his cup to his mouth. And he spoke of the fine bottle of hock he had tasted yesterday. "We'll get ourselves one when next we go into the village. The barkeep says he has a full case o' the stuff." He didn't stay long after that, promising to come fetch the footman that evening.

"Make it late," the man said. "We're working longer hours."

"Whenever you say, I'll be here. The prince don't need me to open the gates for him at night. Don't want to bother no one, I suppose. Decent fellow, that."

His friend's mouth formed into a thin line at Burt's comment, but he only said, "I'm thinkin' 'bout ten."

"Then, ten it is," Burt remarked, coming to his feet. "Thank cook for the tea."

Burt didn't immediately exit the palace, skirting two under maids scrubbing the brass fixtures in the downstairs hall and then slipping into the back stairway when they weren't looking. He met no one on the stairs, although he intended to say he was looking for his friend, the head footman, should he be asked, and in short order, he was peering around the corner of the stairwell on the second floor, taking note of the two guards outside Christina's apartments.

Quickly retracing his steps, he slipped outside and took off for the village at a run. His gatehouse duties would have to wait. The marquis would want to know about the unsettling new state of affairs at the palace.

The small rented house Max was occupying was only a block from the village square, and before Burt could knock on the door, Max had opened it, his expression grave. He had seen Burt racing down the street.

"There must be trouble."

"It looks that way, but no one's talking yet." And on entering the small parlor, Burt quickly detailed what he knew of the sudden departure of the boys and guests, of Christina's detention.

Max listened without interrupting, his head lowered, the muscle high on his cheek visibly clenching and unclenching. "Hans must know something," he muttered when Burt had finished. "I can't wait any longer." He lightly swung his arms as though releasing tension. "If I'm overreacting, I'll take responsibility for Christina's displeasure. But if she's under guard, she's in danger. I'm sending you after the boys, and I'm relying on you to see that they're safely away from Germany. Preferably at Minster Hill. If they want to go to their aunt's, tell them whatever you have to," he briskly went on, "to change their minds. Right now, we don't know whom we can trust. Bring their tutor with them if they wish, if the man wishes, and any of their servants they like. I don't want them to be afraid. You understand. It's absolutely imperative."

"Affirmative, sir. Although, they could already be aware of their mother's peril. Both boys looked frightened; the youngest had been crying. It might be easy enough to convince them to meet her in England."

"The man's a fucking thug," Max growled. "It's about time he met someone who can fight back."

"What are your plans?"

"I was waiting until Tom sent me his latest dispatches on that little trollop Hans has been seeing every night since his return.

The search is on for a marriage certificate. Not that I'd be so lucky. But everything's suddenly changed with Christina's imprisonment, so I'm going in to get her. And if anyone stands in my way, I'll shoot them."

"The palace is well staffed. Are you sure?"

"Do I look like I'm not?"

He looked as though he could take on the devil's host without breaking a sweat. "I wish I could help," Burt said.

"I don't need any help." Max spoke bluntly, fueled by rage and apprehension. "The staff will run like hell at the sight of a weapon. And if I go in after Hans leaves for his nightly fuck, I only have to deal with the guards at her door. You'll have a ten-hour head start, but that's all you'll get. I can't wait to hear that the boys are safe. I'm expecting they will be."

"They will."

Max nodded. "Good." He flexed his fingers, agitated beneath his apparent calm. "I'd like to go in right now, but I can't risk Christina getting hurt if Hans should take it in his head to resist. So, if I wait until he's gone tonight . . ." Max blew out a harsh breath. "Jesus—that's hours away. . . . It's going to be hell waiting. . . ."

Chapter 23

Christina felt ill immediately after breakfast. She threw up after lunch, and when a footman carried in her supper tray, she viewed it with suspicion. Her ears were ringing; her headache had been constant since morning. She had tried to rest in the afternoon, thinking perhaps it was only nerves making her sick; but her stomach burned when she lay down, so she reclined half-seated on her chaise and fought the urge to vomit. Desperately thirsty by supper, she felt like drinking all the water and wine, but was fairly certain by then that she was being poisoned.

The footman looked at her untouched tray later that evening, but didn't comment, nor did she. She wasn't compelled to speak to her jailers.

But her uneaten food brought her husband to her room prior to his departure for the night. Dismissing the footman in the sitting room, he entered Christina's bedchamber and stood at the door, his evening clothes impeccable, his fair hair gleaming, his expression triumphant. "I hear you didn't eat your supper, darling," he murmured, his light eyes bland as he gazed at her lying on the chaise. "You'll have to eat eventually, though, won't you? So take your time. I'm a patient man." He softly laughed. "Or reasonably patient. I doubt you'll last far into the new year, eating or not. I'll think of you while I'm enjoying my champagne tonight. I might even raise a toast to you, my dear, seeing how you won't be here much longer."

"You may not find it so easy to kill me. Someone will take note of my absence."

"Everyone's gone, darling. The boys, my boring relatives—everyone. And with your nerves so susceptible to the least excitement," he jibed, "any caller will understand how much you need your rest. As to your lover, should you expect a heroic rescue, I've armed the staff. So pleasant dreams, darling."

He left the bedroom door open when he walked away so that she could see him speak to the inside guard when he returned, so the handgun the man wore on his hip was visible. And if her despair hadn't been sufficient after Hans's mockery and the nausea threatening to overwhelm her, thinking of the peril waiting him, should Max try to help her, brought on another attack of retching.

Exhausted afterward, she felt half-faint, and as she lay prostrate, the faces of her sons suddenly floated before her eyes. Shaking her head, she tried to dispel the images, but their sad little faces continued to swim in and out of her consciousness, the terror in their expressions heart-wrenching. Tears came to her eyes as the sound of their voices seemed to echo in her ears.

She began trembling.

Maybe she *was* going mad.

Burt and the boys should be on the night train for Paris by now, Max reflected, glancing at the clock in his small rented parlor. His sleigh was outside, the horses fresh in their harnesses. He checked his ammunition, pulling out the Colts from the holsters belted on his hips, spinning the cylinders one by one. Satisfied they were fully loaded, he slid the weapons back into the worn leather. Two single gun belts crisscrossed his chest as well, four revolvers in all, twenty-four rounds in the chambers, not to mention additional ammunition in the belts. He also carried a large sum of money.

Brute force or money or both should be enough to bring out one woman.

The sleigh was piled high with fur robes, two bottles of hot cider wrapped snugly in the corner, and with Hans on his way to his nightly rendezvous, Max expected his rescue mission to proceed without problems.

The moon was hidden, the sky overcast, so he drove with caution, taking his time navigating the narrow back road to the palace. He had been over the route several times in preparation. He knew every bump and curve, every stand of trees and peasant cottage. And at the base of the hill, near the skating pond, he drove his horses into a stand of pines so they would be out of sight. His white sweater blended into the snowy landscape, his pale chamois pants neutral in hue as well, as were the moccasins he wore.

Pausing outside the kitchen, he took note of the staff seated around the table enjoying their evening beer. Keeping well away from the windows, he moved toward the basement door he would be using tonight. Going in or out through the balcony required a degree of strength Christina didn't possess, so he and Burt had quickly gone over the floor plan before Burt's departure. As Max eased open the small door, slipped inside and stood in the dark, listening, he mentally traced his route. The sounds of conversation in the kitchen were audible, so he ascended the stairs slowly, pausing at the top and listening again, before cautiously opening the door into the corridor.

A scullery maid hurried by with a fresh pitcher of beer, and Max slid back out of sight, holding his breath until she passed. When she disappeared into the kitchen, he crossed the dozen yards of hall in a run and leaped up the first level of servants' stairs in two lithe jumps. A pause on the landing while he looked left and right and then quickly moving up another level, he saw what he had come to see. Two footmen stood guard on either side of Christina's door, and surprisingly, they were armed.

He doubted they could shoot straight, although if they discharged their weapons, the noise would be equally dangerous. He could handle two men, but not the entire staff. In the hope they would shift their stances so he would be out of their line of vision, he waited at the top of the stairs. But they stood utterly still, and he wondered at the nature of Hans's threat that they dared not move. As the minutes ticked by, he decided he couldn't wait much longer if he wanted to put some distance between themselves and the palace before Hans returned. Lobbing a coin in a high arch above the guards' heads, he watched them swivel at the sound of metal striking the floor.

The second they spun away, he sprinted toward them, his moccasins a whisper on the carpet. And when the two men turned back from the mysterious noise, they came face-to-face with Max and his Colt revolvers. "Now, if everyone cooperates," Max softly said, "no one will get hurt. This isn't your fight, and I don't want to kill you. So, just hand over your weapons. . . . Put them on the floor and kick them over to me . . . and I'll see that you have enough money to live comfortably far away from here. You're not going to get a better offer than that." His voice was mild, but his gaze was pitiless.

The young men's Adam's apples bobbed as they swallowed, and their eyes bulged in fear, the barrels of Max's shiny revolvers too close, his voice too casual, his killer's gaze terrifying.

"The prince doesn't give a damn about you, but his wife happens to be important enough to me that I'll shoot you without a qualm." His cold gaze flickered from one man to the other. "So what do you say?"

"How much?" The man's voice quavered.

"Five thousand marks—each. It's a hundred years' salary for men like you. I suggest you take it."

"Why so generous?" Such a large amount occasioned suspicion.

"The princess matters to me. How's that? You've got five seconds."

"Show us the money," the other man blurted out.

"Your guns first. And I'm counting."

The smallest pause ensued—a flashing second—and the first footman dropped his weapon to the floor. The soft thud was immediately followed by a second.

Max nodded. "Kick them over."

When they obeyed, Max batted the weapons across the corridor with his foot, holstered one Colt and pulled a roll of bills from his trouser pocket. He dropped the money on the floor. "Now, you tie him up." He slid a rawhide rope from around his waist and handed it to one guard. "He'll get his money and then I'll tie you up."

Neither man mentioned the guard inside the room.

But Max was a seasoned player. He had spent summers with his godfather in the Crow camps where horse raiding was still the warriors' favorite sport. And one never advanced without scouting.

He took the precaution of knocking out the two guards with the butt of his pistol once they were trussed, pulled them out of sight and then quietly tried the door.

It was locked, and a search of the guards' pockets revealed no key, so it was locked from the inside.

He gently knocked.

Softly inhaling at the sound of a key scraping in the lock, he stepped aside, pressing back against the wall.

When the door opened, a man poked his head out, and Max smashed his pistol butt down on his head with such force, the guard dropped in a flash. Leaping over the limp body, Max stood in the doorway, revolvers drawn, his gaze raking the sitting room.

No one. But the door to the bedroom was closed, so he quickly dragged the body of the guard back inside, tied him up and, with revolvers drawn, crossed the sitting room and listened at the bedroom door.

The sound of crying jettisoned all his caution, and rules of engagement be damned, he threw his entire weight against the locked door and burst into the room in a shower of splintered wood.

Christina was curled up in a fetal position on the floor, sobbing, her body quivering in spasms. He was beside her in seconds, and gently lifting her into his arms, he whispered, "I'm here . . . I'm here. You're safe."

She opened her eyes and tried to smile.

Terrified at her weakness, he quickly moved toward the sitting room. "I'm taking you home," he said in a deliberately calm voice, while alarm shrieked through his brain.

Tears welled in her eyes.

"Everything's going to be fine," he murmured, when it wasn't, when she couldn't speak and was pale as death. As they passed through the sitting room, she seemed to stop breathing for a moment, and spurred by fear, he took the risk of descending the main staircase.

And if anyone tried to stop them—he shifted her slightly in his arms and drew out his revolver.

At the base of the stairs, a footman rushed forward, but at the sight of Christina's lifeless form, he respectfully stepped back and signaled the hall porter to open the door.

The old man made the sign of the cross and whispered, "Godspeed, Princess," as Max carried Christina outside.

When the winter wind struck them, she shivered in his arms.

He broke into a run.

Moments later, Christina was lying in the sleigh, wrapped in fur blankets.

"Can you hear me?"

Her eyes fluttered open; but he could see the tremendous effort required for so trifling a movement, and his pulse raced in fear.

"We'll be in England tomorrow."

She struggled to sit up, terror in her eyes. "Boys . . ."

The breathy word was scarcely audible, her frenzied exertion sapping her remaining strength. She fell back, but her eyes held his in a frightened gaze.

"They're safe. Burt took them to England ahead of us."

Her eyes shut and she went still.

Panic gripped his soul.

Jumping into the driver's seat, he snapped the reins, the horses leaped forward and he drove like a mad man down the narrow lane, oblivious to the danger of a headlong pace in the dark. He couldn't lose her. He wouldn't. And urging the team to more speed, the sleigh flew over the snow-covered ground.

Ten miles to the train station.

Ten miles to a doctor.

He began to pray.

Chapter 24

The tavern owner gave him directions to the doctor, and minutes later, with Christina in his arms, he was pounding on the doctor's door, screaming for help.

The servant who opened the door was half-asleep, but at the sharp command in Max's voice, she took off running to wake her master.

Max was building up the fire in the parlor when the elderly physician entered the room, and he quickly came to his feet. "My wife is desperately ill. You have to save her." It wasn't a request or a plea. It was an order.

The doctor glanced at the man, at the gun belt on his hips, recognized the American accent in his German, and moving toward the woman lying on the floor near the fire, he wondered what tragedy had unfolded. The woman was wrapped in sables fit for a queen. He scrutinized the man more closely, his face still partially in shadow. "Who are you?"

"The Marquis of Vale. She's on the verge . . . of death," Max shakily said. "You have to do something!"

The doctor knelt beside Christina's still form, immediately recognized her and looked up, his gaze sharp.

"Did you do this to her?"

"God, no—never . . ."

"I know this woman. You're not her husband." The doctor was taking Christina's pulse, a faint frown creasing his brow.

"It doesn't matter who I am, or who you are, or whether the prince owns you heart and soul. Just do something for her," Max softly said, "or I'll kill you."

The old man's gaze lifted. "Who would help you then?"

Max seemed not to hear or understand, his dark eyes mad with grief as he drew his revolver from its holster and pointed it at the doctor.

"That's not necessary," the doctor quietly said, recognizing a man on the edge. "I'll help the princess in any way I can. She's a good friend."

All the fury seemed to drain from the figure towering over him. "Forgive me," Max murmured, lowering his hand. "I've never been so afraid in my life . . ."

"There's no need to apologize," the doctor kindly said. "Your reaction is to be expected considering what's been done to her." He lifted Christina's eyelid. "Has she been ill long?"

Max shook his head. "She was fine yesterday. That's what I don't understand."

"Let's see what we have here," the doctor murmured, lifting away the fur robes, and as he examined Christina, Max watched him, glancing occasionally at the clock. They couldn't afford to miss the last train.

"It looks as though she may have been poisoned," the doctor finally said, tucking Christina's arms back under the furs. "Although she could have contracted influenza. Its affects are equally alarming, its onset as rapid. However, there's evidence of swelling of the lining of her mouth which makes me suspicious of poisoning, probably arsenic poisoning."

"I'll kill the bastard . . . ," Max whispered.

"That wouldn't be wise right now. We have to see to the princess's safety. And you can't stay here. The prince will find you."

"We're leaving on the midnight train. Please come with us to the coast. You can see how desperately she needs your help. Money is irrelevant now, but you can have whatever you want."

"The princess has always been kind to me and the community, while her husband—" The antipathy in his tone was patent.

"You'll be back tomorrow. She—we would be most grateful for your help."

The elderly man hesitated briefly, weighing the prince's tyranny against Christina's compelling need. "Let me get my bag," he abruptly said, coming to his feet. "I'll tell my servant to cancel my appointments tomorrow."

"Thank you." Max exhaled, relief washing over him. "Thank you very much." He sat vigil beside Christina while the doctor gathered his equipment, and when he returned, the two men worked together to see that Christina swallowed a small glass of water. She opened her eyes once during the process and seemed to recognize Max.

"I'm taking you home," he whispered. "We're going home."

She heard, he thought.

Her pulse rate was dropping, the doctor nervously noted.

They reached the station with only minutes to spare, but a private compartment was procured thanks to the doctor's friendship with the ticket agent. Once aboard, Max settled Christina on his lap, and holding her close, he anxiously watched the shallow rise and fall of her breathing. He knew what a plummeting pulse rate meant, and as the train sped through the night, he silently prayed. In those desperate hours, he bargained with all the mystical spirits and deities who might be listening, begging for their help, offering up extravagant promises if they would see that Christina lived. Stumbling through long-forgotten prayers from childhood, he promised to live an exemplary life if only she wasn't taken from him, pledged his undying gratitude if his prayers were answered, frantically pleaded for their aid.

As they passed through the succession of towns on their journey west, he would whisper their names to her, telling her they were that much closer to England, enumerating the diminishing miles in a soothing litany, wanting her to know she was going home. When they crossed the border into France, he told her he would take her to Paris some day soon and buy out every shop and couturier house she fancied. The slightest flicker of her eyelids as he spoke recklessly buoyed his hopes. "Look, look," he whispered, beckoning the doctor. "She heard me."

In the course of the journey, Christina was plied with liquids, the doctor intent on restoring the fluids to her dehydrated body and in the process mitigating the levels of arsenic in her system. The treatment was a palliative not only to the patient, but to the man who loved her.

Max couldn't bear not offering her comfort.

It was all he could do.

Christina survived the night, and by morning even the doctor had begun to look on the prospects of her recovery with less pessimism. Her pulse had strengthened, her breathing was more normal, and even her color had altered slightly from the grayness of death. And when they reached the coast where Max hired a yacht to take them across the channel, the doctor settled his patient into bed.

After Christina was made comfortable in the small cabin, Max accompanied the doctor ashore. "I'll be forever in your debt," he said, his gratitude already expressed in the extravagant sum he had pressed on the doctor. "If you should ever want for anything, you need but ask. And once Christina is well, I'll see that the prince is no longer a problem for any of us."

"I have sufficient friends in my community. I doubt the prince will cause me harm."

"Then, my vengeance will be entirely personal."

"I don't normally condone violence, but in the case of the prince, I'll make an exception. Take care, though; he's without scruple."

Immune to warnings, Max said, "I'm looking forward to seeing the fear in his eyes."

"Perhaps you should first consider your and the princess's safety."

"I can take care of myself, and Hans won't suffer the loss of his wife and sons with equanimity. Someone has to see that he stays away."

The doctor softly sighed. "Then, I wish you luck."

Max faintly smiled. "My aim is excellent. I don't need luck."

The channel crossing seemed to revive Christina, and whether it was the fresh sea air or the fact they were nearing England—as Max informed her with great frequency—she began opening her eyes occasionally.

She actually smiled when he announced, "I see the cliffs of Dover."

And when the ship came into harbor and the sound of the gulls was shrill on the air, she spoke for the first time. "Thank you," she whispered.

"Thank you for loving me," he whispered back.

And her answering smile had a fragment of the familiar lushness he remembered.

They reached Minster Hill five hours later, and when the carriage rolled up to the door and Christina heard her boys' welcoming screams as they raced toward the carriage, tears came to her eyes.

They tumbled through the carriage door and hugged her as she lay in Max's arms and cried and then quickly rubbed their tears away because they were becoming too grown up to cry.

"Burt said you were coming!" Fritz cried. "So I just knew it was true!"

"He said Max could do anything," Johnnie said, his voice less raucous, but his smile as broad.

"What we should do right now is see that your mother is tucked into bed and fed some warm soup and tea—"

"And blueberry scones, Mama! You have to try some of cook's special blueberry scones!" her youngest son exclaimed, everything right with the world now that his mother was near.

"That . . . sounds . . . won-der-ful . . . ," she whispered, her longest sentence to date.

She was out of danger now, Max realized, as her wispy voice slowly enunciated the words.

She was with her boys.

She was safe.

She was home.

Christina's recuperation was rapid, and each day brought her renewed strength. By midweek, she was able to walk from the bed to a chair, and Max would carry her downstairs for dinner each night, when the boys would regale her with their activities of the day. But by the end of the week, Max could no longer ignore his pressing need to deal with Hans.

Tom Lawson had been to Minster Hill twice since their return, discussing the increasing evidence of Hans's long-ago marriage to his cousin, and he had come again on the evening train with his latest reports.

"While the union obviously resulted in this eighteen-year-old son, the church and civic records are missing from that time frame. The requisite pages are simply torn from each ledger."

"The powerful influence of money," Max cynically murmured. "What of witnesses? Have you found any yet?"

The barrister shook his head. "But I haven't given up."

"Put more men on the case," Max ordered. "Although Christina's physically better, she's frightened to death Hans is going to take her boys away."

"Not with your army in place."

"So I told her, but logic doesn't overcome the degree of terror she feels." He grimaced. "And not without reason. She almost died by his hand."

"A well-calculated act, perhaps. Marlena, it seems, is with child again."

Max sat up straighter. "How do you know?"

"I'm paying off practically every servant in that town. The midwife's maid disclosed the information. The child is due in the spring."

"As an act of Christian charity, perhaps I shouldn't kill him before his child is born."

"Perhaps you shouldn't kill him at all. Dammit, Max, you could spend your life in jail for such a stupid stunt."

"Who said his killer would be known."

Tom let out a frustrated breath; this conversation wasn't new. "It's stupid, however you do it."

"You don't think he deserves to die?"

"I know a hundred people who deserve to die."

"Then, you know the wrong people. But the point is, Hans has to be dealt with, either in your civilized way or in mine."

"Perhaps you should ask Christina if she wants his blood on her hands."

"Never. She's suffered enough for him. She's not to be involved, and I hope you understand that with exceptional clarity."

"Yes, yes, yes," Tom muttered. "Of course. But you may not be able to keep him away forever. He doesn't fight with guns like you, my dear man. He's in London now, about to institute a lawsuit against you for the abduction of his wife. Charles Gordon saw the preliminary papers this afternoon. He's asking damages of ten million."

"Fucking greedy bastard."

"You knew all along he wasn't the model for benevolent ideals. And what does Christina say about this personal army you have guarding the perimeters of your estate."

"She doesn't precisely know the size. I've given them orders not to approach the house."

"You can't stay under siege forever."

Max slumped lower in his chair. "I know. I just wanted her to gain back enough strength so I could leave for a few days."

"To kill her husband."

Max's smile was tight. "Her bigamist husband if we can ever prove it."

"Don't give up. And you have her safe. You should be damned grateful. Forget vengeance. You have what you want."

"But he almost killed her." Max's voice went soft. "He needs to pay."

"And you're judge and jury?"

"Why don't I just thank you for all the fine work you've done so far, and we'll leave the philosophical arguments for some later date."

"When you come back, you mean."

Max faintly smiled. "For then. I think the prince needs to understand there are consequences to his actions."

That night, as Max held Christina in his arms and the moon poured in a river of light through the bedroom windows, he said, "I have to go into London for a day, two at the most. Tom has some business that can't be handled from Minster Hill."

"Must you?"

"I might be away only one day," he parried. "The boys are here; they'll keep you entertained. And you're completely safe. No one can enter the estate without my approval."

"Are you sure?" She still wasn't able to completely forget the terror of her imprisonment. Nor did she expect Hans would allow his sons to be abducted without retaliation.

"I'm absolutely positive. No equivocation. My word on it." He smiled. "Is that sufficient assurance?"

"And you'll be back soon?"

"I promise."

Just as soon as he took care of Hans.

Chapter 25

The following morning in London, Max met briefly with Tom before calling on Hans. "In the event there are problems," he said, "and I haven't returned in an hour, send me reinforcements."

"You're a fool to even consider going in to see him alone. I strongly urge you to reconsider."

"I don't want witnesses. As a lawyer, you have to understand better than most the advantages of doing this myself."

"At least I'm going to see that my men are outside the prince's house," Tom insisted, "and I don't want any arguments. Your courage isn't in question here. I'd just like to make sure you go home to Christina in one piece. And promise me you won't be standing trial for murder."

"You'll be happy to hear I'm taking your advice. I've decided on less lethal—or *possibly* less lethal punishment."

"I'm encouraged"—Tom raised his brows—"I think. You understand the prince's lawsuit will be null and void once we find evidence of his early marriage."

"If."

"We will. It's just a matter of time."

"Good. But this is a personal vendetta," Max softly said. "I have a debt to repay."

"Be cautious, I implore you. The man doesn't fight his own battles as a rule."

"Better yet."

"Perhaps not if he's well guarded."

"He's too arrogant. After a lifetime of uncompromising command, he won't expect retaliation. My father was like that, so I understand."

"Your mother left her husband, too, didn't she? Even then, this may not be the same."

Max gently shrugged. "It's close enough. They're the same kind of men: cold, unbending, unutterably selfish. It never occurred to my father that mother would defy him, nor does Hans think he won't prevail—because both always had."

Tom was aware of Max's history. All London had been atwitter when the beautiful sewing machine heiress from America had taken her young son and walked out on her husband the very day she received news of her father's death. Having inherited his fortune, she could quit the marriage that had been forced on her for the sake of a marquis's title. "Your father exacted payment, though. Hans will as well."

"My mother gladly paid to be rid of my father. And he simply wanted to win; he didn't want either one of us. Once the lawyers handed over the check, he got on with his life as though we'd never existed. Hans expects to do the same—only he wants ten million. Inflation apparently." Max smiled thinly. "I'll see that he changes his mind."

"I can't talk you out of this madness?"

Max merely shook his head.

"Then, I can only wish you good luck in your reckless endeavor."

Max came to his feet. "I don't need luck. I have something better."

"I'm not going to ask what it is, should you require legal defense later."

"I wouldn't tell you if you asked," Max cheerfully replied. "Now, don't worry. This shouldn't take long."

Max surprised the kitchen maid at the Prince of Zeiss's London home.

"This door be for deliveries, sir," she said, bobbing a curtsy at the well-dressed man.

"I *am* making a delivery," he politely said, walking past her into the kitchen.

The cook and servants glanced at him with curiosity, but he seemed unruffled as he strolled through the room and up the servants' stairway to the main floor. They decided he was some well-dressed shop owner here to see the steward.

Max already knew Hans rarely left the house before noon. Burt's colleagues had been on surveillance since Hans's arrival in London. He also understood the prince normally ate breakfast about now in the small dining room overlooking the garden.

Moving undetected down the back hall, Max entered the dining room, pointed the small derringer he held at the footman serving Hans, and softly said, "Out."

The young man dropped the dish he was offering the prince. Coddled eggs and delft china crashed to the floor, and immobile with fear, the servant stared at Max.

"I wouldn't suggest you stay." Max's voice was gentle.

Whether it was Max's voice or the small wave of his derringer, the young man was urged to movement and fled the room.

Keeping Hans in his sights, Max quickly locked the door behind the servant.

"You have dramatic tendencies," the prince disdainfully murmured, putting his napkin aside. "The consequence, no doubt, of having a lowborn mother."

"Speaking of mothers," Max smoothly replied, pulling out a

chair at the table and sitting down, "I saw yours at Christmas, and I'm surprised you don't yodel. She looks as though she might have herded goats in an earlier life." He laid his pearl-handled derringer on the cloth and silkily smiled. "But then, I didn't come here to exchange pleasantries with you. I brought you something to enjoy with your breakfast." Slipping a small porcelain flask from his pocket, he set it on the table beside the pistol.

"You're not actually going to shoot me with that." Hans's mouth curled in a sneer. "It wouldn't stop a fly."

"I disagree. Two twenty-two rounds to the head are quite effective. I've seen men bigger than you drop like a rock."

The lazy indifference in Max's tone occasioned a small tick near the prince's right eye, but his arrogance was undiminished. "You Americans are violent, common rabble."

"I suppose we can't all be moderate, benevolent men like you," Max drawled. "But I never kill a man without cause."

"If anyone has cause," the prince rebuked, "it's me. You seduced and abducted my wife."

Leaning back in his chair, Max gently waggled his finger. "Correction there. Christina isn't your wife, as you well know, considering you married Marlena first."

"You're mad," Hans coldly retorted.

"And you're stupid to think no one would ever find out. I'll soon have proof."

"I doubt it."

"You'll lose on that one. By the way, congratulations on your coming child. Actually, that was what saved your life. I was inclined to kill you. Now I'm going to satisfy my *violent tendencies*," he sardonically murmured, "with something less final."

"You won't get away with this . . . with any of this," Hans blustered. "My servants will be in here any moment."

"Maybe," Max calmly replied, "but then, you're not very well liked, you bloody, inhuman bastard. And of course I'll get away with this, because I'm armed and you're not. Because you're a coward who does battle only with those weaker than you. Because I'm not going to leave until you pay for all the suffering you've caused Christina."

The prince had assumed his staff would come to his rescue, but as the minutes ticked away and no one broke down the door, his nervousness increased. He was dealing with a madman; there was no other word for someone like the marquis who boldly walked into a house in broad daylight and threatened a man's life as calmly as though he were strolling into his club. "I'm sure we can come to some agreement." His sangfroid was slipping; a thin sheen of sweat gleamed on his forehead.

Max uncharitably smiled. "I know we can." Drawing a water goblet near, he lifted the small flask he had placed on the table, unscrewed the top and poured its metallic steel gray contents into the water. He looked up. "I'm sure you recognize this."

The blood had drained from the prince's face.

"If I've calculated the dose properly, this won't kill you . . ." Shrugging, Max softly added, "Unless things go awry. A shame science isn't more precise. You must have faced the same dilemma when you were poisoning Christina. Were you planning her funeral—in a week—a month or didn't it much matter with your cozy love nest so near, you fucking monster," he whispered, his dark gaze so merciless the prince lost control of his bladder.

The stench of urine permeated the air.

"You understand the seriousness of the situation, I see. Although, thanks to my barrister," he grudgingly noted, "you'll be given a chance of survival. If it were up to me, I'd shoot you where you sit, but he tells me an acquittal is more difficult if you're dead. So, hopefully, this won't kill you. Not that I really give a damn," he grimly said, pushing the goblet toward Hans. "Don't spill it or I'll shoot you. The judicial system concerns me less than it does my lawyer since my yacht is at the ready and extradition from the States is uncertain." He tipped his head toward the glass. "But the choice is yours. Two well-placed bullets or arsenic."

Hans was gasping as though he had run ten miles, his face was ashen, and sweat was streaming down his face.

"I'll give you ten seconds to decide. I've a busy schedule today." And Max looked at his watch and began counting—his voice devoid of feeling.

At the count of nine, Hans grabbed the goblet and drank it down.

Max felt a moment of annoyance.

He would have preferred killing him.

"One other thing," Max softly said. "If you should live, you will discuss nothing of this with anyone. If you do, I'll see that you die so slowly, you'll be screaming for the end. It takes a long time to peel off a man's skin inch by bloody inch."

The fear in Hans's eyes didn't offer the deliverance he had expected, and he wondered at his callousness that he could be so unrelenting in his fury.

For perhaps ten minutes, Max impassively watched as convulsions slowly overcame the half-prostrate figure before him. His hand rested on the table near his derringer, an itch to fire still fiercely strong, the less prudent part of his brain hoping he might be given the opportunity to put an end to the prince's life.

But Hans made no aggressive move, only shuddering and gasping in turn, his skin turning a peculiar shade of puce before he lapsed into unconsciousness.

At that point, Max rose from his chair, walked to the windows and, lifting a sash, stepped over the sill onto the lawn.

The woman he loved had been partially avenged.

There would never be restitution enough for the lost twelve years of her life.

Tom's men joined him as he appeared on the street, and a short time later, Max was relating an edited account to his barrister. "I don't anticipate problems, but should the prince find his courage at some later date, I'd be more than happy to kill him anywhere, anytime. In fact, I was hard-pressed not to finish him off today. Until such a time, my mercenaries at Minster Hill should keep Christina safe. Do you have some reasonable estimate on when this marriage certificate or cooperative witnesses might be forthcoming?"

"A fortnight, maybe less."

"Seriously? You're that confident?"

"Someone tore those pages out. We'll find him."

"That must be why you're worth those large fees," Max lazily murmured.

"We're that close." Tom lifted his hand, his thumb and forefinger almost touching.

"Do I dare tell Christina? I'd love to, of course."

The barrister hesitated fractionally, prudence a long-standing habit. "Why not?" he said, grinning. "I've a good feeling about this."

"Your good feeling is my good feeling," Max remarked, amusement in his gaze as he rose from his chair. "And on that cheerful note, I'm off for Minster Hill."

"Did I tell you Burt sent his nephew over last week?"

Max grinned. "So that's your ace in the hole. I hear he can twist arms with the best of them."

Tom's brows lifted faintly. "So I'm told."

"Perhaps I should stop and select an engagement gift on my way home."

"I don't think it would be out of order."

"How about setting a wedding date?"

"After a fortnight . . . there shouldn't be a problem."

"I'm getting the distinct feeling you know something you're not willing to tell me."

"I can't just yet—in good conscience. I don't quite have the documents in my hand."

"So there might be documents."

"It's very likely."

"How likely?"

"Very."

Max grinned. "You're obviously not a gambler."

"I find it doesn't pay in my profession."

"But I can set my wedding date."

"Yes."

"That's good enough for me. I'll see you at the wedding." And with a wave, Max walked from the office.

Chapter 26

"Violet jade—how beautiful . . ." Christina held up the exquisitely large beads, the necklace clasp of pearls and diamonds gleaming in the lamplight. "We'll have matching jewelry," she noted, winking at Max, who lay beside her in the huge Falconer bed that had seen service since the days of Queen Anne.

"To go with our matching lives," he murmured.

"And what does that esoteric comment imply?" Her voice was teasing still; but her gaze had taken on a new directness, and sitting up, she set aside the necklace.

"I wanted to wait until we were alone." Lifting his hand, he gently brushed the soft curve of her arm. "And now that the boys are tucked in and I have you to myself, I'd like to offer you that necklace as an engagement gift." A cheerful buoyancy infused his voice. "A very, very short engagement, I might add."

"No! You don't mean it!" she cried, leaping on him and pummeling his chest. "Tell me, tell me, tell me . . ." She was beating a wild tattoo. "You didn't say anything all through dinner—and not later when you would have had a chance. You wicked, wicked brute—I should strap you, birch you—"

"Reason enough not to . . ." Grabbing her wrists, he smiled up at her. "But we can discuss sex later," he added, his grin roguish. "Right now, darling, I want you to sit real still"—she was straddling his thighs—"because I don't want to be distracted by your delectable wet cunt. I have something of import to disclose." Loosening his hold, he lay back against the pillows.

"Something you should have disclosed sooner," she replied with a pretty pout.

"But I wanted you alone," he politely reminded her. "Now, do you want to listen or don't you?"

She tossed her head in the faintest of movements. "I may or may not."

His eyes narrowed, but a teasing light gleamed beneath the fringe of his lashes. "Maybe I'll beat *you*."

"I don't care to be distracted by talk of sex," she insolently noted.

"Listen to me or there won't be any sex."

Her eyes widened.

"Now that I have your attention," he murmured, and then softly gasped.

"You were saying?" Cheeky and pert, she smiled down on him, her grip savagely tight on the head of his penis.

"You win," he gently said, when he could have broken her hold with ease.

"And you wish to apologize to me."

"Actually, I want to marry you."

She stared at him for a moment, her expression blank. "You don't mean it," she breathed.

"I mean it, absolutely."

She drew in a breath. "When? How? I mean—how in the world—"

"*When* would be after you loosen your fingers a little," he murmured, "and the *how* would be in the usual way," he added with a grin. "In a chapel with a minister, a bride, a groom . . . some guests I suppose, although that's not high on my list of priorities."

"How did you manage it?" she whispered, releasing her grip.

And a second later she was lying beneath him. "You're too trusting," he breathed, settling between her legs. "But cynic that I am," he added with a faint smile, "I find it incredibly attractive—"

"Max! If you don't tell me immediately all that you know of whatever happened to make all this possible, I'll close my legs and make you wait a month at least."

"You could wait a month?"

"I waited twelve years if you recall."

His expression turned grave. "That's what I wanted to talk to you about."

"I hope it's not as serious as you look."

Rolling off her, he came to a seated position and took her hand in his. "Don't be alarmed. It's good serious and happily-ever-after serious."

She softly exhaled. "Go on." But her heart was beating wildly.

"Tom tells me we can set a wedding date. He's very near to having proof that will make you a free woman."

"Hans will give me a divorce?"

"Not exactly." He took a small breath. "It's something . . . more bizarre."

She took her own small breath because he was clearly uncomfortable, and her apprehension returned regardless of his caveat about happily-ever-after. "Tell me."

"You never were legally married to Hans because he'd secretly married a cousin of his earlier."

"Never married?" Her eyes flared wide. "You mean my boys are—"

"No one need know," he quickly interposed. "*They* don't have to know. We'll create whatever fiction best shields the boys from gossip. And I've seen to it that Hans won't discuss any of this with anyone."

"You've seen him?" She suddenly went pale.

"Briefly. He was very cooperative," Max explained in a deliberately mild tone. "I'll have Tom begin adoption proceedings to-morrow, and we'll see that the process is accomplished with all speed."

"You actually *saw* him?"

He felt her small shiver, saw the flash of anxiety cross her face. "Hans is in London, but not for long, I expect. He apologized for what he'd done to you," Max lied, wishing to allay her fear. "Apparently, he's feeling remorse."

"Really . . ." Surprise fluttered through the word.

"It looked that way to me."

"I don't have to ever see him, do I?" Her voice was barely au-dible.

Lifting her into his lap, he held her close. "You never have to see him, I promise."

She looked up, her gaze filled with dread. "What of the boys? Are they obliged to see him if they aren't legally his?"

"No."

He felt her relax in his arms, and she smiled, tentatively at first, until her caution gave way to a broad, bright smile. "My God, Max . . . it truly *is* happily-ever-after. An absolute *dream* come true—the answer to all my prayers and I should ask you how you did it, but I don't want to know . . . I want to never think of him again. Not ever," she joyfully declared.

He smiled. "I can pretty well guarantee that."

"I adore you when you speak as though everything is plain and simple and good and true . . ." She ran her palms down his arms, taking delight in the corporeal bliss of his closeness, so elated with the thought of her freedom she was almost giddy. "There aren't thanks enough in the world to express my gratitude for all that you've done," she whispered, "but thank you, darling, from the bottom of my heart."

"My pleasure, ma'am." His soft drawl was replete with cheer. "I'm happy the princess is finally saved . . . although I forgot my white steed."

"I won't take issue with your lack of a white steed when you made all my dreams come true," she softly murmured, sliding her arms around his neck. "And now that we know dreams *can* come true"—she slowly traced the curve of his upper lip with the tip of her tongue—"I was wondering whether you might oblige me in another kind of dream . . ."

He grinned. "This has a familiar ring."

Leaning back, she raised her brows faintly. "Is it a problem?"

"Definitely not a problem, ma'am. More like *my* dream come true and blue skies forever and paradise arrived at Minster Hill. Did I mention those beads come apart?"

She smiled. "You didn't."

"And some of them have bells inside."

"Whatever for," she purred.

"Let me show you . . . ," he murmured, reaching for the necklace.

"I'm a free woman, you know . . ." Her smile was very close, her voice sultry with suggestion.

"I heard that." He lightly kissed her smile.

She touched the necklace dangling from his fingers. "Which means I can do anything I want."

His brows rose in playful response. "An intriguing thought . . ."

"Now, if I only knew how those bells worked, I could enjoy them."

"We both could enjoy them."

"Better yet," she murmured, licking a warm path down his jaw.

"Would you like a demonstration?"

"If you have time," she said, playful and arch.

He grinned. "If I didn't, I'd sure as hell make some." And lifting her from his lap, he laid her against the pillows and unsnapped the two largest beads from the string. Squeezing the small protrusions on each bead, he caused them to disappear into the smooth contour of the jade spheres. Cupping them in his hand, he gently shook them, and a silvery ringing sound resonated in the air.

"They didn't ring before?"

"I released the springs. Now when you move, I'll hear you."

"What if I don't move?"

"It's highly unlikely."

"These will make me move?"

"They'll make you come."

"You're so sure, I should take offense."

"If you didn't want to come in five seconds, you might."

"That long?" she teased. "Why are you making me wait?"

"With your ready appetite for fornication," he murmured, running his palm up the inside of her thigh, "I foresee a life of blissful content."

"I'm addicted to you," she breathed, her eyes drifting shut at the touch of his hand, anticipation stretched taut in the wake of his upward progress.

"And I to you," he whispered, reaching her pouty vulva, delicately stroking the engorged flesh with the merest brush of his fingertips. "Maybe I'll just keep you here in bed, nude and available and primed for fucking."

"Once the boys are back in school," she whispered, as though she were captive to the lust he provoked, "maybe I'll let you."

"And I'll have you wear these bells"—he slid one large jade bead over the sleek flesh of her vulva—"so I'll always know where you are."

"People would talk . . ." The heat shimmering upward from the smooth friction of jade to slippery tissue spread like molten gold through her vagina.

"They wouldn't dare." He pressed the violet bead upward with a deft twist of his wrist, pushing it along the pulsing vaginal wall, lodging it firmly at the very depth of her passage while she panted and moaned and gently writhed her hips. Placing his hand on her stomach, he quietly said, "Don't move."

It was impossible, particularly with the weight of his hand pressing downward precisely over the jade bead and the sound of tinkling bells was adjunct to her labored breathing.

"We're going to have to practice this—not moving." His voice was husky and low, the smallest hint of admonition in his tone. "As a matter of self-discipline."

As well he held his breath for all the impression his words made on a brain intent on surcease, the sound of the bells quickening her already heated senses, the stimulation of the lodged bead so intense, she lifted her hips in search of release.

Aware of her predilection for quicksilver orgasms, he slid the second bead in, and circling her waist with his hands, he eased her higher on the pillows, bringing her into a seated position. She gasped as the rapture intensified.

"Now you can move," he gently suggested, guiding her hips with his hands.

She groaned as a wild, seething delirium jolted through her vagina, spreading outward in a riveting turbulence that infused every screaming nerve with agonizing pleasure, that made it impossible to define the finite site of fevered response because her entire body was on fire. That brought her to climax in just over five seconds.

He lounged beside her afterward, while she slowly returned to a degree of consciousness that allowed her to open her eyes and survey him with a faint smile. "I adore my engagement gift."

He winked at her. "I had a feeling you would."

"The thought of keeping these—"

"Inside you?"

She softly exhaled. "It's very tempting."

"Once the boys go to school you could indulge yourself. And when you walk into a room, I'll know it's you without looking up," he said with a smile. "Although you'll have to learn to have your orgasms quietly. Not for me, but if you're entertaining your friends for tea."

"Max," she whispered. "How scandalous . . ."

"Walk for me." He held out his hand to help her from the bed. "See if you like it."

She shook her head.

"Come, darling," he cajoled, taking her hand in his and rising to his feet. "If you don't like it, stop."

But even as she slid from the bed and stood beside him, she fought the tremulous excitement aroused by so small a movement.

"You look interested in a walk," he softly said, bending to gently kiss her.

"Maybe just a short one," she said on a suffocated breath.

"We could go to the window and look at the moon."

She followed him as he led her forward; but the first step shifted the large beads, and they came in riveting contact, pressing hard into her throbbing flesh. Panting, she came to an abrupt stop. The bells stopped, but her overwrought passions only quickened.

"Another step, darling . . ." He pulled her forward.

Clutching his hand, she said, "I can't," but she did because he forced her forward one panting step at a time while she came in small gasping exhalations. When they finally reached the window in a slow, halting progress, he slid his hand between her legs, covered her mouth with his and inhaled her orgasmic screams as he pressed his palm upward.

She came countless times as he ground his palm into her throbbing vulva in an exquisitely exacting rotation, her panting pleasure cries sweet in his mouth. But there were limits even to rapture, he knew, and when she grew faint from excess, he lifted her into his arms and carried her to the bed.

She clung to him as he lowered her onto the rumpled coverlet. "Hold me," she whispered, not wishing to relinquish the blissful sense of overindulgence, the basking warmth of his body, his power and strength.

"In a second," he whispered, extracting the beads with a nimble-fingered skill that was lambent rather than arousing, a brief, grazing sensation. "Did you like your engagement gift?" A smile infused his husky tone as he lowered himself over her, bracing his weight on his arms, dipping his head to brush her mouth in a kiss.

"Ummm . . . I'm not sure." She nibbled briefly on his lip. "Maybe we should try it again."

His low chuckle warmed her mouth. "Maybe I should have a turn first, Miss Greedy."

"It's your own fault, you know . . . making me feel so good . . ." Raising her hips, she came in contact with his rigid erection. "On the other hand," she cheerfully murmured, "unselfishness is a virtue."

One dark brow quirked in playful query. "And how do you propose to be unselfish?"

"I was just thinking it really *is* your turn to come."

His grin was cheeky. "Were you also thinking of any particular place I could come?"

"I *am* all slippery wet and, well . . . ready for you . . . if you're interested," she flirtatiously added.

"Does this feel like I'm interested?" He rubbed his hardness against her stomach.

"Marvelously interested," she breathed, undulating her hips in a slow, provocative rhythm. "Did I mention I'm a free woman?"

"I believe you did."

"So as a free woman, I'd like to invite you and your splendid erection to come out and play," she sportively proposed.

"I'll have to check my schedule," he said in a teasing undertone.

"We could play at making a baby tonight if your schedule allows," she softly offered.

The shock of her words strummed through his brain, avoidance of babies more typical of his life. "I suppose we could," he murmured, his hesitation plain.

"I'm sorry. I shouldn't have said that."

"No . . . it's fine." The conceit of fathering a child suddenly flooded his senses. He half smiled. "We could start working on it at least . . ."

"That would mean you'd have to make love to me—a lot," she softly purred. "I mean . . . if we were really serious about it."

His dark gaze was heated. "I think I could do that."

"You'd have to fill me with sperm every day."

"Every day and every night, too—just to be sure." His voice was silken.

"Just to be sure," she quietly echoed, easing open her thighs.

"You're willing, then?"

"Very."

"I'd have to come in you—"

"Often," she interjected, reaching down to stroke the taut crest of his erection. "Early and often, late and often . . ."

"Now and often," he whispered, gliding in with finesse. Slipping his hands under her bottom, he lifted her into his down-stroke and held her immobile for a shuddering moment while a riveting ecstasy raced through their senses. But the wild rapture resonated with a fanatical new nuance, more deep felt, impossible to classify, yet noteworthy and magnificent. "This is love in all its glory," he said, half-breathless.

"In every vivid hue," she murmured.

And they both understood everything was transformed by the wish and hope, the dream of a child.

He moved in the most gentle undulation.

She answered in a more volatile, capricious way.

And when he glided in and out in a silken flux and flow, she arched up into his body, impatient as always, eager, impelled perhaps by her long years of deprivation.

"Are we going to scorch through this?" he teased, holding her hips immobile.

She wiggled against his grip. "You take your time." Her voice was playful. "I'll go on ahead."

"Are you selfishly using me?"

She grinned. "Only a part of you."

"Lord Almighty," he softly exhaled. "You've turned into a feisty little handful."

"And you're perturbed?"

"Au contraire. This feisty little handful fits my cock to perfection." His smile was sinfully wicked, unutterably sexy and deliciously close. "Hang on now, sweetheart . . . I'll race you to the finish."

And he plunged forward with an indulgent, self-indulgent and extremely accommodating zeal.

Chapter 27

The following week, Burt's nephew personally delivered the stolen pages from the civic and church ledgers and presented them to Max. A cleric in the pay of the Prince of Zeiss, it seemed, had failed to destroy them as ordered. Max rewarded the young man with the particular largesse of a man well-pleased and commended him for succeeding where others had failed.

Christina burst into tears when she was shown the unequivocal proof of her freedom and then threw her arms around her husband-to-be and thanked him the way he most liked to be thanked.

The wedding date was now assured, and the estate staff and most of the fashionable shops in London were involved in the rapid deployment of personnel and resplendent materiel to see that the Marquis of Vale and his bride had the wedding of the century. Vast numbers of flowers arrived at Minster Hill, their procurement more difficult in January but not impossible when money was no object. The wedding gown required a dozen seamstresses on the premises, working round the clock. Jewelers and purveyors of fine food and wines set up residence on the estate. In short, Max ordered the world to his wishes.

Two days before the wedding, Christina's family was due to arrive, her mother and father, her sister Charlotte and her two nephews. Charlotte's husband was on safari, not that he would necessarily be available anyway for a family function. He preferred his own pursuits. Max's mother, half sister and stepfather couldn't arrive on such short notice, but would welcome the newlyweds with a reception in New York on their honeymoon trip.

"Invite whom you wish, darling," Max had said. He was quite ready to welcome all of society if Christina wanted, although his preference was for a quiet ceremony.

"I think we'll have only a very few friends," she had replied. "Considering the circumstances," she had added. "And the boys."

He had agreed, and the guest list was limited.

But the day Christina's parents arrived, Max saw his bride-to-be was very near tears at lunch. And when they were alone once again, he said, "Don't worry about what they think. Your life is your own."

"You saw how Mother is. Questioning every little thing. Wondering if I was doing the right thing, for heaven's sake."

"She doesn't understand what Hans was like."

"She doesn't wish to understand. And Father with his comments about leaving Schloss Zeiss behind as though it were mine to leave."

"Perhaps they just need some time to adjust. Admit, darling, we're making some rather abrupt changes in our lives." He was trying to be understanding when his first reaction was displeasure with Christina's parents. But he didn't wish to raise problems when they would be married soon and away from England. "By the time we return from America next summer, your parents will have had time to become reconciled to all the changes."

She grimaced. "You're very optimistic."

"Bottom line is it doesn't matter."

"Easy for you to say. Your family is supportive."

"All we have to do is smile and be agreeable for two more days, darling. Come, sweetheart, you can do it."

She wrinkled her nose and sighed. "I shall try."

* * *

The Colonel and Lady Georgina Grey seemed bent on being disagreeable again at tea, offering their unsolicited advice on any number of subjects that didn't concern them, from the boys' tutor's hairstyle to their dismay that the Earl and Countess of Buxley had been invited when everyone knew the countess had once been a governess. Not to mention, their continuing harassment over Christina's decision to remarry so quickly.

Granted the news given out that Christina had divorced the prince was sudden, their daughter's reasons defined in—if not fully truthful terms—iniquitous enough detail to clarify her decision to all but the most obtuse.

And while they regarded Max with a baleful eye over the cucumber sandwiches and petit fours, he was unfailingly polite to them for the sake of their daughter . . . until dinner that night when Christina's mother again took issue with the suddenness of the wedding.

"Why you couldn't wait a decent interval is beyond my comprehension," she murmured. "A divorce is ruinous enough, but marrying again so soon is inconsistent with good taste. My friends will be appalled."

"By the time we return from our honeymoon, Mother, your friends will have found other gossip to entertain them."

"I'm to blame, I'm afraid, for our precipitous time table," Max interjected, wishing to take the onus from Christina. "I'm at a point where my business commitments in America require my presence, and Christina was kind enough to consent to my schedule."

"Your father didn't believe a gentleman should engage in business," the colonel brusquely said, his military mustache twitching.

"My father believed only in drink and hunting. Fortunately, my mother gave him enough money so he was able to maintain the estate. Otherwise, with the price of land falling during the century, he would have had to sell off."

"Land prices would be up but for all the needless social reform," the colonel peevishly noted. "The laboring class has lost respect for hard work, and the country is the worse for it."

"It's become almost impossible to find good household help with all the young people flocking to the city," Lady Georgina decried. "And the wages they want. It's criminal."

There was no point in discussing social change or the rights of the common man with Christina's parents, so Max said instead, "Tell me, Colonel, do you find the claret drinkable? The vineyard belongs to a friend of mine." The colonel had had more than his share, and a high flush pinked his cheeks.

"Good enough, I suppose," he muttered. "Nothing to compare with Prince Hans's cellar, though."

"Father, for heaven's sake!" Christina's voice snapped with anger.

It required a moment to absorb such blatant rudeness, but Max said with good grace, "Perhaps we could find a wine more to your liking, Colonel."

"Mother, I think Father has had more than enough to drink," Christina heatedly remarked. "Really, Max—there's no need. The claret is excellent."

Fortunately, Charlotte was suddenly announced, and a contretemps was avoided.

Sweeping into the room in her traveling clothes, she apologized for her appearance, for her lateness, and for the ineptitude of her steward, who had made the travel arrangements that brought her to Minster Hill almost a day behind schedule. After kissing her mother and father, she went to her sister with open arms and a broad smile. "Congratulations, darling! Or am I supposed to say, good wishes." Her gaze swung to Max. "You're the one to be congratulated, aren't you?"

"We both are, Charlie," Christina replied, beaming as she hugged her sister.

"I have the better bargain by far," Max noted with a smile, rising from his chair to greet his future sister-in-law.

"That's not what all the ladies you've left behind are saying," Charlotte murmured a moment later as she hugged the marquis.

"Allow me to disagree," he pleasantly said. "Did your sons come with you?" he inquired, wishing to change the subject.

"They wouldn't have missed seeing their cousins. In fact, they're all upstairs at the moment comparing the misery of their respective schools."

"Sit by Christina," Max politely offered, gesturing to the footman holding a chair at the ready. "Might I offer you champagne?"

"Of course. I'm in the mood to celebrate. Such delicious news, darling, when I heard of your plans." She took Christina's hand in hers. "All my very best," she softly said. "Now, if only I could be so lucky," she added sotto voce, winking surreptitiously.

"Charlotte, please tell your sister how unnatural and irregular her hasty marriage," Lady Georgina said in chilly tones. "People will condemn her wickedness. Your father will be forced to withdraw from his clubs until the gossip dies down. As for society—"

"Mother, society isn't unfamiliar with divorce," Charlotte disclaimed, sitting down. "Nor will they condemn Christina for fleeing such a dastardly husband. As for the marquis"—she smiled at Max—"he's sought after by every society hostess of note—for her guest list," she waggishly finished. "Ah . . . my champagne. You may leave the bottle." She tapped the table before her and then offered everyone a smile. "It was a very, *very* long train ride."

In the course of the evening, Charlotte managed to deflect her parents' most patent incivilities while dispensing all the latest gossip from London. She was a welcome buffer and support to the engaged couple, although even with her suave intervention, the conversation turned taut several times. When the last course was served, Max forewent port with the colonel in the interests of harmony—he didn't wish to strangle his future father-in-law before the wedding—and instead invited everyone to retire to the drawing room for tea and sherry.

"Don't drink the bloody stuff," the colonel bluntly said. "Cognac—now there's a man's drink."

By this time, the colonel was well into his cups, and Max quietly gestured a footman to follow him to the drawing room should he fall. As it turned out, the after-dinner sherry and cognac drinking was blessedly brief, for Lady Georgina found it prudent to see her husband off to bed before he passed out on the floor.

"Thank God," Charlotte muttered as Max escorted her parents to the door. "They live in the past century out in Wales."

Christina softly exhaled. "Only one more day . . ."

"And they'll be out of your life, and darling Max will be yours," her sister murmured. "Lord, I envy you—to have found love."

"I thank the fates every day," Christina said, sensible of her sister's lamentable marriage. "I never knew what I was missing."

"Neither of us ever knew."

Christina reached over and patted her sister's hand. "My Lord Duke must be difficult as usual . . . I'm so sorry."

Charlotte shrugged away her moment of melancholy. "At least Percy's in Africa. With luck, a lion may eat him," she said without humor.

"You have my complete sympathy. I wonder now how I endured Hans's tyranny for so long. Mother and Father didn't do us a service—encouraging and promoting our marriages as they did."

"As if titles matter."

"And we knew nothing of the world at seventeen." Christina grimaced; the injustice still stung.

"Not to mention, Mother was a martinet for convention."

"She still is," Christina corrected. "By the way, I'm so very grateful you arrived when you did. It helped to have someone share the parental displeasure this evening."

"I wouldn't have missed your wedding for the world." Charlotte smiled. "Seeing you happy gives me hope."

"Do come and visit us in America. Bring the boys."

"Stay with us as long as you wish," Max added, having heard Christina's invitation on his return.

"You may have a permanent house guest," Charlotte playfully noted.

"We'd be delighted. Wouldn't we, dear?" Max said, sitting beside Christina.

"We'd love it, Charlie!"

The duchess felt a sharp pang of envy as her sister and Max exchanged affectionate glances. But she had had much practice putting on an appropriate face for the world, and lifting her glass, she smiled. "To my dearest sister and the man who brought her happiness and love."

"The luckiest man in the world," Max whispered near Christina's ear.

Christina blushed. "To happiness and love," she softly repeated, lifting her glass.

The following morning, Max came down to breakfast beforehand in the event the Greys were early risers. Christina was still sleeping, the boys were breakfasting with their cousins, and Charlotte had said last night she had no intention of rising before noon. So it fell to him to play host to Christina's parents, an exercise that would require several cups of coffee to put him in a suitably benign mood after their behavior toward Christina yesterday.

Lady Georgina arrived first and, on seeing him, stood arrested on the threshold. "It's you," she said.

Whom did she expect to see? Max wondered, but he rose to greet her with a smile and a bland comment on the weather that would under most circumstances be answered with an equally bland comment.

"My daughter is thoroughly besotted, and I blame you completely," Lady Georgina sharply said instead.

"I'm sorry," Max replied, keeping his voice mild with effort, waving the servants out of the room. "Someday you may understand the great happiness we've both found and be consoled."

"I never shall," she tartly replied.

"I'm sorry again. We're at an impasse, it seems."

She jabbed her finger at him. "You've absolutely *ruined* my daughter's life."

"Damn right he has!" The colonel entered the room, red-faced and looking rather the worse for wear.

"Perhaps this would be a good time to discuss our differences." Max was at his most diplomatic, intent on maintaining his calm for Christina's sake. "We're alone. We may speak freely. Please, sit down."

"There's nothing to discuss. Get out of our daughter's life," the colonel ordered. "Where's the bloody coffee," he muttered, stalking past Max toward the buffet.

"Christina will forget you in time, and I'm sure the prince will take her back," Lady Georgina observed, speaking as though her daughter's reasons for divorce were irrelevant. "You Americans don't understand our world where tradition and custom are held in high regard, where rules matter and etiquette is observed. Christina and Hans had a perfectly good marriage until she met you."

Max had been restraining his temper with effort, but at Lady Georgina's complete repudiation of the misery of Christina's married life, he lost the struggle. "Hans tried to kill her," he said in a voice so taut, the colonel glanced up from pouring his coffee. "For your information, Christina barely survived. So she won't be going back to the prince and their perfectly good marriage," he said in a heated whisper. "Not now, not ever, not whether you want it or all the gods in heaven want it."

"I don't believe you," Lady Georgina sniffed. "You're fabricating this preposterous story to serve your own ends. The prince is a model husband and father."

"Kill her? You're talking damned nonsense!" the colonel blustered. "The man's a prince!"

"He tried to poison her," Max said with awful clarity. "The doctor didn't think she'd live."

"Impossible! You're making this all up!" Lady Georgina cried.

"He's telling you the truth." Christina's quiet tone reverberated in the sudden silence. "And I wouldn't be here today except for Max's courage and love. So I'll be marrying Max tomorrow, and if you don't wish to attend the ceremony, you may leave."

Max immediately went to Christina, who was standing stiffly on the threshold.

Lady Georgina's face had crumpled; her gaze had gone blank. The colonel opened his mouth twice to speak and each time shut it again.

"Hans was unspeakably cruel . . . to me and to our sons," Christina quietly said. "I'd hoped to spare you the details of a further disgrace he imposed on me and the boys, but perhaps you should be told." Christina took a deep breath, and Max knew how much courage it took for her to say what she was about to say. Society was small and incestuous; gossip could be ruthless.

He took her hand in his, and she looked up.

"Do you want me to tell them?"

She shook her head. "It's about time I began speaking for myself." Her gaze returned to her parents. "You may wish to sit down, Mother. What I'm about to say will shock you."

But her mother listened to the full recital without comment, although she turned pale at the horrendous realization that Hans had deceived them all. She rallied with effort as Christina finished speaking, drawing her shoulders back as though she were facing a firing squad, and in shaking accents, she asked her daughter's forgiveness. She even offered Max an apology, the words of atonement so plainly onerous, Max took pity on her. "You couldn't have known," he kindly said, and was rewarded with the first smile he had ever seen on Lady Georgina's lips.

The colonel had turned beet red as the facts of Hans's first marriage were disclosed, and when Christina finished, he sputtered, "I . . . need—a—bloody brandy." After quickly swallowing two large drafts, he manfully expressed his regret to both Christina and Max in a brusque staccato of apology and disbelief.

Breakfast that morning was uncomfortable, conversation stilted, but a process of reconciliation began, each halting attempt at discussion another step forward in the healing of old wounds. By the time the colonel had emptied the brandy bottle, he had recalled a number of defects in Hans he had previously overlooked for the sake of his daughter—the prince's unfriendly family, his pronunciation, the way he sat his horse, his choice of clubs and cravats. "The man can't even shoot worth a damn!" he exclaimed. "My beaters had to send the game birds under his very nose before he could hit one. Now, a real gentleman knows how to shoot straight, bloody right he does! I see you have quite a collection of firearms in the study," he added, casting a friendly glance toward Max. "New models from the looks of 'em. How are you on the target range?"

"Not bad," Max modestly replied. He didn't mention he could shoot a fly at fifty yards.

"Not bad myself," the colonel muttered. "We'll have to give those new rifles of yours a try, eh, my boy?"

Max smiled. "At your convenience, sir."

And so breakfast went on in a mood of increasing good cheer, so much so that when Charlotte walked into the room at—for her—the remarkably early hour of ten, her eyes widened momentarily in surprise.

She shot a glance at her sister, who smiled and winked and said, "Do come and join us, Charlie. Father and Max are going out shooting after breakfast. Should we show them what we can do?"

"Taught the girls how to shoot," the colonel proudly asserted. "And if I do say so myself, they're both tops. Going to give us a run for our money, my boy," he jovially remarked, tipping his head toward Max.

Target shooting after breakfast further cemented the newly

won cordiality, and Max carefully allowed the colonel to win—as did the girls—although he was a fine enough shot that it wasn't difficult. And on their return to the house, they found it in a state of bustle and excitement. A number of wedding guests had arrived.

Dinner that evening was festive with the family reconciled, with all their good friends in attendance, and Max and Christina exchanged affectionate smiles down the length of the table so often, Lulu playfully observed, "If we're keeping you from something . . ."

While they were, the host and hostess knew where their duty lay, and curtailing their ardor, they played their roles with courtesy and aplomb.

The wedding morning was sunny and bright—warm for January—and at eleven o'clock, the guests assembled in the chapel built by an earlier Falconer in the manner of an Egyptian temple. Banks of roses, lilies and early lilac scented the air, sunlight shone through the stained glass windows in gleaming shafts of turquoise and rose, and Max, Johnnie and Fritz stood at the altar, waiting for the bride.

Charlotte and Lulu were delighted to serve as bridesmaids opposite Christina's sons.

When a triumphant bravura roll from the organist announced Christina's appearance, everyone turned to look.

She stood alone at the back of the nave, her gown shimmering with thousands of pearls, the heavy pale satin simply cut, the skirt bordered in ermine, the veil held in place by a wreath of violets. She carried a nosegay of violets as well, counterpoint to the jade necklace she wore, and as she advanced down the aisle, everyone held their breath in awe. Tall, slender, her pale beauty ethereal in the luminous sunlight, she was gloriously radiant, her happiness so plain, it brought tears of hope and joy to many an eye.

As she reached the altar, Max smiled and held out his hand, and when their fingers twined, he drew her close and whispered low, "From this day forward, darling, it's you and me and Digby forever . . ."

There was discussion afterward about the meaning of the phrase, for those in the front rows had heard his murmured comment, but when questioned, Max only said, "You must have been mistaken."

But Lulu knew, and when the wedding breakfast was over and she and Christina were sharing a glass of champagne away from the crowd, she said, "I see Digby holds a special place in Max's heart."

Christina smiled. "It does for us both, and I have you to thank for giving me the courage I needed that morning at Shelagh's. I almost woke you to ask for advice, but decided instead to take a page from your book and just go to meet Max."

The baroness fluttered her lashes in playful raillery. "I'm so glad you decided to dip your toe in the water. Didn't I tell you you'd like it?" She uttered a small sigh. "Now, if only I could find someone as charming."

"Perhaps you will," Christina softly replied, wishing her friend could be as fortunate as she and find the great love of her life. "After what happened to me, I truly believe in miracles."

"I'm not so sure I'm as starry-eyed as you, darling."

Christina laughed. "I never thought I'd be telling you to be open to the possibilities, but *do*, Lulu. Miracles do happen."

As it turned out, Lulu did discover a small miracle of her own, but not in rhetorical toe-dipping water so much as in a very wet bed.

But that's another story.